BIRTH... AND DEATH

Balanced expertly on their back legs, the hatchlings eyed their audience eagerly. Their heads were almost half their body mass, and their jaws were already filled with rows of sharp teeth. With round, flat eyes glaring, they stood in the leathery wreckage of their eggs, they were already as tall as five-year-old humans.

"My God, Phineas, what are they?" Kate said.

"I don't know," Phineas said, "but I think they're little T. Rexes..."

The Saurian warriors weren't waiting to find out. Shrieking and hissing with joy, they unleashed a hail of arrows, and the warm nest became a slaughter pit. Even as the mother arrived...

Praise for the
DRAGONSTAR Trilogy:

"Colorful and vigorous... of a type too little seen."

—*s Weekly*

D1508038

DAVID F. BISCHOFF and
THOMAS F. MONTELEONE

DRAGONSTAR DESTINY

ACE BOOKS, NEW YORK

DRAGONSTAR DESTINY

An Ace Book/published by arrangement with
the authors

PRINTING HISTORY
Ace edition/February 1989

ISBN: 0-441-16676-8

Ace Books are published by The Berkley Publishing Group,
200 Madison Avenue, New York, NY 10016.
The name "ACE" and the "A" logo are trademarks belonging to
Charter Communications, Inc.
PRINTED IN THE UNITED STATES OF AMERICA

10 9 8 7 6 5 4 3 2 1

This one is for
FREDDE LIEBERMAN and
TAD STONES

ACKNOWLEDGMENT

Thanks again to the possibly neotenous
Charles Sheffield

PROLOGUE

A WAILING SOUND pierced Kii's cold-sleep dreams.

Servomechanisms were triggered and slowly brought him to consciousness. The sound of the klaxon initially seemed distant, both in time and space, but gradually its urgent sound became more real, more immediate, and his mind began to clear, to grasp the significance of its message.

It is time! thought Kii as he fought against the effects of the eons-long hibernation.

Slowly the remote tensors were warming him, reviving him. *How long have I slept?* Soon, tactile sensation would be returning to his limbs, his claws, and he attempted to move in the chamber before he was able. He could not stop himself from pressing against the webbed restraints. There was an anxiety, an excitement, boiling in him.

The Returning! A new era in the making!

Summoning up his resolve, he initiated the age-old exercise of *zir*—deep, steady breathing, dilating his nostrils, keeping his jaws clamped shut. He did this to rid his mind of erratic thoughts, of impulsive, nonproductive thinking. There was nothing to do but wait until the automatic mechanisms which monitored his life-forces were satisfied with stable readings. Only then would the machines free him from his self-imposed prison.

Finally the alarm lapsed into silence. The webbing dissolved, releasing Kii from his coffin-like enclosure. Still, he moved cautiously, because he was very old, very weak. In contrast to the electric, scintillant activity of his mind, Kii's body responded with a glacial slowness. Kii stepped down and carefully balanced himself on his thick legs. It was difficult to fight off the dizziness, and he knew that he would require an "assistor"—a motorized exoskeleton—to move about the lab-cell.

Kii sighed and lashed his tongue in the air as he climbed into the assistor, feeling its sensors come to life and begin monitoring his kinetic movements and responses. Each time he moved, the power-assisted exoskeleton would move with him, effectively amplifying his strength and ease of mobility. The amplification was an odd sensation, and required a period of adjustment. Kii took several experimental steps around the cell, anxious to inspect his instruments, but knowing that he must not injure himself.

The thought suddenly struck him that on the entire planet, only Kii was conscious, awake, sentient. It was an oddly frightening proposition to think that the fate of your whole species most likely would depend upon what you did in the next several time units. But Kii did not like to think in such dramatic terms. More simply, he had a few simple tasks to perform. He was no one special, really. His genotype had selected him to be the one awakened. When all was confirmed, he would awaken the others.

That had been the plan.

With confidence, he exited the cryogenic chamber, entering a featureless corridor comprised of dull metallic walls and ceiling. The floor was carpeted in a thick, fibrous synthetic which afforded a firm, yet comfortable purchase for Kii's splayed, clawed feet. Looking down the corridor, Kii calmly observed that it continued to the convergence point of perspective. It appeared to be endless, and after a fashion, it was indeed.

As Kii moved along the metallic passage, he contemplated his location in the vast crisscrossing network of corridors, shafts, and cells. The entire planet had been artificially enclosed, burrowed, and re-formed to assume the shape and function of a gigantic hive. It was an impossibly large data bank, a repository, a library *world*. Each hive-cell resembled a separate neuron, each corridor the connecting nerve-pathways, forming a planetary *gestalt*—a quiescent, nonorganic brain brimming over with data and potential.

With each step Kii gained confidence in his use of the assistor. Although countless eras may have passed, subjectively he was unaware of the occurrence. The cold-sleep had kept him in a timeless void, and he wondered if death was any different from that seemingly endless state. But there would be time enough for death, he thought. Right now, he was about the business of life!

New life, thought Kii. For we are the creators, the progenitors, and once again our greatest dreams are reaching fruition!

The thought filled him with a gladness and a pride that warmed his very bones. Surely there was no better genotype than his . . . to be a Planner was to be the most noble of your species!

With renewed confidence, he moved quickly down the corridor, letting the powered exoskeleton do all the work. Kii passed through the featureless maze of interconnecting corridors as though following the demands of an ancient instinct. He arrived at the entrance to another lab-cell, placed his foreclaw against the entry grid, and watched the field dissipate, allowing him to pass through.

He moved quickly to an interface console and plugged himself into the semiorganic computer by means of a bioneered coupling on the back of his neck, just below his brain stem. There was an icy tingle beside his skull as the interface was activated, and suddenly Kii was informed of all that had transpired.

Initially he was shocked to discover how much time had passed: so many millions of time units! Could it be possible that there had been so many failures? Apparently. Otherwise he and the rest of the Planners would not have slept for such a long time.

Nevertheless, he thought with a great, pleasant expansion of his nostrils, the signal had been received and the response had been triggered. A Returning! Proof again that the plan was as inexorable as the great turning wheels of the planets about their suns.

His warm thoughts were abruptly interrupted by new data.

Impossible! thought Kii. And yet the information which flowed into him was irrefutable. Remote servos were starting up—mechanisms which were somehow *beyond* the interface's sphere of control. Kii pinpointed the location of the renegade devices and was shocked to discover that an entire cold-sleep chamber was being warmed.

This should not be happening, he thought, as he videoed the relevant lab-cell.

The scene filled his mind like a movie screen. He watched an entire wall of cryogenic tanks begin to open. The webbing in all of them was starting to dissolve, revealing the now-awakening occupants.

But this was not part of the plan! It was far too early to awaken the others, and Kii could not understand what could have gone wrong or why this was happening.

There was nothing to do but continue to watch the chamber by means of the remote video. The last of the webbing dissolved from the tanks in the forefront of the scene, an Kii saw with a growing horror what was being awakened.

Turning away from the console, he attempted to secure the control-cell. Interfacing with the emergency defense net, Kii felt blocked at every level, stymied. Another force had tampered with the network—there could be no other plausible explanation. Fighting a wave of panic and sense of impending failure, he continued to search the network for a solution, a means of breaking through the patches and bridges which had been jimmied into the system.

Suddenly behind him there was the sound of two energy fields in flux—the air crackled and sizzled.

Turning, Kii saw the barrier-field to his cell boil away in the final splash of a disruptor weapon. A thin cloak of vapor hung within the threshold of the entrance until it was penetrated by a large, powerfully built figure. Muscles rippled beneath its scaly hide as it stepped forward to regard Kii with flat, pale yellow eyes.

"Do not move," said the Mover.

"How did you do this?" asked Kii. "Why? What do you want?"

The Mover also wore an assistor, although this one was outfitted with combat options. Weapons bristled from gauntlets which braced each forelimb. The Mover advanced and slapped Kii across his lower jaw. The pain spread like white heat up the side of his skull.

"Silence!" said the Mover. More of his genotype poured into the control-cell, all looking as formidable as the first. "We were planted to oversee your Awakening. We must contact our Brethren of this New Time for orders."

Kii gestured his assent and understanding. There was a numbness in his jaw now, and he realized that the Mover could have killed him just as easily. There was nothing to do but cooperate . . . for the moment at least.

Kii would wait until the ship returned. By then, he was certain that he would be true to his genotype . . . that he would have a new plan.

CHAPTER 1

"THEY'RE WAITING FOR YOU, sir," said the Admins Aide who appeared on Gregor Kolenkhov's Deskmate monitor.

"I *know* they are waiting," said the large, beefy Russian. He did not bother to look at the screen as he spoke, but continued to pace back and forth within his private office. "Tell them I will be coming out in several minutes."

In Colonel Kemp's absence, Kolenkhov, as senior member of the Joints Chiefs of Staff at Copernicus Base on Luna, was in charge of all base operations. At present, it was a job he wished belonged to someone else.

Gregor wondered if Kemp was still alive, if he would ever see the man again.

After the catastrophe on worldwide holovision, there was no place to hide. The IASA lunar base was being swamped with media journalists, government agency representatives, and various other political dignitaries all being shuttled up from Earth as quickly as possible. The International Aeronautics and Space Administration had no choice but to allow the whole pack of agency wolves and news jackals into Copernicus Base. After broadcasting the disaster to an audience of more than 4 billion people, the IASA's ass was in one hell of a crack.

Now the world was demanding some answers, and Kolenkhov was the jack-in-the-box, the squirrel in the wheel cage. He would have to face them and answer their questions. It would be a major task, trying to make sense out of the insanity which had been visited upon the IASA ever since the gigantic alien airtifact had been discovered.

Goddammit all! Why could not Colonel Kemp be here to handle this fucking circus?

Of course, there was no telling *where* Kemp might be

now. . . . It was one of those things which Kolenkhov tried not to think about.

Gregor paused in front of the mirror and smoothed down his black hair, combed back and slicked down across his partially bald head. Squaring his shoulders, he assessed himself in his Informal Officer's jumpsuit. For a man of his age and obvious overweight tendencies, he figured he did not look too bad. He exhaled and shook his head slowly, moving toward the door.

No sense putting it off any longer, he thought, palming it open.

He stepped into a corridor and stared into the faces of those who stood waiting to accompany him to the assembly hall. Oscar Rheinhardt, Marcia Bertholde, and an attractive, young female Admins Aide by the name of Fleisher.

"We've been waiting for you, Gregor," said Marcia Bertholde, a tall, greying, no-nonsense woman who looked every one of her fifty years. She had the irritating habit of smoking long, thin cigarettes in public, as if she believed her high rank carried the privilege of making the air rank for others.

"With the three of you huddled outside my door like a pack of simpering dogs, I would have never guessed!"

Oscar Rheinhardt tapped him lightly on the shoulder. "Now, now . . . there's no sense in getting testy, comrade. We're all in this mess together, you know."

"That may be true, Oscar, but it is *I* who must talk to these people."

"It comes with the territory," said Bertholde. She dragged on her cigarette, exhaled the smoke in a tight bluish stream.

Gregor ignored this last crack. To Fleisher he said: "Did you get those notes faxed for me?"

The aide handed him a folder jammed with a sheaf of papers. "Here you are, sir."

Taking the reports and data sheets, Gregor took in a deep breath, exhaled dramatically. "All right," he said. "Let us get down in the mud with these scavengers."

The group walked to the elevators in silence and took the waiting car up to the main concourse of the underground base. Here the corridors were wide and brightly illuminated. There were even occasional skylight shafts which brought in real sunlight from the harsh 336-hour lunar-days. But today, the moon was in its nocturnal phase and no natural light poured in from the light shafts. Bathed only in the artificial glow of the wall panels, Gregor found the passageway dim and full of gloom.

Approaching the assembly hall, Fleisher guided them down a ramp to a set of doors which opened upon the proscenium. As she palmed open the barrier, Gregor felt the wash of a hundred murmuring conversations inundate him simultaneously. It was like plunging into a quiet glade where the trees and shrubs seemed to vibrate with the susurrous life of a million locusts. As he entered the room, he could feel the collective gaze of his audience focusing upon him, pinning him like a butterfly to a piece of cork. As he approached the speaker's console, the other Joint Chiefs took seats behind him.

He looked up, trying to coolly assess his audience of more than three hundred men and women from every conceivable organization and agency, and waited for the inevitable hush to settle upon them. The lenses of cameras, like the multifaceted eyes of giant insects, zoomed in upon him. He cleared his throat as the last murmurs faded away. He could feel their attention drawing a bead on him like a target in cross-hairs.

From the speaker's console, Gregor keyed in the mike and loudspeaker, cleared his throat, and started talking. He had tried to come up with a prepared statement, but now found himself (to use one of Kemp's favorite phrases) "winging it."

"Good afternoon, everyone. For any of you who may not know me, I am IASA Colonel Gregor Yurianovich Kolenkhov, senior member of the Joint Chiefs of Staff here at Copernicus Base. I will attempt to make some sense out of the terrible tragedy we have all witnessed within the last thirty-six hours, and will, if possible, answer any questions you might have." Gregor cleared his throat and signaled for Fleisher to get him a flask of water, wishing that she had the presence of mind to substitute a liter or so of vodka.

Looking up, he continued: "I have here a prepared report, and I will be happy to present it to you intact. You will also receive copies of the report as you all leave the assembly hall. Or, if you wish, we can forget about the report for now and carry on like a regular press conference. I leave it up to all of you. . . ."

Gregor paused and looked off to the right where Fleisher had returned with a flask and small glass. He nodded, and she brought it quickly to the podium, then moved back into the wing of the proscenium. As Kolenkhov poured some of the clear liquid into the glass, then raised it to his lips, he detected the familiar bouquet he had first smelled in his father's *dacha* many, many years ago.

Vodka! Fuck-your-mother, the girl had done it!

Despite the crowd staring at him, he almost broke into a smile as he threw down several fingers of the crisp, clear burning liquid. Hah! Several of those and he could handle anything! He shot a raised eyebrow and the slightest of grins to Aide Fleisher, who smiled, then looked shyly down at the floor.

Looking back to the audience, Gregor spied a man near the back of the stepped bank of seats who was raising his hand.

"Yes, sir?"

"Ashley Littlejohn from the *Smithsonian*, Colonel. We are filming this entire presentation, and for the sake of history and posterity and all that sort of thing . . . would you mind summarizing the events which have led up to this point in the whole *Dragonstar* affair?"

A collective groan rose up from the body of the crowd as Gregor held up his hands for silence. "What? You mean all the events? From the very beginning?"

Mr. Littlejohn scowled at the crowd, then nodded. "Yes, I'm afraid so. . . ."

Actually Gregor did not mind this request as much as one might expect. Summarizing the events leading up to this point would at least give him a chance to "warm up" to the audience, to relax, and to allow the vodka time to do its job.

"Very well," he said after a decently dramatic pause. "But I promise you: I will be very brief."

Mr. Littlejohn nodded perfunctorily and sat down. There was a low murmur running through the assemblage, which faded away as Gregor began speaking.

"Seven months ago, the Lunar Observatory on Copernicus Base discovered an alien artifact which became known as the *Dragonstar*. The artifact was an immense cylindrical ship, more than three hundred twenty kilometers in length and sixty-five kilometers in diameter. The cylinder rotated on its longitudinal axis once every three hundred sixty seconds. It was moving in a highly stable cometary orbit with a period of two hundred ten years.

"First visual intercept was made by a survey/prospecting vessel just as it entered the asteroid belt. A boarding party from the IASA *Heinlein* successfully entered the alien vessel, and discovered the enclosed Mesozoic ecology lining the interior of the cylinder. Lakes, rivers, mountains, plateaus, and valleys perfectly re-created—an exact duplicate of the Earth more than one hundred sixty million years ago. However, the boarding party was not very prepared to deal with the carnivorous dinosaurs which soon attacked them, and only Rebecca Thalberg and Ian Coopersmith survived."

Gregor paused for a short sip from his glass. The vodka blazed a new path of confidence through his chest as he continued:

"A second, specially equipped expedition soon arrived on board the *Dragonstar* and established a permanent base of operations. Colonel Phineas Kemp headed up the team which intended to attach outrigger impulse engines to the alien vessel, break it free from its comet-like orbit, and ferry it back to the Earth-Moon system where it could be placed in a stable Lagrange Point orbit. While this operation was being completed, Kemp organized a search party through the Mesozoic Preserve to find Thalberg and Coopersmith.

"Meanwhile, these same two survivors trekked across the hostile terrain until they discovered the equivalent of the Great Wall of China ringing the interior of the cylinder, effectively isolating the last forty klicks of environment before it abutted against the flat end of the enclosure. Beyond this artificially constructed barrier lay the civilization of a species dubbed the Saurians by Coopersmith and Thalberg. The creatures were a species of bipedal dinosaurs which evolved to intelligence during the last fifty million years within the sealed universe of the ship. The Saurian technology was based partly on biological as well as mechanical innovations, and operated roughly on a level equivalent to eighteenth-century Earth.

"While Thalberg and Coopersmith established contact with the Saurians, Colonel Kemp and his crew succeeded in bringing the *Dragonstar* back to the Earth-Moon system. After defeating an attempted hijacking of the alien ship by terrorists of the Third World Confederation, the IASA expedition rescued Thalberg and Coopersmith and began the long project of unraveling the mysteries of the *Dragonstar*."

Gregor risked several additional fingers of vodka before pressing onward:

"Several uneventful months passed in which a large team of scientists established permanent installations within the alien ship. Finally succumbing to combined pressure from the media and various world governments, the IASA agreed to open up the *Dragonstar*'s doors, so to speak, by producing an epic documentary to be broadcast on a worldwide basis. While the production was being prepared, scientists began detecting changes in the radiation levels on the ship. The radiation caused cancer-like mutations in some of the Mesozoic fauna and began to affect the mental stability of the Saurians, too.

"Despite warnings from various members of the scientific community on board the *Dragonstar* that something might be wrong, the decision was made by Colonel Kemp to go ahead with the scheduled broadcast of the documentary. And it was during the final live segment that the current disaster occurred—the massive riot of the Saurian population, and the slaughter of hundreds of Saurians and humans while the holo-cams rolled. Several small groups of human survivors managed to escape from the radiation-maddened Saurians and await rescue from Copernicus Base.

"There was only one problem—the one for which you have all gathered here today. When the IASA dispatched rescue teams aboard shuttle craft, they found that they could no longer gain access to the *Dragonstar*. The last messages we received from Colonel Kemp and his people on the inside reported that the alien ship seemed to be 'coming to life,' turning itself on, and operating on its own. All outside hatches were sealed and all communications frequencies from the interior were either jammed or in some other way blanketed."

Gregor paused and looked at the clear liquid in the flask. His head was beginning to feel a bit light, and his tongue felt loose and limber. The temptation to take another drink passed over him, but he knew he had reached his limit. What the hell, he thought, he was almost finished, anyway. Drawing in a breath, then exhaling with an almost audible sigh, he wrapped it up:

"Soon after that, we observed an aura, a kind of force-field, begin to form around the exterior of the *Dragonstar*. Unable to identify the nature of the field, but fearing for the safety of our people on board, we sent several rescue ships out to forcibly board and enter the vessel. And, as you know, they were disintegrated by flare-like extensions from the field. And then it was not long after that before the on-board engines of the *Dragonstar* ignited.

"The ship accelerated away from the Lagrange Point at a constantly increasing velocity, leaving the ecliptic plane of the solar system. We continued to track the vessel as it accelerated until it achieved a speed of more than three hundred kilometers per second. After that, there was a brilliant flash of light, and then nothing. . . ."

Gregor paused, and the audience took their cue, exploding into a shattering wave of questions and comments. He had already carried the summation past the point of what most of them already knew. That last bit about the flash of light and then nothing had not yet been released. Looking out at them, Gregor could see hands waving frantically like a sea of wheat in a strong breeze.

"Please, everyone!" he boomed through the P.A. "We must do this in a more orderly fashion!"

The frantic atmosphere seemed to calm a bit, then surged again. Gregor pounded on the podium console, and the pickups resonated the sound through the hall like thunder. Things started to calm down in a hurry as he grabbed their attention.

"Yes," he said, pointing to a woman in the second row, who had held her hand up with dignity and an absence of body English. Gregor hoped that others would take the cue.

The woman stood up. "Michele Jordan, NBC. When you say 'and then nothing,' what exactly do you mean? Did the *Dragonstar* explode?"

"I am afraid I cannot answer that question. Visually the ship appeared to simply vanish in a flash of rainbow-colored light. It *looked* like an explosion, because of the brilliant flash, but our instruments do not confirm this."

A man in the middle tier raised his hand and Gregor nodded at him. The rest of the assemblage remained orderly and respectful. This was more like it, thought Gregor.

"Gary Leventhal, CNN. What do you mean by that last line? What *do* your instruments confirm, if anything?"

"Well, an explosion has a particular 'signature,' if you will, which is well identified in terms of electromagnetic patterns. The final images of the *Dragonstar* do not fit this pattern. In fact, if anything, our scientists feel that we have witnessed an *implosion*."

A distinguished-looking gentleman with silvery grey hair raised his hand and was acknowledged. "Al Tyler, BBC. What the bloody hell does *that* mean? Did the *Dragonstar* collapse *in* upon itself?"

"We do not think so," said Gregor. "From the initial analysis of our data, it appears that the *space* surrounding the vessel did the collapsing. Let me explain. You see, what we are talking about is all highly theoretical, but the observable evidence suggests that the *Dragonstar* entered that region of reality which has been referred to by various names—hyperspace, null-space, tau-space, or whatever. In other words, the vessel made the jump into the realm of faster-than-light travel, and the brilliant flash we saw was the impact of normal space rushing in to occupy the . . . uh . . . 'gap,' shall we say, left by the starship when it jumped."

Countless hands shot up now, and Gregor pointed to one at random. "Cho Su, Chinese Sat-Net. How can this be so? Did not all earlier studies conclude that the engines of the *Dragonstar* were inoperable?"

"Yes, that is true," said Gregor. "But I think it is safe to say that such findings reached the *wrong* conclusion."

A burst of tension-breaking laughter filled the room. Gregor waited till it subsided before speaking again.

"Prior to the sudden on-board activity, our technical people had no indication that the engines could be fired. Having never seen a star-drive, our scientists did not know what to look for. In fact, we still have no conclusive proof that an FTL jump was accomplished. The *Dragonstar* may have been indeed destroyed in some kind of strange implosion. Please be warned that I am speaking hypothetically about all of this ... we simply *do not know* what actually happened."

Gregor pointed to a familiar face in the first row.

"Wallace Michaels, ABC. If the ship *did*, as you suggest, enter hyperspace, do we have any means of tracking it or communicating with it?"

"None whatsoever. . . ."

"Do we have any idea where it was headed?"

Gregor smiled. "Well, it was pointed toward the center of our galaxy, but this could be meaningless when applied to the 'Wu Li physics' of FTL theory. In hyperspace, direction, as we currently understand it, may have little or no meaning."

Buoyed by the vodka, Gregor Kolenkhov fielded their questions with a boundless energy and solid professionalism. The group asked some very intelligent questions in addition to the inevitable silly ones. And they kept it up for almost another two hours. When it was over he felt like an old dishrag squeezed dry. But overall, he believed that he had not alienated the media and had not given them any reason to believe that IASA was holding back any information. Granted, he had painted the picture a bit more cheerfully than his staff felt the situation indicated, but Gregor saw nothing wrong in giving the public the impression that there was probably more than a fifty-fifty chance that the occupants of the *Dragonstar* were still alive.

"Good show, Gregor," said Rheinhardt as they left the assembly hall and walked quickly back to the Joint Chiefs conference room.

"I thank you. Although I must give credit where credit is due!" he said, holding up the empty flask and winking at his young aide, Fleisher. "As much as I love those wonderful California wines, they do not give a man the fortitude of a good slam of vodka!"

Rheinhardt laughed and slapped his shoulder. Marcia Bertholde's expression remained grim. Gregor had always thought the
woman was a pain in the ass. A real anal-retentive personality.
Ever since this business with the *Dragonstar* began, at the first
appearance of each new complication, Marcia Bertholde played
her cards closer and closer to her vest. She would only speak to
voice alarm, to push an ultraconservative action, or to express
displeasure at any attempt to break the mounting tension. Gregor
found her to be about as warm as your average lizard.

Aide Fleisher opened the door to the conference room and
everyone entered. There were two lab-coated people already
seated at the table. The man was lean and good-looking in an Ivy
League sort of way. His face was smooth and unlined, and only
his penetrating eyes belied his age of around forty. The woman
had the body of an athlete, lithe and graceful. Her dirty-blond
hair had been tied back in a pony tail. It was a purely functional
style, but it made her look young and coltish to Gregor.

He recognized both of them. Dr. Bill Baker was Chief Engineer at Copernicus Base and Victoria Wendt was a physicist who
had been serving as liaison for Dr. Takamura, who was now
among the missing on board the departed *Dragonstar*. Baker and
Wendt stood up as the Joint Chiefs entered, and Gregor waved
them back into their seats.

"Good afternoon, Doctors," he said. "More bad news, no
doubt . . . ?"

Baker shrugged, tugged at the cuff of his white coat. "That
depends on whether we're right or not," he said in a deep son-
orous voice.

"I've been collecting the data-trans from the *Dragonstar* for
Dr. Takamura since the beginning," said Dr. Wendt. "Along with
the last few reports concerning the radiation levels, his initial
work had been on the structural integrity of the vessel and the
radical engineering design employed in the alien ship's design."

Gregor nodded, looked to his colleagues, and then gestured
for the scientists to continue.

"For the last month or so, Vickie's people have been running a
lot of 'what if' games with the data we've been getting," said Dr.
Baker. "Lots of standard, Hudson Institute stuff . . . and we came
up with one model which might bear some attention."

"Go on," said Rheinhardt.

Victoria Wendt produced a decahedron crystal from the pocket
of her lab coat and carefully inserted it into the holographic pro-

jector sitting in the center of the table. "Here, let me show you," she said as she flipped on the machine.

The room darkened and a 3-D image of the interior of the alien control-section of the *Dragonstar* appeared to float over the conference table.

"This is a typical bulkhead running longitudinally along the outer hull," said Wendt. "Note the cross-hatching patterns which seem to be a central alien engineering signature. At any rate, the stress tests we performed on the hull sections indicate that the immense age of the metals and bonds used in the ship has severely limited its intended functionality."

"In plain language, what are you saying?" asked Bertholde.

Dr. Baker cleared his throat. "The *Dragonstar* is not as structurally sound, not as *strong*, as it originally had been. As with all things, time has taken its toll."

"Of course," said Dr. Wendt. "This routine test was not thought to be significant or important because the vessel was in a permanent orbit, and there were no plans to subject it to the undue stress of extended space flight."

"What are you trying to tell us?" asked Gregor, although he suspected that he already understood.

"If what we witnessed was indeed a jump into hyperspace," said Dr. Baker, "then the *Dragonstar* might not be strong enough to withstand the kind of tidal forces we expect to be present in a jump to FTL speed."

"Not strong enough?" asked Gregor. "What do you mean? What would happen?"

Baker shrugged again. "This is all theoretical, you understand . . . but the forces implied in such a maneuver could possibly crush the hull of the *Dragonstar* like an egg."

CHAPTER 2

THEIR NAMES WERE NORMAL ENOUGH.

Alexandra Marshall.

Timothy Linden.

Two solid American citizens, who had excelled in their respective colleges—UCLA and Yale—they joined the IASA in scientific capacities, and excelled, serving their country Earthside and in space. They seemed absolute studies in American physical and mental values: she of the blond hair and blue eyes, with a computer-sharp mind that danced amid the tricky planes of astrophysics, he of the brown hair and dark brown eyes, with an IQ and test scores off the map, and a love of baseball, with a degree in xenobiology.

It was natural that the IASA should assign them to duties aboard the vessel known officially as *Artifact One*. They seemed tailor-made for such duties, and in fact their work had been absolutely sterling aboard the already fabled *Dragonstar*, that 200-million-year-old alien vessel, complete with its bizarre complement of a Mesozoic interior and array of dinosaurs. The IASA was modern enough not to mind that they seemed to have a sexual and emotional relationship: this seemed natural. These were good-looking, healthy adults, with adult needs and attractions. Certainly their relationship did not seem to interfere with their work. Perhaps it even helped it. What was the harm?

However, if all had continued as planned, their work would indeed have harmed the IASA.

For they were sleeper agents of the Third World Confederation, studying the likelihood of another hijacking, a takeover of the *Dragonstar*.

But, the *Dragonstar* had other ideas, apparently. It had taken off—into hyperspace—long before it could be taken over.

15

It had taken off with the fresh-scrubbed "American" sleepers Marshall and Linden aboard, leaving them with no way to contact their superiors.

Still, they had their orders, and they had original minds and could easily improvise. Which was just what they were doing as they drove out from their base camp, dispatched by Dr. Robert Jakes himself to investigate a source of intermittent radiation that had been popping up on the base screens.

"It is fortunate," said Marshall, her long blond hair blowing, "that we were able to dissuade them from sticking another guy aboard."

"Fortunate I could let them talk me into letting me take you along," said Timothy Linden as he downshifted the omni terrain vehicle to deal with a steeper grade. "Glad you've got that good marksman record."

"Well, if there was still the problem with the 'natives,' I think they'd have wanted another gun along." The "natives" that Alexandra was referring to were the dinosaurs. Somehow they had been changing lately, often with murderous results. The scientists aboard conjectured that they were affected by the radiation the *Dragonstar* was giving off in certain places after the arrival of human beings. But in the last few weeks the reports of aberrant behavior in the beasts had lowered. Certainly the predators were just as nasty as ever—but the others seemed to have settled down after the abrupt insertion of the *Dragonstar* into hyperspace—

—even if the radiation had not.

"With my smooth tongue? Never." Linden turned the vehicle slightly to avoid a ginkgo tree that had grown apart from the forest. "We have to talk, Alexandra," he said. "I have been having serious doubts."

"Yes, I know what you mean," she said, peering about at this primeval world. "The training certainly never prepared us for anything like this. Loyalties to factions on Earth seem to fade, so many light-years away, with dim likelihood of returning."

"And yet, we must remain faithful, to our religion and to our calling. The opportunities are not present now, but if they should arise . . . we must pounce."

"Yes, that is quite correct." She shook her head dismally. "Should we ever return to our solar system, that is."

"Our mission keeps us alive, I think," said Timothy Linden. "And our love . . . We are not as the others. . . ."

"I'm not sure about that, Timothy. We are, after all, in the same boat together . . . so to speak." She smiled and stroked his shoulder. "A threat to them is a threat to us . . . like this radiation we are investigating."

"I don't think it's a threat, but it is well that we are checking into it. Dr. Jakes believes that these radiation outbursts could be the key to understanding what makes the *Dragonstar* tick. We must learn as much as we can . . . for our survival, and most important, for our mission."

They had both been planted into college with fake backgrounds. Both had been born in the United States and grew into the culture and language. . . . But both had parents who were fanatical Muslims. During pilgrimages to Mecca, the Jiha—the state-of-the-art terrorist organization run by the TWC—had seen their potential and convinced their parents that their formative years should be spent in the Mideast, receiving vital training and indoctrination. It was all much in the tradition that the notorious KGB had established in the twentieth century. The result: almost foolproof sleeper agents, with airtight backgrounds. They had not been activated until the business with the *Dragonstar*. And their masters could never have known what was going to happen with that vessel they so desired. Of course, despite the failure of the expert terrorist Marcus Jashad to secure the alien ship—a failure he paid for with his life—doubtless the TWC were having the last laugh now. For it was they, not the IASA, who would have been trapped aboard the ship when it clamped up tight and dived like some space whale into hyperspace. And the TWC knew, after all, that if there was any hope that anything could be done on their behalf, then their agents Alexandra Marshall and Timothy Linden could be counted on to act in their interests.

The day was hazy with tropical humidity, even though Linden kept the open OTV away from the jungle areas. He knew that he could be stuck in this hell for a very long time—and he knew that he would never get totally used to the oppressive heat, pulsing down from the Illuminator rod . . . the shaft that bisected the interior of the *Dragonstar* and created an Earth-like day/night cycle, switching on at "dawn" and dimming at "dusk." Even now, with the breeze created by the OTV's speed, he sweated. It was not at all like this in the desert. The heat there was dry and omnipotent, like the presence of Allah, and the body adjusted to it. No, here was a great deal like hell.

"That juncture of hills up there," said Alexandra while she consulted the screens on the dashboard in front of her. "The overlay map is picking up the type of radiation we've been reading. From behind those rocks, Tim."

"Excellent," said her partner, adjusting the direction of the OTV accordingly. "I must admit, this does intrigue me. The spectrum readings on this radiation have been quite interesting."

"Do you think that this is the sort of radiation that's been escaping and affecting the beasts?" asked Alexandra.

"That's what Jakes thinks. See any strange-looking creatures about, my love?"

"Absolutely nothing," she said, after a survey of the area with her field glasses. "Which *is* odd."

"Could be smart—could be avoiding this radiation. Maybe we'd better get the life-support suits."

"I don't see anything on the screens that would warrant that," said Alexandra. "Nothing the suits would keep out, anyway."

"Oh, that's nice to know!"

"Hey, cheer up. Those things can be hot!"

"So, my dear, can be radiation!" They were approaching the rocks. "Looks to me like the terrain up there is going to be too rough for the OTV."

"Which means we walk?"

"Which means we walk."

He stopped the vehicle and got out his rifle. He wore a portable analyzer, which by now was going crazy with blinking arrows and numbers.

"I kinda think that old Jakes is going to like what this thing is recording," she said.

"Should I radio back and tell him to get out here?" Linden asked, checking his weapons.

She laughed. "Oh no. There may be things we find that we may want to keep to ourselves."

"Funny, you don't look like an A-rab spy," said Linden, affecting a southern twang.

"Funny, you don't, either," responded Marshall. "And you TWC people ain't supposed to have a sense of humor, either!"

Alexandra Linden shrugged. "Allah chuckles from time to time, I suppose."

"If Allah truly exists, I suppose indeed he does."

"Oh, come off those stupid doubts of yours!" she said, suddenly harsh. "You really can't afford them, Timothy."

"I don't know. I suppose it was a perverse luxury back a couple of years ago . . . enjoying the luxury and life-style of the

West, while nurturing a big secret in your heart. But after getting called up—" He gestured expansively at his surroundings. "And certainly after all this—one begins to wonder."

"Too true. But there are too many oaths, too many duties and obligations . . . too much inside us that is of the Old Lands to allow doubts to have any effect. Who is to say, my Hasan"— which was her secret name for him—"we may have truly been swallowed by a djinn, and we walk in some desert mirage. . . . This perhaps is some test of our faith!"

Linden looked at her skeptically. "Stow it, daughter of the desert. We do what we do because we've been trained to. I don't need to hear the damned theology."

She shrugged, her face all business again. "All right. Now, I think that if we take that pathway up there, we can get to the source of these readings."

"Okay. I'll go first."

They threaded through a couple boulders, then found the narrow stony pathway that Marshall had indicated.

"I figure only about fifty meters," she said, looking up from her board.

"Yeah, but with this kind of zigzag path, it will take a little while."

Which it did.

Nor was it truly a pathway. They found themselves often having to climb and crawl over considerable obstacles, from rocks to boulders.

"I hope that Jakes is damned grateful," said Linden, sweat dripping down his face. "This is work!"

"And let's hope the TWC is grateful!"

"I didn't know they *got* grateful."

"If we ever get back, we'll get our reward, I'm sure."

"I'll just settle for staying alive right now, thank you."

Finally the pathway opened up into a large clearing, perhaps forty meters in diameter. Marshall's readings indicated that the radiation emanated from the other side. But what lay between them and it was of much more obvious interest.

It seemed, at first sight, to be an allosaurus, stretched out on its side. It appeared also to be dead. But no scavengers were present, feasting on its flesh . . . and upon further inspection, it proved to be still breathing, its thick sides rising and falling regularly.

"Be careful," said Linden, holding up a warning hand after

clicking off the safety of his rifle. "What do you make of it? Think this radiation has affected it?"

"Nothing indicates the radiation is harmful. . . ."

"Doesn't have to be harmful to affect something . . . Damn! Do you see that?"

The allosaurus spasmed a little, twitching as it rolled over, revealing its true nature.

It was an allosaurus, all right . . . both Marshall and Linden had seen them before.

But it was an allosaurus with two heads.

Two heads, to say nothing of the extra limb that grew from its side, and the rudimentary tail that sprouted midway from its original tail.

"Some kind of freak?" wondered Linden.

"I don't know," said Marshall. "But whatever it is, I'm getting a picture of it." She pulled out her special Leica for a shot. "Mikaela Lindstrom will certainly want to see this!" The device clicked twice. Alexandra Marshall adjusted it, and then moved closer to get better shots of the creature's extreme abnormalities.

"Alexandra, you don't have to get too close."

"Don't worry," she said. "I'll be careful. Fascinating, isn't it? Like something in a horror movie!"

"This whole month has been like something in a horror movie," said Linden. "Okay, that's close enough. We're going to have to skirt the thing to check out the radiation. . . . I don't like it being here. Maybe we can just get the necessary readings—"

The thing moved with lightning speed.

In less than a second, it had thrashed its way onto its feet. The heads moved in amazing synchrony, swiveling around, both sets of eyes leveling fiercely upon the exploration team. Those eyes were pure red, pupilless, seeming to flare like a double set of glimpses into hell.

"Get back, Alex!" Linden cried as he jerked his rifle up to eye level, aiming.

But his companion seemed frozen in her tracks.

Linden pumped a round into the beast's chest. Flesh and blood spurted, but it only seemed to madden the monster. It lunged forward, straight for Alexandra.

Linden fired again, wildly, running at an opposite angle in hopes of distracting the allosaur, but his shot missed.

However, the explosion did bring Alexandra to her senses. Her training had her gun in her hand instantly, and she fired two blasts into the dinosaur before trying to run away from the thing.

But it was too late.

The allosaur took an incredible leap into the air. It landed just meters from her, and dipped down with one of its heads, even as another rifle shot from Linden slammed into its larger tail.

Alexandra screamed as she saw the thing's jaws close down on her.

There was a loud snap as teeth crushed bones and human blood gushed from the allosaur's mouth.

"No!" cried Timothy Linden.

He fired the last of his ammo into the beast's neck, still in shock over what he'd witnessed. The death of his lover . . . the end of his companion . . . It was too much to take.

The allosaur jerked about with his new sting of pain, and its pair of heads seemed to have a single mind. A severed arm and a hank of blond hair hung from one set of jaws; the other set snapped in Linden's direction.

He threw down his rifle and pulled out his handgun. The allosaur was already advancing as he fired at one of the beast's heads, but only grazed the skull.

The allosaur charged on toward him.

Desperately Timothy Linden ran for the cover of the rocks. On fire with adrenaline, he did not even think this was where the radiation emanated. He became a soldier, retreating for survival.

The rocks formed a crevice and instinctively Linden ran for this cover. The allosaur snarled as it bore down upon him. Linden took a moment to fire into one of its eyes, rupturing it. The allosaur roared with pain, halting for a moment and digging with a claw as though to pluck the bullet from its extra head.

Linden seized the opportunity to retreat farther into the crevice, into the shadows, back-first, watching the great wounded beast that wished to kill him. Blood trickled from the ruined eye as the allosaur jumped after him, just able to squeeze its large body into the crevice.

Again, Linden fired into the wounded head, and didn't wait to see what damage he'd done. He moved back farther into the dimness, sensing an emptiness.

The cry of the allosaur echoed into the darkness behind him.

A cave!

It was some sort of small cave—protection enough, surely, from this abberation. Linden ducked into the small opening, moved back into darkness, away from the allosaur.

The creature knew he was there, no doubt about that. It could smell him still. But there was no way now it could get at him. All to the good . . . at least for the time being.

Linden leaned against a cool wall and rested, letting the reality of his situation sink in. The place was curiously dry for a cave, and Linden sensed it went farther back, which meant there might be another exit. He could wait here for a while—he knew that the beast wouldn't linger long at the entrance—or he could try another way out.

The former method seemed the safest. But then, as he sat there, his grief for Alexandra began to build to a point past bearing. No, he thought. Better to keep moving.

Besides, this cave virtually invited exploration—and he was here, after all, to discover the source of the radiation. Too bad he didn't have the necessary gear . . . but he did have a small flashlight on his belt.

He unclipped it and turned it on.

The small cone of light played over moistly gleaming rock, over stalactites and stalagmites in the distance, over a narrow path that dived down into further darkness like a gullet into the ground.

The pained roar which echoed through the narrow cave reminded him that a pair of gullets waited for him outside.

He decided to use this opportunity to explore.

After checking to make sure all of him was in order and he didn't have any wounds he was unaware of, he did just that, cautiously moving down the steady incline. He was quite aware there might be other creatures down here—but this was far better than sitting and listening to the growls of the thing that had killed Alexandra, wrapped up in his grief and fear. Besides, he was here to explore, to discover the nature of the radiation. He didn't have the equipment, but he did have his own superior observational abilities and intelligence. That would do for now.

That beast, thought Linden as he carefully navigated his way down the incline. That beast was quite remarkable. They'd seen nothing like it. . . . Was it an older mutation . . . was it *born* that way? Or was it like the others—had it been a normal allosaurus affected by the changes in the *Dragonstar*'s interior so that it grew new limbs, grew that extra head? God knew that *something* was going on . . . something, for example, that had rendered a whole portion of the saurian populace into bloodthirsty savages who had killed and eaten that science fiction writer.

If he could be the one to discover this secret of the *Dragonstar* . . . If he alone knew what was going on in the depths of the machinery that ringed this cylindrical ancient world, then that secret might help him get back to Earth. And that secret might be used for the benefit of the Third World Confederation.

All these thoughts buzzed in his head as he descended, working hard to keep from thinking about Alexandra in those awful jaws.

Then, below him, he heard a buzzing sound.

It was more a subliminal bass hum than a buzz, actually . . . and Linden could feel it in his feet, beginning to travel up his legs like an attenuated shiver.

Oh yes . . . by God, there was something down here. . . .

It gave him a spooky feeling . . . a feeling of the numinous. If he left everything up to his natural instincts, he knew he would turn tail, go back up to the mouth of this tunnel, and just wait until the two-headed allosaur was gone. But Timothy Linden had above all a strong training and a strong sense of duty . . . to say nothing of his natural scientific curiosity.

So after only a short pause to strengthen his resolve, he continued downward.

The walls at this point began to widen, and the stalagmites and stalactites on the floors and the ceilings began to disappear, creating more the resemblance of an esophagus.

And then, Linden no longer needed his small flashlight.

Faintly at first, and then more strongly as he descended, the walls began to glow.

He switched off his light as the tunnel angled abruptly and he walked into greater luminescence.

He realized then that the tunnel was no longer of rock.

It was of metal. A dull grey metal that at first could easily be mistaken for stone, but metal nonetheless. The light emanated from strips in the walls and it shone softly, perhaps even gloomily.

This continued on for some meters. Then, up ahead, it steepily angled down. Linden progressed cautiously, unable to make out what lay ahead because of all the angling and uniformity.

Then suddenly the floor slipped from underneath him. With a yelp, he fell and began to slide down an abruptly steeper angle, feet-first.

It seemed as if he slid for only a short time, but he wasn't sure, he was so involved in trying to stop himself.

The chute dumped him all asprawl in a small round chamber.

It was the end of the tunnel. There seemed to be no other way out. The walls around him were curved and shiny, almost of a translucent glassy nature now.

He stood, and just as he began to despair from the thought of dying down here of thirst and hunger, unable to clamber back up that chute, the walls began to change.

And then Timothy Linden began to scream.

CHAPTER 3

LOOKING OFF TO HIS LEFT, Mishima Takamura took a moment to appreciate the way the terrain of the Mesozoic Preserve in the distance faded away, misting into muted, pastel colors. Like the work of a Kyoto artist, nutshell-browns and minted greens dappled with watercolor oranges and greys. But instead of ending at the horizon, it surged upward, curving in upon itself and rising skyward until it hung suspended over his head, sixty-five klicks distant.

Inside the closed world of the *Dragonstar*, there was no such thing as a horizon.

Like time in a bottle, a piece of the Earth's history had been locked away within the immense cylindrical vessel. Mishima looked out upon a perfect reproduction of the Mesozoic Era.

Takamura maneuvered a four-man omni terrain vehicle down a rocky hillside toward an artificially created stream. Seated in the back seat was a muscular black man—James Barkham, an IASA small-craft pilot, who held an HK-99 heavy assault rifle at the ready, scanning the nearby foliage for any unwelcome predators. In the front passenger seat sat Rebecca Thalberg, monitoring readouts on a portable scanning device.

Becky was the most attractive biomedical specialist Mishima had ever seen. Long, curly hair, shining blue-black like a raven's hood, and naturally thick lashes accenting her dark almond-eyes. Smiles came easily to her full lips, and her wit gleamed sharp and bright. Mishima found her totally captivating, and he wished that she would eventually notice how he felt.

Sure, it looked like he might be able to have something going with Kate Ennis, the holo-journalist from NBC, but there was something about Becky Thalberg which made her special. Mishima couldn't pin it down, but it might have been her mental *toughness*, her ability to survive under some of the worst conditions any of them had so far endured. Not that she was not a gentle person, though. Rather, Becky possessed a will, a *spirit*, that was seemingly unbreakable. Whatever the world wanted to throw at her, she always appeared ready to catch it and throw it back with equal force. Mishima liked that quality in people, and when combined with a woman so sensuously attractive, it made Becky irresistible.

"Something up ahead," she said, not looking up from the screen of the scanner.

"Animal, vegetable, or mineral?" asked Barkham. He wiped some sweat from his shining black forehead with his sleeve.

"Animal. Looks like a carnivore from the size of it. Moving pretty fast, too. Coming this way."

"You want to put up the dome?" asked Mishima. He had cleared the rocky slope and was moving along an alluvial plain toward a crisply running stream. The plan had been to follow it toward its source in the hull, or at least discover how its fluid dynamics had been constructed.

"No, not yet," said Barkham. "We're out in the open, so it can't surprise us. Where is he now, Becky?"

"Starboard side, less than a hundred meters into those trees. He's slowing up. Maybe he's picked up our scent and he's trying to recognize it."

Mishima slowed the OTV and peered into the copse of cycads and ginkgoes off to the right. He had very little experience roaming about in the Mesozoic Preserve, and he had a great fear of the carnosaurs. Riding about with the protective dome up seemed foolish to him. He wondered if Barkham was like a lot of guys who only wanted a chance to pull off the macho deal of bagging a dinosaur. The idea of killing living creatures just for "sport" or, worse, to prove one's self-worth, was abhorrent to Mishima. If there was a predator out there, he would just as soon have the dome up.

"Looks like he's veering off a bit," said Becky. "Still coming this way, but up ahead of us."

Just then, there was a burst of color and sound breaking free of the lush greens of the forest to the right. Looking that way, Mishima watched a yellow-and-brown-speckled gorgosaurus wade into the clearing. Its snout was smeared with the dark red crust of drying blood, and it had apparently just finished feeding. Less than four meters tall, the dinosaur was hunched over, its head thrust forward while it balanced powerful hind legs by keeping its thick tail rigid and parallel to the ground. Mishima stopped the OTV and watched the beast hop-skip past them, less than thirty meters distant, and hunker down by the stream bank.

Plunging its snout into the water, it slurped water noisily and scrubbed at its blood-crusty jaws with its small foreclaws. It ignored completely the humans who watched warily.

"Just washing up after a meal," said Becky. "I's mom taught it well, I guess."

"Just keep an eye on it, anyway," said Barkham.

"God, that thing's hideous!" Mishima couldn't help feeling the fear and revulsion well up in him.

Becky grinned. "Oh, they're not so bad once you get used to them. Dr. Lindstrom says they're fairly predictable."

"Right," said Barkham. "Eat. Sleep. Eat. Sleep. That's pretty easy to predict, don't you think?"

Becky giggled softly. "Oh, there's more to them than that, Jim. . . ."

The gorgosaur finished his drinking and washing routine, and pushed away from the bank still hunched over. It looked awkward leaning on its foreclaws as it lashed out with its heavy tail, using it as a counterweight. The practiced movement seesawed the creature's head upward, and it attained its normal bipedal stance. The entire maneuver had occurred in an eye-blink. Mishima found the carnosaurs to be surprisingly agile, and as he stared at the gorgosaurus, he could not keep from thinking of what it would be like to be snapped up in its terrible jaws. . . .

The dinosaur stood upright now, tilting its head so that it could view the OTV more squarely. Its tongue slithered in and out as though tasting the scented air.

"Watch it now," said Mishima.

"I got him covered," said Barkham, apparently in no great hurry to rip the beast's hide with a banana clip of slugs.

"If he's just finished eating, we don't have anything to worry about," said Becky. "The only thing he probably wants right now is a place where he can flop down and go to sleep."

"You're sure about that?" Mishima had pulled the OTV to a full stop. It was probably a good idea to wait until the meat-eater made his next move.

"Don't forget that Ian and I spent a couple of weeks running away from these boys," said Becky. "We learned a few things that kept us alive."

"You know . . . every time I think about what you've been through, I am amazed," said Mishima.

"I can dig it," said Barkham. "I was only out here a coupla *days*, and I was freaked by it. You're one tough cookie, Dr. Thalberg."

Just then the gorgosaur turned his head away from the OTV, apparently not finding it very intriguing. Taking ponderously slow steps, it ambled away from the river and plopped down under a shady stand of cycads within twenty meters of the stream bank. The beast rolled over on its back and leaned against the base of the largest tree trunk. Its hooded eyes closed to slits and it was quickly torpid.

"That's great," said Mishima. "He has to pick that particular spot! I wanted to follow the stream right up that way. . . ."

"We can get past him," said Becky. "He's going to be out for a while—getting in some serious digestion."

Mishima looked at the dinosaur warily. It looked like a miniature tyrannosaurus, a very dangerous-looking creature. To roll the OTV so closely past its sleeping hulk seemed crazy, foolhardy. If it awakened, it could easily pounce on the vehicle before Mishima could escape. The thing's head seemed to be more than half jaws and teeth. Just looking at it made chills race up Mishima's spine.

"I'll keep it right in my sights, man," said Barkham. "If it makes the slightest move, it's done for. . . ."

"Let's go, Dr. Takamura," said Becky. "It'll be okay."

Mishima swallowed with some difficulty and keyed in the OTV's forward engines. The low-mass turbines whined and the vehicle surged forward across the flat terrain. As they drew even with the torpid beast, its left eyelid fluttered and its nostrils flared instinctively, but it did not move. Mishima keyed in the highest velocity available and the OTV zipped away from the gorgosaurus. As they moved off he felt the twisted fist in his gut begin to relax.

"Okay," said Becky. "We're clear. . . . Just keep an eye out for anything else."

"Yeah," said Barkham as he wiped his high forehead again. "This water probably draws all kinds of things down for a drink."

"We have to follow the stream," said Mishima. "The scanners indicate that the water is forced through bulkheads between the inner and outer hulls. There *must* be pumps and reservoirs mak-

ing the water run. That means there has to be *access* to that
machinery."

"Don't bet on it," said Becky. "There's no real way to figure
on the logic of the aliens who built this ship. You should know
that, Doctor."

She was right, Mishima knew. But his strongest suit was probably his unquenchable optimism, and he had vowed that he
would never let the engineering mysteries of the *Dragonstar* defeat him.

"I'm not betting on anything, Rebecca," he said after a pause.
"I'm just playing out a hunch. After all, we don't have any alter-
natives."

"He's right," said Brakham. "There's no way we can break
through the temple hatches to the control-section."

"I just keep thinking that those hatches were sealed for a very
good reason," said Becky. "That maybe we shouldn't mess
around with something we don't know anything about."

"Of *course* they were sealed for a reason," said Mishima. "To
keep us out! And that tells me the alien intelligence which is
controlling this ship feels we might be able to alter its flight!
That's why they are trying to keep us out of there. And that's why
I want to get back *in*!"

"But we don't know anything about faster-than-light travel,"
said Becky.

"There are theories . . .," said Mishima. He glanced at her for
an instant, then back to the ever-changing landscape ahead. As
the stream wound its way through a marshy strip and shining mud
flats, he guided the OTV along its banks relentlessly.

"Theories? This ship isn't running on any of your theories!
Even if we *could* figure out where this ship is taking us, do you
really believe you could alter its course and navigate us back to
Earth?" Becky shook her head at the thought of such an improba-
ble outcome.

Mishima did not immediately reply, pretending to be studying
the proper course ahead. As much as he would have loathed to
admit it, Becky was on target. After several months of hands-on
study and tinkering inside the alien control-section, Takamura
and his team of engineers and physicists had been able to learn
very little about alien technology. Under the harsh light of rational thought, Mishima's plan of somehow sneaking back into the
control-section and jury-rigging the hyperspace navigational system with some chewing gum and bailing wire seemed pretty ab-

surd. Maybe Becky was right: perhaps Mishima was just bull-shitting himself. . . .

Then why was he pursuing his hunch, his Rocky-Jones-and-the-Rocket-Rangers plan, so doggedly? The question had occurred to him more than once, and he probably didn't want to answer it truthfully. But the motivation was actually quite simple —it gave him something to *do*!

The thought of being trapped inside the giant ship, hurtling through the absolute nothingness of tau-space, and *having no control*, was an especially scary one for Takamura. He had lived his life by keeping things orderly and *very* controlled, everything planned in advance, everything functioning within well-defined parameters.

That all went down the tubes when the *Dragonstar* sealed itself up and kidnapped everybody to hell-knows-where.

"What's that up ahead?" asked Barkham, pointing over Mishima's shoulder.

He had been driving in that semiconscious state where your eyes are seeing and your brain is responding but your *thoughts* are off in a faraway land. Barkham's voice brought him all back to the present situation and he looked up to see a large outcropping of rocks which seemed to jut straight up out of the earth. The stream flowed into the rocks through a dark aperture which took on the familiar configuration of a cave mouth as the OTV moved even closer to it.

"Looks like this might be something interesting," said Mishima. In front of the entrance to the cave, spread out across a sere plain to the right to the stream, milled a small herd of triceratopses. Several of the rhino-like beasts looked up from their grazing as the OTV rumbled into their territory. Two of the larger males started to lumber up for a closer look.

"Better put up the dome," said Becky. "They probably won't hurt us, but they're gong to sniff us out a little."

Mishima keyed in the smoked Plexiglas dome which eased up out of the body and sealed them inside the cabin. Mishima slowed the vehicle down until it matched the heavy gait of the closest ceratopsian, which was now abreast of the OTV and giving it a cursory once-over. Several times it tilted its bony, flanged head and nudged the side of the vehicle, more out of curiosity than hostility. All the same, Mishima felt uneasy with the armored dinosaur keeping pace with them as they closed in on the cave entrance.

"He probably thinks we're just an odd-looking cousin or something," said Barkham.

"They're not *that* stupid, are they?" asked Mishima.

"Hard to tell," said Becky. "I'm no expert, but the 'tops *do* seem to be of the dumber beasts in this place."

No one spoke as Mishima guided the vehicle slowly toward the stream bank and the cave mouth. When he stopped by water's edge, the two male triceraptopses circled them several times, snuffling and snorting a bit before losing interest.

"In a few seconds, they'll have forgotten all about us," said Becky.

"If you say so," said Mishima.

Becky smiled, pushed an errant strand of long dark hair away from her face. She wore a headband, but in the humid, tropical atmosphere, perspiration still runneled down her cheeks, giving her whole face a vibrant, healthy shine. She was one of those people who seemed to flourish in the hot, sticky climate, who managed to look good under any conditions.

No one spoke for another moment as they watched the two armored beasts trundle off to rejoin their herd. One of the males began snuffling about the hind legs of the closest cow and attempted to mount her several times without success.

Barkham chuckled. "Now, that guy's got the right idea," he said.

"Make love, not war, right?" asked Becky, joining in with a soft chuckle of her own. She glanced over at Mishima and smiled, and he felt a low-level electric shock course through him. This woman was causing one hell of an effect on him, that was for certain.

He cleared his throat and looked away with some difficulty, gesturing toward the moth of the cave. "You think it's safe to get out and check things out?"

"Yeah," said Barkham. "Looks okay to me. What about it, Dr. Thalberg?"

"Just keep those males in your sights until we reach the cave itself," she said. "If one of them charges us, it's going to take a couple of shots to bring him down."

Mishima nodded and retracted the dome.

"Let's wait a few seconds to see if our scent is going to disrupt them again," said Becky.

The larger of the two males continued to follow one of the cows about the grazing area. He had sex on his lemon-sized brain, and the smell of a few sweaty humans wasn't going to change things. The other male had commenced feeding and had his flanks turned away from the OTV. If they were going to move off toward the protection of the cave, this seemed like the best time to do it.

"C'mon," said Mishima. "Let's go!"

The trio gathered up their equipment and weapons and climbed down from the cab. Keeping the OTV between them and the herd, they moved to the edge of the stream and then quickly south toward the cave from which the water issued. Mishima manned a lightweight, portable holo-cam, which gave him a visual record of their explorations, and Becky carried the mini-scanner, which would accurately map and monitor their location as they moved along. Barkham kept his Heckler & Koch ready for anything.

As they silently approached the cave entrance, Mishima once again marveled at the utter *realism*, the perfect reconstruction of the environment which the builders of the *Dragonstar* had achieved. The bank to the stream, the flat rocks, the lazily churning water . . . everything not only looked "right," it simply *was* right. Unless you were to look off into the distance where the horizon should be, unless you took notice of the upward-curving inner hull, you would never imagine that everything was artifice, that it had been as carefully planned and built as a Japanese garden. He tried to imagine the kind of technology required to accomplish an engineering feat such as the *Dragonstar*, but it only made him feel foolish and insignificant.

His plan was madness. He was wasting his time, and needlessly risking the lives of his colleagues with this bone-headed expedition. They were like insects thrumming about the hold of a cargo freighter, secretly plotting to take over the bridge.

Fat chance, thought Mishima.

"Is there something wrong?" asked Becky as she touched his arm. The warm press of her fingers jacked him back to the present, and he realized that he had been woolgathering—standing at the cave entrance, staring off into space.

"No, Becky . . . sorry, I was just thinking of something, that's all. . . ."

"I'm getting some interesting readings on the beta band," she said.

"Like what?"

"Looks like there's another level beneath this one once we get inside the cave."

Mishima paused and looked back over the terrain they had recently covered. "Makes sense. Look—we've been gradually following a rise in the landscape. See how it slopes down behind us, real easy-like? There *should* be some space beneath us at this point and the outer hull."

"We goin' in?" asked Barkham.

"You bet we are," said Mishima, smiling, his excitement renewed in a sudden burst of enthusiasm. "You know, maybe my ideas are right, after all!"

As if in reply, one of the female triceratopses honked loudly as she was successfully mounted and entered. Everyone laughed at the near-perfect timing.

"Follow me," said Mishima, turning and edging along the bank of running water, leaning into the cave's shadowed entrance.

"Watch out for the nests," said Becky. "It's just occurred to me that this might make a perfect place for something small to want to keep its eggs protected."

"Somethin' small to us . . . or *them*?" asked Barkham.

"It's all relative," said Becky. "Just watch out, okay?"

Nodding, Mishima stepped into the shadows and allowed his eyes to adjust to the drop in light intensity. He was expecting to see the rocky path and walls of a cave, and was surprised to find that just beneath the surface the artifice had been abandoned so quickly.

Instead of rocks and dirt, he stood on a metallic slab leading off into the darkness. Above his head, the grey cantilevered struts and supports of the cave's interior held up the curved roof. It reminded him of a movie set on a studio's sound stage. Incredible. And yet, not to be unexpected. For a moment, everyone stood quietly, and he could hear the hum of machinery, punctuated by a softer thumping sound.

Barkham stepped up beside him, panning the barrel of his weapon back and forth. "Everything look okay?"

"Yes," said Mishima. "But let's get a little light on the subject before we go any farther."

Barkham unsnapped an electric torch from his utility belt and flicked it on. Adjusting the diameter of the beam, he directed its light on the expanse ahead of them.

"What's that?" asked Becky as the light touched the leading edge of some superstructure in the distance.

"Let's take a look," said Mishima.

As they walked slowly and carefully through the darkness of the artificial cave, their boots slapping loudly on the metallic flooring, Mishima could hear the sounds of machinery growing more distinct, rising in volume as they obviously drew closer to it.

"What's that, you think?" asked Barkham.

"Probably some kind of pumping system to keep this water flowing, to keep it recirculating."

"Yeah, you're probably right," said the pilot.

"Just be careful," said Becky. "You can't assume anything about this place. That's when you get your worse surprises."

"So I've heard," said Mishima. He again thought of how Becky had trekked through a big piece of the vessel's interior forests and jungle when the initial exploratory team was attacked by a pack of carnosaurs. It was Becky and Coopersmith who had actually discovered the Saurians and their walled-in culture. She was indeed a competent woman. Mishima found himself wondering how he would have handled things in the hostile terrain . . . if Becky would have fallen for *him* the way they all said she had for Coopersmith.

And to think that she had been Colonel Kemp's lady! Mishima grinned to himself. Old Coopersmith must have been quite a guy—a thought that was doubly profound when Mishima recalled how Ian Coopersmith had sacrificed his own life so that others would survive. And he wondered if he had enough of the right stuff to ever do the same. . . .

"Something wrong?" asked Becky, touching his arm.

"What? No! I was just thinking about something, again, sorry. . . ." Woolgathering again! She was going to think he was an eccentric-old-professor stereotype. . . .

They walked closely together as they approached the object up ahead. It soon resolved itself into a gangway or catwalk, which appeared to be attached to the outside bulkhead of the hull itself. It ran longitudinally along the hull, headed directly toward the engines and the control-section end of the gigantic ship.

"Bingo!" said Barkham. "Looks like we found something, Doctor. . . ."

Mishima clambered up onto the catwalk. It appeared to have been built to carry creatures wider and taller than humans. Look-

ing off, the metallic path led off into darkness, farther than the
strength of the torch's beam could penetrate.

"I wonder if this is it?" he said softly.

"Looks like it goes on *forever*," said Barkham.

"It would almost *have* to," said Becky. "We're more than
forty-five kays from the control-section."

"Yes," said Mishima. "It's a long walk if this thing goes all
the way. . . ."

"We gonna check it out now?" Barkham's distressed expression belied his feelings concerning such a possibility.

"I don't think so," said Mishima. "We were out here just to
map out the area. I think we should go back and plan this out.
Get together a group of volunteers who want to make the trip."

"You're going to need technical people who can help you once
you get in there," said Becky.

"Hey," said Barkham. "I just thought of somethin'. What happens if you get all the way down to the end of this thing, and
there ain't no door into the ass-end of this can?"

"I'm hoping that the gangway runs along the bulkhead right
into the control-section," said Mishima. "If it does, then there
won't *be* any hatches . . . we'll simply *be* where we want to be."

"Are we heading back for now?" asked Becky.

"I think so," said Mishima. "We've done more than I expected
already."

The trio turned and retraced their steps, back out into the
artificial sunlight of the Mesozoic Preserve. The ceratopsian herd
had moved off to graze farther away from the stream bank, and
the area appeared to be quite safe.

Mishima watched Becky as she walked ahead and entered the
OTV. She was a beautiful woman, and he wanted her. Yet it was
not all that simple—he also wanted her to want *him*. And that
might take some doing. . . .

But there were more important things to be thinking about,
and he chided himself for letting his glandular system override
his neurological one. He must compose a report to the other Ruling Council members, enlist their support, and get a team organized. Regardless of how small his chances of success might be, it
felt *good* to be finally *doing* something about their plight.

As he reached the operator's side of the vehicle, Mishima
turned and looked back at the stream, the cave entrance, and the
landscape in general.

"Anything wrong?" asked Becky.

"No," he said, climbing aboard. "It just hit me all over again how incredible this whole ship actually is . . . what an engineering achievement it is. I keep wondering what kind of minds could have conceived of such a thing, and to what purpose . . . ?"

Barkham chuckled. "Yeah, you and everybody else, Doc."

Becky nodded. "I have a feeling that sooner or later you're going to have some answers to those questions," she said.

Keying in the ignition, Mishima looked at her grimly. He new what she meant. The *Dragonstar* was not passing through hyper-space on a lark, or by chance. The unspoken feeling of almost every human in the Saurian Preserve was that the ship was heading toward its destiny. . . .

CHAPTER 4

THEY WERE ON THEIR WAY BACK when the message came over the radio.

"Takamura? Jakes here."

Takumura took the OTV transceiver from Barkham, let the big man take the controls.

"We read you, Doctor," Mishima Takamura said.

"That other OTV party we sent out this morning."

"Oh yes. Linden and Marshall, checking out that radiation. A minor excursion, I thought."

"Problem. They haven't reported back. I thought since you're heading back that way, you might be able to stop and check to make sure they're okay."

"Just a second. Barkham... take down the coordinates that Dr. Jakes gives you... we're going to have to make a stop." His face assumed a serious cast. "I want everybody's weapon out and ready by the time we get there."

Barkham obeyed, and the others readied their weapons.

"Think there might be trouble?" asked Becky Thalberg, studying him carefully as though taking his measure.

"Linden and Marshall know enough to report back at regular intervals. There must be trouble—and we have to be ready for it."

"In that case," said Becky, "I think maybe we should put the dome up as we approach. That way we won't get plucked out of our seats by strolling dinosaurs."

He raised an eyebrow.

"Don't look at me like that—it's happened. And Mishima—remember, I _know_ this place. I've been here far too long." She looked away with a sigh. "And I'm probably gong to be here for a long time more, it would seem."

"Not if I have anything to do with it, Becky," said Mishima, quite sincerely.

"Hey, man," said James Barkham, putting down the transceiver after recording the coordinates. "Now, that's the kind of talk I like to hear. Don't count me out till I'm dead! I say if this ship can get us into hyperspace or whatever, it can get out, too!"

"Well, I suppose a little positive thinking never hurt anybody," said Becky, smiling wryly. "So okay . . . how long do you figure it will be until we get to the pit stop?"

"Oh, give it an hour, hour and fifteen," said Barkham, "unless you want me to put on the pedal, sir."

"Yes. Do so, please. A pair of lives may be at stake."

"That's right, James," said Becky. "No traffic cops here. You can go past the limit."

The handsome black man rumbled out a laugh and stepped on the accelerator. The OTV shot forward quickly along a fairly clear path, gaining speed at a remarkable rate. "These mothers can move if you give them half a chance," said Barkham, eyes shining with glee at the discomfort his passengers clearly were undergoing.

"Very gratifying," was all Becky Thalberg said, while Takamura held back an order to slow down. This was, after all, an emergency, and he had just given the man leave to do all the speed he could muster. His leadership would not look good if he changed his mind, even if Barkham's driving was rather breakneck. Doubtless, the man would slow down eventually, even if just a little.

And Barkham indeed did, as soon as they hit rougher terrain —but not by much.

So they barreled through the Mesozoic Preserve, frightening herds of iguanodons and flocks of pterodactyls, collecting a wealth of smashed insects on their windshield.

They made it to the designated coordinates in just over forty-five minutes.

"Look," said Becky. "There's the OTV."

"Seems undamaged," said Barkham. "And I don't see any beasties about."

"Nonetheless, I want your weapons ready for anything," said Takamura. "Barkham, you stay here while Becky and I check this out."

"I'll have my motor running and my rifle cocked," Barkham said, still excited from the ride.

"You just do that," said Becky, her eyes taking in the surroundings carefully.

"Let's go check that OTV," Takamura said.

The walk to the vehicles proved uneventful, and the OTV was quite empty.

"You say they were checking out radiation?" Becky said. "Shouldn't we be wearing our suits?"

"Jakes says it's not harmful radiation." Mishima examined the interior of the car. "They've taken their measurement devices . . . and their weapons. They must be in those rocks yonder. . . . That's consistent with the coordinates from Jakes."

They made their way through the rocks, to a clearing.

"Oh my God," said Becky, pointing. "Look, Mishima!"

In the middle of the clearing was a large pool of blood, a smashed piece of equipment, and a severed leg.

She turned away from the sight, hiding her eyes against Takamura's chest. He put an arm around her to comfort her.

"It looks as though we know what happened to at least one of them," he said, his gun raised, carefully looking about for the perpetrator of this horror. He noted the shell casings and splatters of blood all around. "Looks as though they certainly put up a fight!"

"How do we know one didn't escape? There are plenty of hiding spots in these rocks, surely."

Takamura nodded grimly. He released Becky and put a hand to his mouth. "Hello!" he cried. "Is anyone there?"

No response.

"Linden!" called Becky. "Marshall!"

"Looks like there's some sort of cave over there," said Takamura. "Cover me, Becky. I'm going to take a look at it."

"Right," she replied tersely.

It was a small opening, just visible between a pair of upthrust rocks. Takamura approached it with the safety of his weapon off. It was dark inside, and he could make out nothing.

"Anybody in there?" he called.

Abruptly a shadow parted from the larger shadow and a man stepped out.

"Takamura," said the man. "Thank God you've come. I was petrified . . . I couldn't move for a while. I don't know what came over me."

Takamura recognized the man. It was Timothy Linden. He lowered his weapon.

"What happened?"

"An allosaurus. Sneaked up on us somehow. Grabbed Alexandra . . . and—"

Linden began shuddering. "I'm sorry. . . . You were close, weren't you."

"Yes . . . yes. I fired God knows how many bullets into the thing and it didn't stop it. I fled into this cave. The creature didn't stay long."

Takamura nodded. "A great tragedy about Marshall, but I am glad you are still alive." He nodded to the cave. "What is beyond there?"

"Nothing. It only goes back a few meters."

"But this is the source of the radiation that you and Marshall were investigating?"

"I can't say. . . . Marshall had the equipment. It was somewhere around here. The readings should still be on the central memory unit of the device, I think. God, I just want to get out of here!"

"Yes. We shall go. Go and sit in the car. I will deal with the sensor device. . . ."

And with what is left of your companion, he thought grimly.

Takamura drove the extra OTV back to base camp, refusing Becky Thalberg's offer to ride with him. He wanted to be alone for a while, to think and to renew his spiritual strength. It was difficult to lose a crew member. Especially a woman. There was no telling how long this group of human beings would be out in space together. It would be necessary to start families, and women were high priority, for only they could produce children. From now on, he thought, women would go on such expeditions only when absolutely necessary.

He also had a funny feeling about Linden. He couldn't put his finger on it, but the man just didn't ring true. Oh yes, he believed the story of the allosaurus. . . . There was just something else that didn't seem quite right.

Jakes, of course, was horrified when he heard about the incident via radio. But he was also clearly eager to obtain the memory module from Marshall's equipment. This radiation business was bizarre stuff, and it was vital that they get to the bottom of it.

When they got back to the camp, Linden told his story again to Dr. Jakes, and then was dispatched to sick bay, complaining of sickness and headache. He had to be checked out, anyway, and the man certainly needed a rest.

Thalberg and Barkham went about their business, and when they were gone, Dr. Jakes spoke to Takamura.

"The reason I needed this was that this seems to be the same kind of radiation readings we were getting just before the disaster—with some variations of great interest."

"The memory module will be sufficient, then?"

"It seems intact. I'll tell you what we find."

"Odd. When the last recordings of this radiation were made, the natives went insane. Yet they seem quite well now . . . and well behaved and cooperative."

"What can I say? I'll report to you as soon as possible," said the doctor.

"Oh, and Dr. Jakes . . . please keep an eye on Linden, too. I have this weird sense that he's not telling us everything."

Dr. Jakes nodded solemnly, then went about his business.

CHAPTER 5

COLONEL PHINEAS KEMP, IASA, and formerly Chief of Deep Space Operations at Copernicus Base, entered the large tent which served as home for him and the noted paleontologist Dr. Mikaela Lindstrom. He had been in the nearby arboreal park of Hakarrh gathering wood for their cook stove, and while performing the nearly mindless task, spent the time *thinking*.

A dangerous habit, that.

Kemp smiled ironically as he loaded fresh wood into the stove's open maw. *Chief of Deep Space Operations*. Well, they were certainly in *deep* space, all right, but neither Phineas nor anyone else was "chief" of *any* of it.

Deep space. So deep, in fact, that they had been traveling at hyper-light speeds for almost three weeks and were now incalculable light-years from the Earth's star system. Phineas shook his head and grinned. Whenever he started feeling bad about being voted out of power, by being excluded from the survivors' choice of Ruling Council members, he tried to remind himself that there were far *worse* things to fret about. . . .

Like the number one concern on everyone's mind: *Are we ever going to get back to Earth?*

Phineas Kemp, forever the optimist, believed that the surviving band of humans would indeed make it back to Earth. The means of achieving this feat, however, was a complete mystery to him. His unflagging optimism was reflected in his decision to retain living quarters in the tent which only weeks ago had been a part of the Saurians' continuous outdoor bazaar. After the Documentary Riot (as it was now called) and the eventual realliance with the Saurians, the humans had been given the bazaar tents as temporary housing until more permanent quarters could be built by joint teams of humans and Saurians.

But Phineas Kemp wanted no part of "permanent housing." He didn't like the sound of those words, and so, despite the still-lingering Saurian redolence of the tent, he and Mikaela made no effort to secure more comfortable digs.

The stove's flames accepted the new cuts with warm gratitude, and Phineas now began preparing for the evening meal. He was a member of several committees, but today was his day off, and he was playing house husband for Mikaela, who was attending a round of meetings with the Ruling Council, of which she was an elected member, and various committee chairmen and chairwomen.

Phineas frowned as he stood up and began pulling goods from their ration larder. Already the bureaucracy of their normal world was beginning to creep over their survival camp like an unstoppable fungus, like Georgia kudzu, and to choke off all recognizable signs of life and accomplishment. He had never liked trying to do things by committee, but it seemed as though it was the only way to mollify some of the more liberal and idealistic factions among the Human Enclave. He believed that too many cooks spoiled many a stew, and that there was no replacement for singular, decisive, one-man-in-charge kind of leadership.

Phineas Kemp serving as a committee-person! The idea seemed ludicrous, and he loathed being a part of not one, but *several* of the damnable things! But he had no choice. . . .

Mikaela was always telling him that he suffered from a John Wayne complex, but he didn't think it was very funny. Phineas had not risen through the ranks of the IASA to the rank of Colonel, before reaching the age of forty, by being a chumpy, cautious, indecisive wimp.

Hell no!

Very quickly he gained a reputation as a take-charge guy. A guy with what the Italians called *cogliones*—balls. In fact, he had always known that his nickname among the IASA officers was "Iron Balls," but he'd never let any of *them* know it.

Well, it would be a cold day in hell before anybody could say that Phineas Kemp threw in the towel, that was for certain. He'd never quit on anything in his life and he wasn't about to quit now. Wherever this giant tin can was going to end up, Phineas vowed that he would be ready for it.

As he placed the rations in their cook-pak containers onto the stove, Phineas heard footsteps on the loose gravel outside the entrance to the tent. Turning, he saw Mikaela Lindstrom enter.

She wore her usual loose-fitting khaki jumpsuit, with her long, sparkling blond hair piled up on her head. It was totally functional, but when errant strands started to fall out of the bun-like construction, Phineas found it sexy as hell.

"Hello, my dear," he said with a smile. "How did it go in the office today?"

"Meetings bore me," said Mikaela.

She moved close to him, hugging him, letting her head linger on his shoulder. Being at least ten centimeters shorter than Phineas's less than imposing height, Mikaela always made him feel quite tall. He kissed her long, delicate neck and relished the smell of her freshly washed hair. A sudden rush of desire surged through him like an electric shock. He wanted her as strongly as he ever had.

Mikaela, backing away from his embrace, must have felt his sudden wanting, too. She looked at him with a wry smile.

"Feeling inspired all of a sudden?" she asked.

"You might say that. Can't help, Mickey. It's what you do to me."

"Don't call me Mickey. You know I *hate* it."

Mikaela sat down at the small table by the stove. She tilted her head back and began unfastening her long hair. Phineas watched as the blond tangle fell about her shoulders, reflecting the dim light with a singular brilliance. He watched with admiration. She was a fetchingly sexy woman, and he was damned lucky she had thrown in her lot with him. She was like Becky in so many ways, and yet so different, too.

But wasn't it like that with *all* the women in a man's life? It seemed like you were always finding characteristics in current lovers which reminded you of past ones. It made Phineas think about how similar we all really were, and how silly it seemed to get into such rows about such trifling matters.

"God, that feels better," said Mikaela, tossing her head slowly from one side to the other, letting her hair swing free and loose. "I feel like a schoolmarm with that bun all the time."

"Form follows function," said Phineas, attending to their now-warm rations. "Beef stew sound all right to you?"

Mikaela grimaced. "Whoever selected the menu for these survival kits must have owned stock in a cattle ranch. What about some variety, for God's sake?"

Phineas shrugged. "Sorry, love, I have to cook them as I get them. . . . We could be dining on ceratopsian steaks, if either of us could get up the nerve, you know."

"I think I'll wait until it's a necessity. . . ." Mikaela drafted cups of water from a five-liter container.

"So what happened today? Any news of import?" Phineas served their cook-paks, handed out some utensils, and sat down opposite her.

"Maybe," she said, telling him of Takamura's discovery.

"I admire that guy's tenacity. Even though I think he's all wet about changing things, I'm glad he's not giving up."

"Do you really think it's a waste of time," she asked.

"Oh hell, I don't know. I mean, we'll probably end up learning something if he takes an exploratory team through there. It seems like we're constantly learning new things about this ship, but . . ." Phineas shook his head.

"But *what*?"

"I just keep getting the feeling that we don't have any choice but to wait for the ship to emerge from hyperspace and see where it brings us. Takamura doesn't have a bloody chance of figuring out how to fly us back to the solar system."

"Then maybe we shouldn't okay the expedition he wants to mount?"

"Oh no, don't do that! Then he'll just have to dream up some new scheme to keep himself busy." Phineas grinned. "No, this one is good enough."

Mikaela grinned. "You know, it's funny. . ."

"What's that?"

"Well, everybody was so upset with the mess we've gotten into, and they blamed *you* for it, then they 'punished' you by not voting you into the Ruling Council, right?"

"That's what you call *funny*?" What the hell was she getting at?

"Listen," said Mikaela with an impish grin. "I mean, wouldn't everybody be surprised to know that I come home from my meetings of the Ruling Council and base my decisions and votes upon opinions garnered from you? I just think it's ironically funny, that's all."

Phineas nodded, took a swig of water. "You mean Phineas Kemp as Northumberland, as the 'power behind the throne' and all that crap? Yes, Mikaela, I suppose that *is* kind of humorous."

"Oh, Phineas, don't be such a stick in the mud!"

"Maybe you're right," he said, breaking into a smile. "Wasn't it Thomas Jefferson who said that people always get the government they deserve?"

"American history isn't one of my strong points."

"Take my word for it. And in this case, I think the people on this ship deserve to be commanded by a certain Colonel I know very well."

"Despite the recent bruisings, I see your ego is still reasonably intact."

"Aren't you glad? I mean, isn't that part of my charm? Part of the reason you fell for me?"

"I suppose so."

"So, you're going to approve of Takamura's mission, then?"

"Why not? I think everyone else favors it, anyway. I was just curious as to what your feelings were." Mikaela cleaned up the empty paks and utensils.

"Now that you mention it, I think I'll volunteer for his little team."

"You'll *what*?"

"You heard me," said Phineas.

"Yes, but *why*? You just said it was probably silly for Mishima to even *think* he might be able to change the course of the ship."

"Of course, but it will keep me off the streets, so to speak. It will give me something to *do* all day."

"But you're on the reconstruction and salvage committee," said Mikaela.

Phineas rolled his eyes. "Ghack! Need you remind me? We've just about salvaged everything that can be used. The ornithopter's being worked on by Barkham's crew and some of the men from Tactical Engineering—nothing much I can do except stand around handing people tools. Great fun, that."

"But Phineas . . ." Mikaela was grinning in spite of what she felt.

It gratified him that she wanted to keep him safe and out of any potential danger, but he just wasn't the kind of person who would be satisfied with that kind of arrangement. Years ago, Becky Thalberg had told him that he was doomed to spend his whole life proving his worth to *himself*. She was undoubtedly spot-on correct.

"I know what you're thinking, my sweet paleontologist, but it's all rather silly, don't you think? I mean, I worry my *ass* off when you're out in the Mesozoic, studying the beasts, but I just tell myself that it's your *job*, and that's *that*."

"I know you're right, Phineas, it's just that this place is always surprising us." She walked over to him, put her hands on his shoulders, and administered some of her special Swedish massage. "I'm afraid you might be walking into something dangerous. At least I know what I'm dealing with out in the Preserve."

"Mikaela, you're beginning to sound like a wife." He laughed softly, but she did not share this particular jest.

"What's wrong with *that*?"

Phineas Kemp paused, considering his reply. Had to be careful here, since he knew that Mikaela was very much interested in more of a commitment than their adventurous relationship in the midst of possible chaos. One night in their shared bed, she had even wheedled a half-promise out of him that if they ever made it back to Earth, he would probably consider marrying her.

"Oh...," he said finally. "There's nothing wrong with it, really. I was just kidding."

"I sincerely hope so, Phineas." She came round and faced him, sat on his lap. "I really love you, you know. . . ."

He nodded. ". . . and I love you, too."

Phineas kissed her, and she shot her tongue into his mouth. Instantly he wanted her. Incredible how women had such ultimate power over their men, he thought in a flash. Reaching down under her legs, he picked her up, preparing to whisk her off to their bed when another woman's voice intruded upon the moment.

"Hello? Anybody home?"

Recognizing the perfect pronunciations of Kate Ennis, Phineas stopped in midstride and slowly eased Mikaela to the floor. "Just a moment," he said hastily. "Be right with you."

"Expecting someone?" asked Mikaela, who had stiffened a bit in his arms at the sound of Kate's voice.

"No," he said softly. "Of course not."

Mikaela turned away and moved quickly to the front flap of the tent, pulling it back to reveal the lithe figure of Kate Ennis.

"Good evening, Ms. Ennis," said Mikaela with just a slightly perceptible tinge of sarcasm in her voice. "Please come in."

Kate was tall and leggy, with shining dark hair that was a subtle blend of brunette and auburn highlights. Her face was angular, accented by large, glistening doe-eyes. She had a perfect media-smile, and even Mikaela had been known to admit that Kate projected a great image for NBC news. There was no denying that Phineas found her extremely attractive, although up to this point their other-than-professional relationship had progressed no further than the flirtatious smile, the double entendre, and the occasional, semiaccidental touch of the hand. Phineas knew he was entering dangerous and uncharted waters, but there was a thrill about it which kept him from shutting down the operation.

"Sorry to interrupt anything," said Kate, "but I had a few things I wanted to check out with you, Phineas."

"No, no, it's fine," he said, gesturing Kate to a chair by the table. "Would you like some tea or coffee? We were just about to make some."

Mikaela shot him a look which said: *Oh, were we, now?* Then she moved to the stove and prepared a pot of water.

"Coffee would be fine," said Kate, taking a seat opposite Phineas.

"So what's up, newslady?" He attempted to be light and casual, especially under the harsh examining light of Mikaela's attention.

"Well, I was just contacted by Mishima Takamura," said Kate. "I guess you've heard about the expedition he's planning."

Phineas nodded.

"He's planning to take a band of Saurians along, did you know that?"

"No, I hadn't heard," said Phineas, looking over at Mikaela. "Did he mention any of that to the rest of the Council, my dear?"

Mikaela shook her head as she began pouring the water for coffee and tea. "No, nothing at all. But why does he want the Saurians along?"

Kate shrugged. "Something about engendering a 'spirit of cooperation' is what he said to me. He also thinks the Saurian Warriors would be a great advantage in case the team runs into trouble."

"What?" said Phineas, only mildly surprised. "I've had a bunch of the warrior-caste working in salvage and reconstruction. Rough, brutish types. Rather difficult to keep in line, don't you think?"

"Of course! That's why he wants me to come along. . . ."

Phineas nodded. "Because you've been working with them in . . . oh, what*ever* committee name they dreamed up, right?"

"Yes, the Cultural Exchange Committee," said Kate.

Phineas smiled. He loved the officious names someone had

conjured up to describe all the foofaraw that was going on. Because of her investigative and journalistic skills, Kate had been selected to work on the committee to try to establish better lanes of communication with the various biological "castes' among the Saurians. Phineas knew that Kate had been working with digital translators and several of the members of the priest-caste Saurians. Bridging cultural and communications barriers with the Merchants and Priests had been easier than with the Warriors and the Agrarian Workers.

And yet, in a relatively short time, Kate had made significant strides, enough to qualify her as an "authority" on Saurian culture—if there could *be* such an entity.

"And so . . . let me guess," said Phineas. "Takamura wants you along to act as an interface between the humans and the Saurian Warriors?"

Kate smiled and batted her long lashes in mock-dramatic fashion. "That's right, and that's why I thought maybe I should talk to you first."

"Me? Whatever for?" Phineas tried to act surprised, but he was inwardly pleased that she had thought to seek his advice.

Mikaela served the mugs of coffee and tea, then took a seat next to Phineas. She sat very close and reached out to casually touch his forearm. The cat establishing territorial imperatives, thought Phineas.

Kate paused before replying. Then: "Because I trust your opinion, Phineas."

"But *I* can't tell you whether or not you should go along with them! You've got to decide for yourself, Kate."

"Is it safe?" she asked, then sipped from her mug.

"Safe?" interjected Mikaela. "Is *anything* safe on the *Dragonstar*? I mean . . . *really*, Kate."

Kate Ennis seemed a bit embarrassed by the silliness of her question. She looked away from Mikaela without acknowledging what she had said. To Phineas, she said: "I don't mean to sound silly, but after working with the warrior-caste, I'm *scared*. I just don't seem to be getting through to them, and I can't let myself *trust* them. They're weird, Phineas!"

He smiled and nodded his head in a fatherly way. "I understand what you mean. To be honest, I never did much care for any of the Saurians—they *all* kind of give me the creeps. But I've had one of the Warriors' leaders on my salvage team—we call him Visigoth because he's such a damned brute!—and I don't trust the son of a bitch any further than I can throw him."

"That's great advice, Great White Hunter," said Mikaela. "You sound like the bad guy in one of the old Tarzan movies."

Phineas shrugged. "Sorry, but that's how I feel." He looked at Kate. "My advice is simple: if you don't want to feel trapped on a mission with any of the Warriors, then tell Dr. Takamura you can't go, that's all."

Kate seemed relieved and a smile gradually appeared on her face. She stood up and reached out to shake his hand. "Thank you, Phineas. Suddenly I don't feel like a whiny baby about this."

He shrugged. "Despite all the frigging committees, this is *still* a democratic process we've got going here. Nobody's going to make you do anything you don't want to do."

Kate nodded. "I'm glad you don't think less of me because of the way I feel." She turned toward the entrance, then paused to look back at him and Mikaela. "I'll go tell Takamura I can't make it. Thanks."

"No problem," said Phineas. "See you later, then."

"Good night," said Mikaela.

Kate said her good-byes and walked off into the darkening evening. Phineas returned to his seat and stretched out, gesturing for Mikaela to come back to his lap.

She stood for a moment eyeing him oddly.

"Something wrong?" he asked.

"I wonder if she would be so afraid of going on that expedition if she knew *you* were planning to volunteer?"

Phineas laughed. "My God, I do believe the paleontologist is jealous of the journalist!"

"Jealousy has nothing to do with it, Phineas."

He was still grinning at her. "Then what is it?"

"I can tell from the way she looks at you—that woman's in love with you." Mikaela spoke as though she were recording an observable phenomenon.

"That's ridiculous!" he said, although he was inwardly flattered at the thought of such a possibility.

"You might think so," said Mikaela, "but just watch what happens when she finds out you're going with Takamura...."

I will! thought Phineas, feeling like a mischievous school kid. I will indeed!

CHAPTER 6

IT WAS A TYPICAL EVENING within the *Dragonstar*. Hanging in the zero-gravity center of the immense cylinder, the Illuminator —a 200-mile-long fusion-reactor kernel—began to cast off its daytime brilliance, creating the perfect illusion of twilight. The close, humid atmosphere seemed a fright more bearable as the temperatures slowly dropped. It made Becky wonder if maybe she was finally growing accustomed to feeling sticky and always in need of a shower.

Riding in one of the only operable IASA vehicles, the trusty OTV, she and Mishima left the wide boulevard which flanked the Human Enclave in the Saurtan city of Hakarrh. They entered a smaller pathway, which gradually snaked up to higher ground, toward the ruined Temple and its Potemkin steps. Beyond the squat architecture of the Saurian Priests' headquarters lay the steel-grey wall which soared upward into the ever-present clouds at the end of the vessel's interior.

The wall behind the Temple. The Saurians called it the End of the World, and it was certainly that. Beyond the wall lay the alien crew section, the control-section of the *Dragonstar* where Drs. Jakes and Takamura, and all the others in the IASA research team, had been carrying out their initial investigations. But when the ship prepared itself for the jump into hyperspace, it automatically sealed off the hatches to the control-section, and thus began Takamura's latest mission.

They passed few Saurians in this part of the city. As evening drew on, there were a few lamplighters out riding ostrich-like dinosaurs from post to post, lighting the oil lamps, and only a few pedestrians. That was to be expected, thought Becky. They were entering the domain of the priest-caste, and it was forbidden territory to all other Saurian castes. She didn't like being out on the Hakarrh streets after dark. There was something about the Saurians that would forever make her uncomfortable. It was not only their temporary insanity caused by the start-up radiation of the *Dragonstar*'s command systems which scared her . . . but also their *coldness*, their lack of emotional bonding to each other as well as to their human allies.

As guilty and ashamed as it made her feel, she honestly believed she could never trust them as a group.

"The meeting went very well, don't you think?" asked Mishima Takamura as they approached the cliff wall of pueblo-like dwellings carved into the rock. He drove the OTV past the end of the Temple steps, following a route which would take them directly to the base of the cliff-face dwellings.

"Yes," said Rebecca Thalberg automatically, although her private assessment of the recently adjourned Ruling Council meeting was markedly less enthusiastic than his.

Joy Davison, the Chair of the Council, had expressed reservations about Mishima's idea—as had his department head, Dr. Robert Jakes. However, Mikaela Lindstrom and Dennis Patrick, the remaining members of the Council, had not really expressed any negative opinions. Since Mishima was a member of the ruling board himself, his own vote tipped the Council's decision. Maybe *that* was why he felt things went very well. . . .

Becky had no interest in the lines of power and the attendant politics which were being drawn up by the very formation of the Ruling Council. She found politics a thundering bore, and the people who pursued its ramifications to be shallow fools. Not that Mishima was getting into the inherent politics of his position . . . moreover, it seemed that he only liked the power because it gave him the chance to pursue his own private interests.

From what she had seen of Mishima, he did not seem to be an authoritarian type, getting his cookies off by bossing other people around. Rather, he seemed genuinely driven and fascinated like any good scientist should be. He was open and generally cheerful. His intelligence was ever present, shining out from behind his dark almond-eyes. His Beatles haircut enhanced his "little boy" image even though he was taller than the average man.

She found herself liking him in spite of her unspoken, practically un*thought*, decision to call a moratorium on relationships, feelings, emotional entanglements, and all the baggage that went with it. Since Ian Coopersmith's death several weeks ago, Becky had been trying to cope with the finality of it, the deep sense of loss, the anger and frustration, and the seeming pointlessness of ever allowing oneself to fall in love with *any*one.

And now she could tell that Dr. Takamura was definitely interested in her. Just what she needed right now. . . .

Of course Mishima couldn't possibly know of any of this, and she had no intention of telling him or anyone else how she truly felt. Really, now, who *really* knew how they truly felt about everything? Here she was sounding like she was getting ready for the convent at the not so terribly old age of thirty-three. Looking over at him, he was grinning to himself, obviously pleased to have received the go-ahead to put together his expedition. He *was* like a little boy.

A silent chuckle passed through her mind. There wasn't one man she'd ever met that did not, at some time or another, remind her of a little boy. Maybe there was a part of *all* of them which was incapable of growing up. If that was true, then she envied them at least that part of their nature.

A loud groaning sound interrupted her from her thoughts. It was a low-frequency howl not born in the throat of any living creature.

The groaning increased in intensity, like the straining sound of wood rafters being twisted away from their support beams in an old house. The sounds echoed and rolled across the landscape like thunder, setting up vibrating resonances beneath their feet. Then just as abruptly, there was silence once again.

"My God, what was *that*?" said Becky.

Takamura had maneuvered the OTV to a halt at the onset of the sounds, and was listening with his head slightly tilted.

"I'm not certain," he said. "At first I thought it might be the engines! Changing their status in some way—accelerating, braking, whatever. . . ."

"But now you don't think so?"

Mishima shook his head. "No, that was a *different* sound. This was like a . . . a *groan*, a crying out of pain, if you will allow me the metaphor. Do you understand what I am trying to say?"

Becky smiled at his attempt to describe what they had heard. And she nodded because she, too, had felt a straining, almost painful quality in the sound. "Yes, I do," she said after a pause.

"Something is putting structural pressure, or some other kind of stress, on the hull," said Mishima. "That was the sound of metal trying to do things it is not intended to do—such as stretch and bend."

He looked up into the cloudy sky, as if to penetrate the murky clouds and coming darkness.

"Any good ideas?" asked Becky with a tinge of childish hope in her voice. Despite her close association with real, "hard" scientists over the years, Becky, like most people, still half-believed that *real* scientists could come up with the answers to just about any goddamned question.

Mishima shrugged. "It could be any number of things. Don't forget, this ship is very, very old—two hundred million years at the outset, maybe much older. Nothing lasts forever, so maybe it is finally beginning to wear out."

"Great timing," she said. "Just when it decides to take us all for a ride across the galactic rim, it also decides to start falling apart . . . !"

"Now, don't start quoting me! The last thing we need right now is a panic situation."

Becky shook her head and grinned. "We already *have* a panic situation. . . . We're just getting used to it, that's all."

Mishima laughed in spite of himself, then tried to assume a more serious countenance. "My expedition through the bulkhead area might be more fortunate than we could have imagined."

"What do you mean?"

"If the superstructure of the hull is indeed undergoing severe stress, we can run some tests to check it out."

Becky nodded but did not respond, and Mishima fired up the vehicle again. They approached the base of the cliff dwellings called the Priests' Rookery and climbed down to the red-clay soil. Walking to the face of the rock wall, they entered a staircase which had long ago been cut into the stone. Like an immense fire escape, the staircase scaled the cliff, switching back and forth as it angled from landing to landing, level to level. At each landing, a stone catwalk stretched in both directions, allowing access to hollowed-out interiors in the cliff. These were the dwellings of the priest-caste, the biologically superior subspecies of the Saurians. The higher a priest lived in the Rookery, the higher his social and biological status was perceived by his peers.

Becky and Mishima were climbing to the highest level to see Thesaurus, one of the oldest, wisest members of his race.

She remembered first encountering Thesaurus with Ian Coopersmith, back when they had first discovered the Saurian Preserve by simply stumbling out of the jungle and seeing the Barrier. It was the great wall which protected this race of evolved dinosaurs from their more primitive relatives, the wall which Ian eventually died protecting.

Mishima had wanted to enlist the aid of Thesaurus in hand-picking a detachment of Saurian Warriors for the expedition. Since Becky was probably the closest human to the old priest, she had agreed to accompany him for an audience.

"I must be getting old," said Mishima as they approached the second-to-the-last landing. "This is going to kill me."

"We're almost there," she said.

"Do you think he'll give us any static?" asked Mishima.

"I don't think so. He's very intelligent. Nobody wants to give any of the Saurians credit because of the way some of the other castes act, and the way they're treated, but you'll see."

"I hope so."

They reached the final landing, more than four hundred meters from the surface. Becky looked over the railing and stepped back as a wave of vertigo crashed over her. Heights usually did not affect her. Maybe it was just her nerves. . . .

Thesaurus was awaiting them as they approached the entrance to his dwelling. He was tall and thin, almost fragile in appearance, and his smooth greenish-brown skin was mottled from age and a bout of radiation poisoning. Like all Saurians, his long neck flowed upward from his shoulders to support a reptilian/bird like skull. But his stereoscopic eyes, high forehead, and large brain case were all indicators of sentience. He wore the loosely flowing, bright lemon-yellow robes of the priest-caste, cinctured by a thin waist-high belt.

He also wore a digital translator which allowed Saurians and humans to communicate. Their language sounded like a series of clicks, barks, and hisses, which were not easily produced by the human throat and tongue. English was equally impossible for the Saurians, and the digital translator would forever be one of the primary ways of the two species to exchange ideas.

The only hang-up with the translating devices was the inherent delay in all interspecies conversations. But, thought Becky, you could get used to just about anything, and after a while, you didn't even notice the delay—it became part of the whole ritual.

"Greetings, my Rebecca," said Thesaurus, holding out both hands to touch her own.

"Hello, Thesaurus. This is one of our scientists, Dr. Takamura. He is here to seek your advice."

The Saurian Priest took Mishima's hand and welcomed him.

As Becky watched the two of them, she was reminded of how Ian had first tried to talk with Thesaurus, how the always witty Englishman had given the Priest his funny name as a joke and how it had simply "stuck." It occurred to her that she'd never actually learned the Priest's "real" name. . . .

"Whatever I can do to help," said Thesaurus. "Please come in and tell me."

They entered the spacious front room, which was filled with odd-shaped pieces of furniture, shelves, and cabinets. The walls were decorated with various woven tapestries and macramé-like "hangings." Becky also noticed ordinary IASA items such as a canteen, a calculator, a cam-corder, even a jumpsuit insignia. These were also placed on display proudly. It was a warm room, even in its alienness, radiant with the personality of Thesaurus.

Calmly, but with the deliberate manner of a philosopher, Thesaurus began their conversation with a question about the groaning sounds just heard. Mishima explained his theories about their possible origin, and watched the old Priest as he accepted the information in silence. Becky imagined the concern which must have filled him, but the Saurian did not allow it to manifest itself.

Briefly then, Takamura outlined his planned expedition, his intentions, and his wish to have a detachment of Saurian Warriors included in the party.

"It is admirable that you wish to involve my people in the quest for a solution to our plight," said the Priest. "But I wonder if it is also *wise*."

"Why do you say that?" asked Mishima. He was sitting on a wide mushroom-shaped fixture which served as a chair, but did not look at all comfortable. Becky continued to stand by the entrance, watching them.

Thesaurus flickered his large amber eyes—a gesture which translated as a rough equivalent to a human shrug. "The warrior-caste is . . . unpredictable . . . around humans. Visions of the riot and the scent of Warrior blood still linger in their memories. I mean no offense when I tell you that as a group, they still do not really trust humans."

"I understand that," said Mishima. "But perhaps this mission will help foster goodwill between us and their caste."

The Saurian clapped his hands once—a gesture meaning agreement. "Yes, that is possibly just so. However, I think it would be best if you also brought one of my own caste along. A

Priest among them would be a stabilizing influence, I assure you."

Mishima smiled. "Of course! You are most welcome to come with us!"

"No, I do not ask this for myself." Thesaurus opened his mouth to awkwardly display a lower jaw full of teeth. It was his attempt to emulate a human smile, which, to Becky at least, gave him an oddly fearsome aspect. He'd never make it as a holovision personality with a look like that. Thesaurus continued: "I am too old for such adventures. I would send one of our younger, stronger caste members."

"Very well," said Mishima. "That will be fine. Now, tell me, please . . . do you have any members of the warrior-caste which you might recommend for the mission?"

The Saurian clapped his hands once. "There is the one Colonel Kemp calls Visigoth. He is one of the caste generals, and is very respected by his men. He has worked very much with the human salvage crews, and it seems likely that he would be agreeable to gather up a band of young fighters."

"Good. Very good. You will arrange this for me?"

"Yes, of course." The Saurian paused, tilted his head a bit to the left, and stared at Mishima for a moment before continuing. "Do you really expect any trouble?"

Mishima shook his head. "Not really, no. But we have learned that we cannot ever *expect* anything on board this ship . . . other than the *un*expected."

"Just so . . . ," said Thesaurus.

Mishima spent the next few minutes finalizing the details of the mission, and Thesaurus promised him a platoon of four Warriors and a leader. They would join his team at the main gate the following morning.

Finally Mishima stood and stepped toward Becky, still standing by the entrance. Thesaurus accompanied him and reached out a hand to touch her shoulder. The Priest towered above her, and one less familiar with his species might find his posture threatening. But as he looked down at her with a saturnine expression in his eyes, she could sense the concern and sincere friendship in his gaze.

"Your Ian Coopersmith is still in my thoughts," he said.

"Mine, too." It was all she could manage.

"It was a strange and beautiful thing he did. As much as my

people cannot understand *why* he did it, they will still remain forever grateful."

"Thank you," she said, fighting back some tears. Damn it! How could this utterly alien species touch her so deeply, so quickly? It didn't seem possible, but it was happening.

Thesaurus flickered his eyes. She recognized the wistful quality of the Saurian shrug. "It is so difficult for both of us, is it not? My caste has tried to educate our people, and I fear that so few of them truly understand. . . ."

"I know," said Becky.

"How do you tell that their universe is really a great carriage hurtling through a night so deep, so dark, that it has no end?"

"You simply tell them," said Mishima. "Eventually they will understand. But if they cannot do that, then they will at least accept it as a fact."

"Or explain it through their myths," said Thesaurus.

"Perhaps that may be the best way," said Becky.

"It is getting late," said Mishima. "We should be going back."

"Very well. Thank you for the honor of your visit." The Priest inclined his head in imitation of a bow.

"Good-bye, Thesaurus. We'll come see you when we return," said Becky.

"With good news, let us hope."

"Let us hope," repeated Mishima.

Takamura had not spoken for several minutes as he maneuvered the OTV down a dimly lit path toward the boulevard. The domes and spires of Saurian architecture hunched and squatted in deep shadows on either side of them. The city was settling in for a quiet night, punctuated only by the whine of a single methane-turbine engine. He eased the machine into the field next to the tents of the Enclave and killed the power.

"Want to stop by my tent for some coffee?" he asked softly, not looking at her.

She stared past him, then quickly around the dark field where the shadowed hulk of a partially assembled ornithopter lay amid scattered scavenger parts.

"Well?"

"Oh," she said, chewing on her lips. "I don't know. I'm awfully tired."

She wasn't ready for this. She really wasn't. Not now. Not so soon. . . .

But what was she waiting for? It was funny how you had to remind yourself that there might not be any more tomorrows, that you could, as Ian used to say, wake up tomorrow morning and find yourself *dead*.

"I just want to talk to you. I need to talk to someone once in a while," said Mishima.

"Well . . ." In the mood she suddenly found herself in, it wasn't going to take much persuading.

"Look, I won't try anything. . . ." Mishima's eyes were big and pleading.

She smiled. "You *won't*? What're you trying to do—scare me off?"

He laughed. "I take that to mean yes, you will come?"

She reached out and touched his smooth cheek, looked into his eyes. "For coffee, yes. And anything else that might pop up. . . ."

CHAPTER 7

KATE LAY IN HER COT, listening in the darkness. She could hear her tent-mate, Joyce Kinsey, stirring in her sleep. But there was *another* sound.

The groaning, twisting noise resonated in Kate Ennis's head, waking her from a deep, dreamless sleep. Its subsonic vibrations seemed to touch the marrow in her bones, and yet it was dull and loud like distant thunder, echoing through the ship's interior.

It was an awful sound, like the creaking wood in an old sailing ship, the windswept rafter of an old house. The lower-caste Saurians were terrified by the "ship-quakes" as they were already being called, and Kate was having no success in quieting their fears. Some of the merchant-caste members were becoming surly. They were circulating a familiar prejudice among themselves: that their world had been nothing but turmoil since the arrival of the humans, that perhaps the Saurians would be better off without the humans around. . . .

Kate knew there was more than a little truth in that sentiment. She thought of the Hawaiians several decades after the Europeans had found them: talk about *Paradise Lost* . . . ! We were doing the same kinds of destructive things to the Saurians, even if there was no one person or policy to actually blame. Maybe it was an unwritten law that when two cultures first meet, the more primitive is going to have to suffer the most.

"What was that?" asked Joyce sleepily. Kate could hear her sitting up in her sleeping pouch, fumbling for her cigarette pack.

"Another 'quake,'" said Kate, looking over to see the flare of the self-lighting Virginia Slim as Joyce brought it to her lips.

Leaning out to the small crate which served as a nightstand, Kate turned on a power-cell lamp, and the shadows ran off into the corners.

"Jesus! Why didn't you warn me you were doing that?" Joyce chuckled in mock-anger.

"Sorry . . . I figured as long as we were up and we were talking, maybe we should have some light."

"Those noises scare me," said Joyce. "It's like the whole ship could be twisting apart."

"I've heard that it's because of the age of this ship, that the hyperspace flight may be putting . . . some stress . . . on . . . things." Kate chose her words with care, so that Kinsey would not become more anxious.

Kate worked with Joyce on the Cultural Exchange Committee, and she seemed to have a natural, intuitive gift for communicating with the Saurians. Her job as a lab technician with the IASA Paleo Survey Team was now nonexistent, and she had volunteered to work with the Saurians because it offered her a chance to be doing something at least halfway related to her real vocation. During the past few weeks Kate had become quite friendly with her.

"They seem to be happening more frequently, don't you think?"

"No," said Kate. "Not really. I think that's just people talking —you know, exaggerating."

"Maybe, but it still scares me." Joyce dragged deeply on her cigarette, exhaled a long thin plume of blue-grey smoke. "I mean, I try not to think about it most of the time, but this whole *thing* scares me!"

"I know what you mean," said Kate.

"I mean, really—what's going to happen to us, Kate? *Where* in hell are we going? And *who* wants us there?"

Kate didn't answer because there were no answers available. For a short time, the two women sat in the half-light of their little lamp and listened to the madness of their own random thoughts. Kate knew that if she continued the conversation, there would be no more sleep tonight, and she could not afford a full day without enough rest. Being around the Saurians required that she be as alert and involved as possible.

"Well, maybe we should be getting back to sleep," said Kate.

Joyce nodded and stubbed out her cigarette. "One more thing . . . I forgot to tell you earlier because I got in so late. . . ."

"What?" asked Kate. She hoped it wasn't going to be a long, involved story. She really did want to get some rest.

"While I was at the wine-making class, I heard Joy Davison

remark about Colonel Kemp volunteering for Takamura's little exploratory mission."

"You're kidding." Suddenly her pulse quickened, and she felt totally awake. Kate tried to put a lid on her shocked reaction to the news.

"No, it's true. At least, that's what I heard." Joyce paused. Then: "So . . . are you going to tell Takamura you've reconsidered?"

"I don't know. Do you think it would look kind of funny? This late, I mean. They're supposed to head out the day after tomorrow."

"You really like him, don't you?"

Kate propped herself up on one elbow, grinned sheepishly. "I guess I do . . . I *think* I do."

"Then go on! Do it! There's certainly nothing exciting going on around here."

"You're right," said Kate, trying to sound nonchalant. Inside, her heart was racing as she thought of being close to him again. Sister, you've got it bad.

"Of course, I'm right," said Joyce.

"All right," said Kate. "Maybe I'll go talk to Takamura."

Joyce chuckled. "Yeah, right . . . and *maybe* this is all just a bad dream!"

CHAPTER 8

MIKAELA HAD WAITED for him to mention it.

It was the night before the expedition was heading off "along the bulkhead trail," as Phineas had phrased it, and she decided to lay out enough rope to see if the Colonel could manage to hang himself.

He had spent the afternoon in meetings with Takamura and the other volunteers, and it was after dark when he returned to the tent. She could tell he was feeling randy, and had most likely planned a romantic send-off, because he arrived carrying a bottle of Robert Mondavi 2007, appropriated from Bob Jakes's private cache.

She served him a late dinner. And she waited for him to say something. The rope seemed to be getting shorter . . . because it was slowly wrapping itself around his neck. No, that wasn't quite right: the rope ws innocent; Phineas was the one doing the wrapping, thank you.

Mikaela smiled to herself as they cleaned up from the meal. Phineas seemed full of small talk, as though he were avoiding mention of the mission. And that was not like him at all, because prior to going to the final briefing, the prospect of some new adventure filled his sentences.

She wasn't really certain *how* she felt about his silence. It wasn't that she was really angry with him, or even hurt by his sudden avoidance of the subject. Maybe she should give him the benefit of the doubt. Maybe he was thinking of a way to bring up the subject. Perhaps the news had been so *meaningless* to him that he was not even *thinking* about her.

God, she went round and round! What was it about relationships that made us all so crazy?

An hour passed, and the wine had been poured, glasses

clinked, and lamps turned low. Considering the romantic limitations of a baggy vendor's tent, redolent with Saurian exudations, Phineas was giving it his best shot. After kissing her along her arm, and all the way up her neck into the fragrant blond nest of her hair, he reached for the front zipper to her jumpsuit. Mikaela lay back on the cot, arcing her back, presenting herself to him, letting the wine perform its magic. She could confront him later.

Soon their clothes had fallen away, and without speaking they had both decided to make this one last. Each touch, each kiss, lingered and teased. At one point she lay back away from him, tracing a wet fingertip up and down the length of his body. He was short, but not compact; muscled, but trim and sinewy rather than bulky or heavy. As he edged toward his fortieth year, she could detect the first hints of softness, of creases and tucks and rolls, but he would battle them for many years to come. His face was still unlined, and his sandy-brown hair still thick. He was classically handsome and always would be.

When he finally entered her, it was with a gentle confidence. He was always attentive, and careful not to be too rough, too quick. They moved together in the humid night, their sweat mingling, making them deliciously slippery. He cried out when he reached orgasm, and she held him at her breast like the little boy he often seemed.

Afterward, as she lay in his arms, and the wine threatened to carry them off to sleep, she broke the silence with a single, direct question: "Why didn't you tell me that Kate Ennis is going along?"

At first he acted like he may have already drifted off, but his eyes popped open and he looked at her drowsily.

"For Christ's sake, Mikaela, are you serious?"

"Just tell me *why*?"

"Because I assumed you already *knew* it. And it sounds like I was right."

He turned over, stretching out, as though very tired—which he most likely was. She had to admit his answer made sense, and he certainly was not acting like a guilty man. Still, she thought she might press it a bit further.

"You think you're so smug, don't you, Colonel . . . ?"

"Smug? No, just tired. Good night, my dear."

"Phineas—"

"Look." He was starting to sound more irritated and less sleepy. "I just found out Kate had changed her mind—women have been known to do such things—and it was not that big of a deal to me, all right?"

"Yet it must have been enough of one for you to figure I would already know about it."

"Christ, you're on the bloody Council! Of *course* you'd know about it!" He paused, drew a breath, then exhaled dramatically. "Listen: I am not interested in Kate Ennis and have no intention of becoming so—even if she *is* interested in *me*, and demonstrated same by signing on for the mission . . . and, oh yes, you were absolutely correct in your prediction, assumption, knowledge aforethought, or whatever you want to call it, and can we finally *end* this silly discussion and get some bloody *sleep*!?"

Mikaela almost laughed aftter his performance. He could be *damned* charming and funny when he wanted to be.

"Very well, Phineas. Maybe I was being a bit too hard on you."

He harrumphed through the haze of half-sleep. "Maybe you were just being a bit *jealous*, why don't you admit it?"

"Oh, is that what I was doing? Thank you, my love, I would have never known."

She waited for a reply, but he had already slipped into an unfakable deep slumber. Not exactly the demeanor of a guilty man. Maybe he was right: she was acting jealous.

And yet, she thought as she reached out to cancel the lamp, I just don't trust that Ennis woman. . . .

CHAPTER 9

TIMOTHY LINDEN LAY in the cot, sweating.

Outside, a rare breeze fluttered the flap of the large tent. No light seeped through; it was the middle of the night. Beside him on a table was a pitcher of water and some medicine. Linden made an effort to reach for them, then fell back into the cot, exhausted, feverish, shaking. He teetered on the edge of delirium, but fought to retain his consciousness.

He'd done it. He'd fooled them. They believed him. Only he knew that the allosaurus was two-headed. Only he knew what lay at the bottom of that tunnel. And the secret would be safe for his people—this astonishing secret that would bring them the glory in the world—no, the universe—that they desired so much. Oh, how the name of Allah would be glorified.

I was predestined for this, Linden thought. *Glory be to God and the Prophet, this is the reason I was placed upon the* Dragonstar!

He lay back, and the night seemed to fold in upon him, but there were stars in that night, wonderful stars that shone with glory and with hope, and he felt again the burning and cleansing radiation that had shot through him there in that chamber.

He stifled a scream. No, they must not hear him scream. They must not realize he was changing, until it was too late to do anything about it. They might try to stop it, they might try to kill it, they might try to kill *him*.

Yes, he thought. He could feel it. He could feel the changes flowing through him, like strong currents twisting in his body. Would he grow another head, another arm or leg like that allosaur had? That would be difficult to hide, surely. Yet Linden suspected something more would happen. . . . Something even wilder . . . Something wonderful. Something . . .

66

A spike of pain suddenly shot through his spine. He opened his mouth to cry out, but nothing came forth. He twisted and contorted atop the cot, his hands shaking spastically, and he could feel a deeper darkness closing in.

Light exploded all around him.

He was back in the desert again.

Back in training. Back with his brothers, learning the holy ways of terrorism.

The sun beat down upon the exercise like the blessing of Allah as he ran across a tarmac toward a bunker, firing blanks from a laser-aimed pistol, scoring points with each hit. He and his comrades took the hill, and when they occupied it, the great man himself, Marcus Jashad, strode to the bunker to congratulate the men on their expertise.

Only when he arrived, Timothy Linden could see that there was something wrong with the feared assassin, the great Muslim leader. He wore a turban and a beard and had a rifle slung across his back, looking much like a warrior of the Mahdi in the nineteenth century.

And the whole of his chest was riddled with bullet holes.

Blood seeped from his mouth as he opened it to speak.

"Allah bless you, my son," he said, and Linden knew he was speaking to a dead man, a ghost. "Allah bless you on your mission aboard the Dragonstar, *that vessel of the Deep Dark that cost me my life."*

"Marcus!" said Timothy Linden in his vision. "Marcus Jashad! I am doing the correct thing, am I not?"

"You are working amid our enemies, and your prize in heaven will be great."

"But my secret!"

"Ah yes! The secret of the cave! Glory be to Allah, it will be his Gift to His People!"

"Yes. Yes, then I shall keep it to myself."

"Oh, indeed. You shall make the universe ring with the Glory of the Faithful. Allah's name shall echo down the corridors of the Deep Dark. And his enemies—" The eyes in the man's head glowed like coals. "His enemies and mine enemies shall know the edge of the sword, and shall be stricken down like stands of wheat, and this chaff shall burn in hell for Eternity!"

"Praise be to Allah," said Linden as the specter faded away into a dust devil and swept off into the dazzle of the sun and the

dunes. "His Holy Name shall be made manifest unto all the Nations of the Earth—and of the Stars!"

A sense of divine purpose swept through him like a scouring wind. He saw it all clearly now. He could feel himself transforming toward the blessed purposes of Allah and Mohammed, his Prophet. And perhaps—just perhaps—

Perhaps he was the next Prophet. . . . Yes, just as Mohammed was the Prophet of the Earth, he would be Mohammed, Prophet of the Stars!

Then the desert faded away—a mirage within a vision—and darkness bloomed again.

He was back in his cot, sweating and shaking.

He was back in his cot, quite out of his mind.

"Jashad," he muttered, the sweat blubbering from his lips. "Jashad, I will avenge you. The unbelievers shall perish!"

His eyes closed, as though in sleep, and his muscles seemed to relax.

But then the eyes shot open, and he sat stiffly upright, the cords in his neck drawn tight as steel.

"Jashad! I shall avenge you, my departed brother, in the name of Allah." He stood up from the cot shakily. "I shall avenge you this very night!"

Corporal Jacob Darlington hated night duty.

It wasn't so much that he was alone. He'd had plenty of periods in the service when his weapons were his only company. No, it was the night duty here at the base on the *Dragonstar* that he hated so much, because of the sounds that crept and crashed out of the night, like live things themselves. Night duty was constant adrenaline, night duty was anxiety, night duty was . . .

Well, it just was pretty miserable, that's all. Not that anything was super peachy keen anymore, since the *Dragonstar* had gone haywire and wrested its passengers away from Earth, from their home solar system. He really hadn't had a decent night's sleep since then, anyway, which was why it was just as well that they stuck him out here regularly to watch the camp's periphery. He missed his wife, Josie back in Tennesee, terribly, and it was just starting to dawn on him that he'd probably never see her again. And her pregnant and everything! It was just a bitch, that's what it was—a real bitch.

His station was by a ginkgo tree standing separate from a cluster of them. Nearby was the hum of a force screen, which proved fairly effective when it was kept on, but couldn't be 100 percent effective, especially against one of those big mothers out there if it really had its mind on getting at the camp. From here, Darlington could see just about half the periphery, and he'd rest here just a few more minutes before he patrolled the other side.

That was the one nice thing about the duty, he supposed, smoking on a cigarette with a kind of local tobacco the botanists had discovered. You got to move around a lot, exercise, work off the anxiety.

A shrill reptilian scream pierced the faint hum of the force-screen and Darlington jumped despite himself. Goddamn things! Used to be he was in awe of the creatures, and a little bit fascinated with them. Now he just plain hated the bastards.

He shivered, blew out some smoke, shouldered his rifle, and was about to step on out and continue his patrol when he heard a noise.

A noise that seemed to come from the *inside* of the periphery.

It sounded like footsteps.

Too early for my relief, thought Darlington as he looked around. What the hell—

And then a figure stole out from a tree. It ran for him, and before Darlington could bring his rifle to bear, it jumped on him, pulling him to the ground.

"Hey!" Darlington screamed, wrestling with the man—it *was* a man, that much was apparent. "What the hell!" Before the man could get his hands around Darlington's windpipe, the Corporal yelled, "Help! Help!" for all he was worth.

Then he set about keeping alive.

It wasn't easy. His attacker fought like a madman. His grip around Darlington's throat was like iron. They rolled about in the dirt, and the madman seemed to be growling something about "revenge, revenge." Darlington managed to get in a few good blows, but they didn't seem to deter the man much. Plus, he was getting weaker and everything was getting darker and his last thought was, Well, at least I'm not going out inside the jaws of one of those bastards out there—

And then suddenly there was a *thump*. The attacker stiffened and then fell off to one side, quite unconscious.

Stars swam into Darlington's vision, but he managed to keep hold of things long enough to get slapped gently on the face.

"Corporal. Corporal! You okay? What was going on?"

"Dunno."

"Who is this guy?"

"I dunno."

Groggily he managed to get up. His savior had a flashlight, and he recognized him. It was Private Gonzales, his relief. Gonzales, he knew, also had insomnia problems. Thank God!

"Let's get a look at him," said Gonzales. "Didn't know you had any enemies, Jake."

"Didn't know I had any, either."

"Shirt's all torn up. Let me see if he's still alive. Don't think I hit the bastard that hard."

Gonzales kneeled down with the flashlight, examining the man. "Oh yeah, still breathin' and—" He took in a breath, then stepped up and back. "Jesus Christ!"

"What's wrong?" Darlington said, still woozy and bleary-eyed.

"That's Linden, the guy that's been in sick bay. And—and Christ, what's happened to him!"

"What?" Darlington got up and stared down at the fallen attacker.

Oh yeah, it was Timothy Linden, all right, though it was damned hard to tell for sure, what with the way his face had turned all rough and scaly. But that wasn't the worst of it, no sirree.

For his chest, exposed by the torn shirt, was just as hard and shiny and scaly.

And growing from under his right arm was the beginning of an extra arm!

CHAPTER 10

DR. DANA LOMBARDY looked up from the patient to Mishima Takamura with pure bafflement in his expression.

"I gotta tell you, Doc, I've never seen anything like this in all my born days," the doctor said, holding an examination light between three fingers, his stethoscope dangling from his short neck.

"I think it's safe to say that no one here has, Dr. Lombardy," said Takamura. "Now please proceed with the examination."

They were in the sick bay. Lieutenant Timothy Linden lay on a table before Dr. Lombardy, securely strapped and thoroughly knocked out by drugs. His shirt and his pants had been removed, revealing the scaly, shiny epithermal covering that had set in over all his body. Takamura found it difficult to take his eyes off the beginning of an arm—a vestigial hand and wrist, rather like that of a thalidomide baby—protruding from the side of Linden's chest. Wrapped around the man's arms and legs were sensors, leading to a central diagnostic machine, quivering with readings.

They'd brought both men in last night after the fracas—Linden and Darlington—but they'd released the sentry with a couple of aspirins tucked into his palm.

Linden, of course, was going to take more work. This morning, they'd made a cursory examination and Dr. Lindstrom had taken a subcutaneous cell sample for examination in her makeshift lab. Kemp and the others had taken a quick look at Linden, scratched their heads, shrugged their shoulders, and allowed that they just hoped it didn't spread. Dr. Jakes was the most interested—so interested, in fact, that he lingered now, watching the proceedings.

Takamura eyed the silent man, then decided to ask the question he'd put off for a while.

"Well, Dr. Jakes, do you think it's the radiation that did it to him?"

"Hmm?" Jakes roused up from his reverie.

"The radiation. Do you think it was the radiation that's making Linden like this?"

"Hard to say," said Jakes. "I'm no medical doctor."

Dr. Lombardy looked up from the examination. "Well, I am, and I must say, this doesn't look at all like radiation sickness to me—and I've seen the effects of radiation!"

"Yes, but only certain *kinds* of radiation, correct, Doctor?"

Lombardy blinked. "Well, yes, I suppose you could say that."

"What are you saying, Jakes?"

"This radiation was quite peculiar—that's why I wanted Linden and Marshall to go out and make a quick check of it up close. All kinds of wacky wavelengths. I can't even begin to tell you—"

"Perhaps, when you make the analysis, you can give me the exact spectography."

"Yes, of course. In any event," said Jakes, "it's pretty weird, and it's quite similar to some of the readings we got about the same time the Saurians went wild—only that was not localized, like this case."

"But there's no sign of activity of concern among the Saurians?"

"Nothing. They're very cooperative now, as you know. And why wouldn't they be? They've not been torn away from their home system. *This* is their home. Always has been and probably always will be!"

"Gentlemen, if you please," said Dr. Lombardy. "I believe I'm finished."

"What's the verdict, then, Doctor?" Jakes requested eagerly. He turned to Takamura. "This could key us in to exactly what this radiation is."

"Well, I admit I'm still baffled. To begin with we've got a temperature of a hundred ten degrees. Blood pressure at 310 over 170, and from all signs there are unusual activities going on in this man's endocrine system, to say the least. What I want to do is to get some X rays, with your permission."

"Yes, of course. Why do you ask?"

"A different form of radiation, sir. Might influence the patient."

"Ah. Jakes?"

"I think we ought to know what's going on inside this guy."

"What's going on, Doctor," said Lombardy, "is that basically Timothy Linden should have died several hours back."

Takamura and Jakes exchanged glances of disbelief.

"A normal human body cannot tolerate this kind of internal strain," continued Lombardy. "I've never seen anything like it . . . and I wish I knew exactly what was happening here. All I can say for sure is that there is a great deal of change going on in the musculature, the epidermis, the skeleton, the organs . . . and, God help us, even the brain."

"And that extra limb, Doctor?" said Takamura.

"Just the tip of the iceberg," said Lombardy. "Give it a day, Doctors, and I think we'll see much more than that. This hardening of the epidermis, for example—I've observed a spread across the whole body just in the period that I've been examining the patient. And also, it seems to have hardened . . . become thicker."

"It's as though some kind of hide were forming over him," said Dr. Jakes.

"Or some kind of cocoon," murmured Takamura.

"Exactly my thought, though it's a very unmedical thing to say," said Lombardy.

"Doctor, we're in a very unmedical atmosphere," said Mishima.

"Too true. Ah, but wouldn't I like to have him back on a decent lab on Earth."

"Take us along with you, please!" said Mishima, and they all chuckled, breaking the tension considerably.

At that moment, Mikaela Lindstrom came in.

"Well, I'm glad to see that levity is not a forgotten commodity aboard the *Dragonstar*," she said.

"What have you found?" Jakes said eagerly, speaking for them all.

"Plenty," she said. "And nothing."

"Care to explain that?"

She took out several lab photos. "I did a mounting of the cell sample I took. I checked it out under the electron microscope in the portable lab we so fortunately had installed on the base before our departure. I immediately saw the resemblance."

"Resemblance? Resemblance to what?" demanded Jakes.

"Do you recall that incident with the iguanodon a few weeks before chaos struck?"

"Sure," said Jakes. "The patrol you took with Dr. Penovich where Lieutenant Hagerman was killed."

"That's right," said Mikaela grimly. "Well, afterward we took a sample of what we could find left on the dead iguanodon."

"The one that was all distorted," said Jakes. "Like Linden here."

"He didn't have any extra limbs. . . . But also you may recall that iguanodons are herbivorous and seldom attack. This one was deranged . . . quite crazy. Much perhaps as Linden was deranged when he attacked Darlington."

"You think they were both exposed to the same sort of radiation—both the iguanodon and Linden?"

"It's a possibility . . . a strong one. Take a look at these photos." She handed them over. "Both show highly abnormal cellular activity—and there are similarities."

"Yes, I see," said Lombardy.

"But what does it mean?" asked Mishima.

"That's something we're going to have to wait and see," said Jakes. "But in the meantime we've got Linden here to watch."

Suddenly, as though he heard his name being called, Timothy Linden groaned, low and long. They turned to him. His face was a mass of discolored scabs, cracking at the lips as he opened his mouth.

"By God," said Lombardy. "I think he's trying to speak."

The moans slowly became more articulate.

"Don't get too close," said Mishima.

"What's he trying to say?" Mikaela said, craning curiously.

"Hungry," said Linden roughly. "Hungry."

They looked at one another. "I thought we'd have to feed him intravenously. Looks like that won't be necessary," said Lombardy.

"Can you tell us what's happening to you?" Dr. Jakes said lamely to the strapped-down Linden.

"Hungry," repeated Linden. He opened his eyes, and they shone red. But there was a dullness to them, an unawareness. "Hungry." He made no effort to try to escape from his bonds.

"Maybe after he eats," suggested Lombardy.

"Yes," said Mishima. "Perhaps after he eats."

"But then what?"

"We'll just have to wait and see," said Mishima. "Just like everything else."

CHAPTER 11

IT WAS A SURPRISINGLY SMALL contingent of humans and Saurians which gathered outside the main gate in the Mesozoic Preserve. Besides himself, Phineas counted Mishima Takamura, his old friend Becky Thalberg, Greg Krolczyk and Frank Cavoli from Tactical Engineering, and "the green-eyed monster" (one of Mikaela's more endearing monikers), Kate Ennis. The Saurians were headed up by his co-worker in Salvage, Visigoth, and four slope-browed members of his warrior-caste—none of whom Phineas could recognize.

A wispy, ground-hugging mist swirled about them as they inventoried their gear. An early-dawn fog leaked from the edge of the jungle, sending finger-like streamers across the clearing, which formed a DMZ between the Barrier and the Mesozoic Preserve. The air hung damp and humid, and it would soon be oppressively warm—business as usual inside the *Dragonstar*. Phineas had never grown accustomed to the climate, but he had long ago refused to let it bother him.

"All right, everyone," said Dr. Takamura. He spoke slowly, pausing between each phrase or short sentence so that Visigoth's digital translator could provide him with the gist of all conversation. "I do not expect trouble, but we should be prepared for anything. Colonel Kemp, Krolczyk and Cavoli, and of course the Saurians will handle any emergency encounters. The rest of us will fill in if necessary. Any questions?"

There were none. The briefing the previous evening had been extensive and god-awful boring. Phineas hoped that Takamura was a better physicist than he was a leader of men. The man lacked the character-dynamic, that ineluctable quality that made others look up to you and be willing to follow you into hell's mouth. Takamura was too soft-spoken, too polite, simply too nice a fellow for any of that.

Phineas liked him, but he knew it might be difficult taking orders from him. Well, they'd be seeing what transpired along those lines soon enough.

As Dr. Takamura headed up the group and started leading them off into the jungle, Phineas waited until everyone had filed past so that he could take up his prearranged position as the rear-flanker. Using the opportunity, he studied each member of the group as they filed past him. All the humans wore standard-issue, khaki jump-fatigues with survival-paks on their backs. The doctor, Becky, and Kate carried additional bags of tools and instruments, and everyone carried a 9mm side arm with C-4 explosive hollow-points. Cavoli, Krolczyk, and Phineas also carried HK heavy assault rifles, plus plenty of spare clips in their utility bags. Phineas hadn't seen anything in the Preserve that could stand up to a volley from an HK.

The Saurian Warriors were dressed in their usual scant attire: dull red tunics which ended at hip level, a bandolier-type belt across their broad chests, several dangling pouches of dried strips of meat, and a sheathed hunting blade. The Warriors wore no pants or leggings of any kind, probably because of their still-prominent, though vestigial, tails. Their sexual organs were kind of folded up and protected by scaled plates. Modesty wasn't a word in their vocabulary, anyway. The Warriors' weapons were simple, but surprisingly effective: each carried a heavy, pike-like spear and a devastatingly accurate crossbow. The bows could be loaded with either barbed shafts or *squaves*—tiny sleek-bodied reptiles which the caste had trained centuries ago as "organic weapons." The squaves sported pointy, hard-bone snouts and shark-like jaws full of tiny, razor-edged teeth. Phineas had seen the squaves impact their victims and then burrow into the flesh like ore drills. The lowest-ranking member of the Warrior contingent carried a large pack on his back filled with dormant squaves. It looked like a lousy job, but, as Phineas knew well, somebody had to do it.

The rest of the team was now moving single file through a copse of young redwoods and protofirs; Phineas fell in behind them. The Mesozoic forest thrummed and vibrated with the sounds of insect life. The low-level din was occasionally punctuated by the cries of beasts either eating or being eaten.

Directly in front of Phineas strode Visigoth, the large, very tall "General" of the warrior-caste. The leader was distinct from the others because of his bright yellow eyes, his immense size, and a helmet covered with the orange-and-yellow-striped hide of an allosaurus. Visigoth presented a rather fearsome image to all, and Phineas would not like to get the fellow upset.

They tramped through the green-shadowed world for more than an hour without incident, although Phineas was careful to keep a trained eye behind them. Most of the carnosaurs spent the morning and midday propped up against the bases of big trees, sleeping off the effects of a nocturnal kill and meal. Sometimes, the really big bastards would gorge themselves and remain torpid for days on end. But then there was always the chance that one of them hadn't scored the night before and might be rampaging through the Preserve ready to eat anything that moved.

And Phineas had seen men minced in their steam-shovel jaws, or smeared into jelly beneath their hind claws . . . .

Thoughts like that always reminded him of what a nightmare place the Mesozoic Preserve actually was. And that made him think of the *Dragonstar* itself, a monster-sized ship full of monsters, which, since its first appearance on the Copernicus Base instruments, had been like a curse on his very soul. When Phineas considered the facts, *very little* had gone right in his life since the alien artifact became a part of it. Everyone had crosses to bear, but why in hell did *his* have to be more than three hundred klicks long?

His thoughts idled about his mind as he kept a vigilant watch. The team moved ahead with a deliberate, slow pace which was unavoidable when passing through the thick flora. Looking up the line, Phineas was somewhat surprised to find Becky waiting for him. She fell into step as he drew even with her, and he found her dark good looks as appealing and riveting as ever.

"I've been meaning to ask you, but I never got the chance . . . ," she said, followed by a sly, familiar grin.

"Exactly *why* I would volunteer for this hare-brained little trip, right?"

"Yes," she said. "Although I wasn't going to put it just like that."

"Why not? It's apt, isn't it?" Phineas smiled, continued to scan the rear flank as he walked with her. He found himself wondering if she and Takamura were an "item" yet. He'd seen the way they looked at one another during the briefing, and even earlier this morning when they were assembling the group. He'd

bet his ass they were getting it on. He also wondered why he was
thinking such thoughts. Did he *still* care for Becky? Could she
ever be "just a friend," as she had once suggested?

Who the hell knew . . . ?

"I guess so," said Becky. "It's just that, well, knowing you as
well as I do, I can't help but imagine that you might have some
trouble doing things Mishima's way."

She used his first name. That probably meant something. But
he quickly told himself he didn't really give a damn, and enacted
a good "smile for the camera" kind of smile.

"I just had to get away from all that boy-scout crap," he said
firmly. "I wouldn't make a good pioneer, Becky. And I can't
stand this *waiting*. Waiting for something to happen."

"I know what you mean. You'd rather try and *make* something
happen, wouldn't you?"

The smile had left her face now, and she was analyzing him,
as she had always done. Some people could never accept what
you said at face value. They always had to search for the "real"
meaning, and Becky belonged to their ranks.

"It's funny," he said, "but I have a feeling this little excursion's going to be a bust."

"Really?"

He shrugged. "It's just a feeling . . . what can I say?"

"I'd better go back up the line. I'm probably distracting you."

"That's one way of putting it." He chuckled and regarded her
with a mock-leer. "All right. Talk to you later."

She nodded and double-timed it up the line. As Phineas
watched her ass bob and weave beneath her jump-fatigues, he
noticed another face turned out of the line, looking back at him.

Angular features, dominated by large, sparkling green eyes,
and framed by a coif of long curls, it was the face of Kate Ennis.
She only glanced back for a moment, but it was long enough for
her gaze to lock in with his own.

I'm watching you, said her gaze. *I'll always be watching you.*

She turned away just as Phineas thought of flashing her a
roguish smile, and it died on his lips. Mikaela had been spot on
in her assessment of the NBC journalist. On one level, it made
him feel good to be attractive to Kate, but on another, her interest
just meant more complications in his life. And his life was complicated enough, and he had no idea how he might deal with this
latest twist.

He followed the column as they cleared the heavy foliage of

the forest and entered a prairie. It was punctuated by rising blades of rock, which gradually sloped down to a riverbank. The cave mouth, he recalled from the briefing, should be close at hand. Scanning the area, he saw a grazing herd of triceratopes, but they were far away and posed no threat to the group. Still, it would be a good idea to watch them. Any panicky movement from the herd might be an early warning that a predator was about.

Phineas remained alert as the group crossed the prairie and gathered at the edge of the stream. The dark entrance to the cave yawned in front of them.

"The floor slopes downward once you get inside," said Takamura. "There's some machinery—probably pumps for the water—and then it's clear until we reach the catwalk. Are we ready?"

Everyone nodded. The Saurians shuffled their feet, snorted, and hissed a reply.

Takamura looked at Kate. "Do our friends have any problems? Any questions?"

"No," said Kate. "If you want to know the truth, I think they're itchy for some action. . . ."

Takamura seemed put off by her reply, but he forced a smile, anyway. "Well, I hope they don't get their way," he said stiffly. Then: "Okay, everybody . . . let's go."

Phineas followed the entire file into the cave, now flooded with the beams of torchlights. The interior dirt and rock soon surrendered to a metallic flooring which ran past an array of machinery. It pulsed with a rhythmic, low-register *thunk-thunk*. The floor gradually sloped down to join a catwalk, or gangway, as Takamura had described it.

As everyone climbed upon it, Phineas tried to keep himself oriented. The group was headed toward the control-section of the ship, and from the looks of the superstructure which surrounded them in the darkness, it appeared that Takamura's observation had been correct. They were walking along a bulkhead, a pocket between the outer hull and the interior boundaries (actually, the *ground*) of the Mesozoic Preserve.

The almost total darkness of the bulkhead passage was broken up by small utility lamps spaced every thirty meters or so. Their dull amber glow cast long shadows across the burnished metal walls, imparting a spooky atmosphere to the place. The farther along the group trekked, the more agitated the Saurians seemed to be getting. Several times, both Kate and Visigoth were forced to stop and discuss the matter with the troops. The second instance ended with Visigoth suddenly smacking one of his charges alongside his head. Discipline was not much of a problem in the warrior-caste.

After exchanging a few words with Visigoth, Kate moved back to join Phineas. Her harried expression was something he had not seen much.

"Problems?" he asked.

"Maybe. They're not exactly wild about walking down this narrow, dark passage. It's very alien to them. Making them restless." Kate looked at him with those big eyes as green as the sea. She had the eyes, no doubt about it.

"Well, you can't blame them, can you?" he said. "They're just a bunch of dumb grunts, and they've never seen anything like this before."

"I know, but it scares me. . . ."

Phineas grinned. "Well, try looking at it their way: how would you like it if all of a sudden somebody took you down *beneath* your basement, and you found out that what you always thought was the good old solid Earth was really just a bunch of *stage props*, held together with some chewing gum and bailing wire?"

"You're right," said Kate. "It's got to be more than unsettling. It's probably got them terrified."

"Of course it does. That's why they're hot for a fight. At least that would be something *familiar* to them."

She sighed and glanced up at the Warriors as they trudged onward. "I guess I'm not being much help. It sounds like you understand their cultural problems a lot better than I do."

If she was fishing for compliments, he decided not to bite. "Well, I've been around them longer than you, that's all. Plus, I have a feeling that all soldiers think alike—no matter what the species."

Up ahead, Takamura was signaling for the column to halt. His voice echoed along the passageway. "Let's take a rest right along here. Any objections?"

Visigoth passed along the message to his troops, but the Saurians remained standing in the center of the gangway, nervously looking back and forth in the dim, amber light.

"I'd better see if I can help the General," said Kate. "See you later."

"Right," said Phineas. "I'm going up and see how things are going with Takamura."

He edged past the Saurians, unable to ignore their pungent

body odor. They smelled particularly foul when they were in a fighting spirit. How in hell did Kate stand it? Cavoli and Krolczyk nodded as he passed, but Becky and Takamura did not look up from the portable instruments they had unpacked.

"What's going on?" he asked.

The professor looked up for a moment, then back at the readout panel on the betatron scanner. "See this buttress right here?"

Phineas looked at the metallic brace which Takamura had indicated and nodded. "Sure."

"Its molecular bonding is breaking down."

"Why?"

Takamura shrugged. "Hard to tell. Age. Radiation. Stress from the FTL jump . . . who knows? I'm going to test other points along the hull superstructure as we move through here to see how widespread the weaknesses are."

"Which means?" Phineas hated the way scientists always assumed you knew what the hell they were talking about.

"Well, for one thing, I think we've found the cause of the ship-quakes. It's like the tectonic plates in the Earth, with opposing pressures building up and building up and finally the plates slip a little . . . and I see the same things happening here, but on a smaller scale, of course."

"But large enough to cause problems," said Becky.

Phineas wondered when she had become an expert in physics, but caught himself for being so damned petty.

"But how can parts of the ship be 'slipping'?" he asked. "Isn't it all connected together? Welded, or whatever?"

"Yes, of course," said Takamura. "But that does not keep the ship from being subjected to various stress-vectors and torques. Imagine the hull being twisted along its longitudinal axis. Instead of actual slippage, the molecular bonding in buttresses such as this one get 'stretched,' and therefore weakened."

Kemp nodded. "I'm going to have to take your word for it, Dr. Is the ship in any danger because of it?"

Takamura shrugged. "Possibly. It depends upon the extent of the bonding damage."

"You mean this tub could just break apart at any moment?" The idea stung him deeply. One more thing to worry about when things seemed like they might be going too well.

"Well, it's not likely . . . but it *could* happen, yes."

Becky had slipped on a communications headset. "You want me to relay back to Dr. Jakes and the rest of the Council?"

Takamura nodded. "Yes, give them our position and the latest data. Tell them we'll keep them posted."

"How far along *are* we?" asked Phineas. "Now that you mention it."

"We're under the Saurian Preserve, about halfway till we reach 'World's End.'"

"And then what?"

Takamura grinned thinly. "I don't know."

"You about ready to find out?"

"Yes. Let's get them moving again."

The group pushed ahead for another two hours. Occasionally they paused to run instrument surveys on pieces of the hull's superstructure; twice they encountered banks of machinery, which Takamura inspected. The alien machinery had a familiar "look" or design to it, but Phineas didn't have the foggiest notion as to what any of it was. Bob Jakes and Takamura's research team had supposedly been learning about the alien technology back when they still had access to the control-section of the ship. He had no idea what they had learned or not learned.

Phineas was tiring of the monotonous walking, with an infrequent glance over his shoulder. There was nothing to see back there, other than an endlessly long pathway, defined by amber pools of light which grew ever smaller and weaker in the distance. He considered calling out to Kate, to invite her back for some small talk as they walked along. He needed something to help pass the time. He considered the situation with Linden's strange condition, but like Lombardy and Takamura, came up blank on the subject.

The Saurians seemed to have settled down. No longer were they snorting and hissing and turreting their heads back and forth almost constantly. They seemed to have accepted the alienness of the passageway and its apparently harmless nature. For the past hour or so they had been shambling forward, heads slightly bowed, shoulders hunched, and tails hanging low.

Abruptly that all changed.

Phineas watched all five Warriors' heads snap up at once, immediately alert. They stopped walking, and Kate moved on ahead for about ten paces before noticing that something was happening. She paused and looked back, then signaled to Takamura.

"What's the matter?" Phineas asked as he approached Visigoth. A redolent aura of Saurian odors wafted over him. Was it the smell of fear? Of a fight? He could not discern it.

For a long moment, the caste leader did not acknowledge him. The Saurian remained rigid, like his mates, as though they'd risked a look at Medusa.

Kate was suddenly by his side. She reached out and touched his arm, and Phineas could feel the warmth of her hand penetrate his sleeve. It was a pleasant warmth.

"What's going on?" he asked.

"I don't know. I've never seen any of them like this." There was the first hint of panic in Kate's voice.

Now Takamura and the others were crowding along the gangway, everyone looking from the Saurians to Kate and Phineas.

"What is it?" asked the professor.

"I don't know," said Kemp. "They were walking along and they all just stopped, got real tense."

"It looks like they're listening to something," said Becky.

Phineas touched Visigoth's muscular shoulder. "Hey, big guy . . . anybody home?"

"Careful," said Kate. "That might be the wrong thing to do . . . we don't know what's wrong with them."

Phineas nodded and stepped back several paces, raising the HK to his waist. If any of those lizards made a wrong move he'd cut them in half.

Slowly then, Visigoth lowered his head, blinked his eyes, and spoke to Kate. The other Saurians were in an agitated state again, and Phineas could see their nostrils flaring, their fingers tightening upon their pikes.

What the hell was going on?

"They *were* listening to something—" Kate said as soon as her translator completed the message in her headset.

"What?" said Takamura, interrupting her.

"Something up ahead," she said. "Something coming this way."

CHAPTER 12

SOMETHING WAS COMING this way.

Kate's words lingered in his mind like an unwelcome guest.

There was a fist tightening in Mishima's throat, and at the same time, he felt as though he might have an attack of diarrhea. Just what he needed—to crap his pants just when things were getting complicated. Everyone was looking at him, waiting for his command, and here he was worrying about letting loose in his jumpsuit. . . .

But none of them could know that, and he *was*, after all, in charge of the expedition. He was responsible for everyone. That was what their looks were telling him. He had to *do* something.

"What is it?" he asked in a soft voice. "Did they tell you what it is?"

Kate shook her head. "No. They don't know. But they hear its footsteps. 'Goth says it has 'hard feet,' like our boots, only harder. Like the walls."

"Like metal?" asked Kemp. "Is that what he means?"

"Phineas, I'm not sure. He's having a hard time expressing it. There might not be a Saurian word for it. I don't know."

"Great," said Kemp.

"How far away?" asked Mishima as he addressed the Saurian General.

Visigoth tilted his head, listened to the translation, then barked out a reply.

"Too far for humans to hear," said Kate.

"That doesn't tell us a hell of a lot," said Kemp.

"You want we should go on up ahead and see what it is, Doc?" Cavoli stepped forward, sporting an incongruous grin.

Mishima hesitated, wondering what might be the best decision in this case. He looked quickly from the tactical man to Kemp,

84

who nodded almost imperceptibly. Mishima then turned back to Cavoli.

"Yes, do it while we still have the element of surprise. Take 'Goth and a couple of his friends along. I'll come with you."

"You got it!" said Cavoli. Patting the stock of his heavy assault rifle, he started forward.

Visigoth's translator rattled off the last pieces of the conversation. The caste leader then selected two of his charges and gestured that they follow him.

Mishima looked at the rest of the group. Maybe it was just his imagination, but they all looked rather stunned that he was going along. He was a bit stunned himself. His stomach was ablaze, his bowels churning like a mill. He should face it: he was not cut out to be much of a hero.

But there was no turning back now.

Looking at Becky, he said: "I'll keep in touch by radio. Just keep your channel open."

"No problem. Be careful," she said.

Mishima nodded, looked over at Kemp. He wanted to say thanks, but he knew it would be inappropriate. "Colonel, you and Krolczyk can keep an eye on things back here."

"I should think so," said Kemp.

"All right, then. Let's go."

Mishima headed up the small group as they moved quickly down the gangway. Soon, they had left the rest of the team far behind, wrapped in the dull shadows of the passage.

What were they rushing forward to meet? A beast, somehow lost in the bulkhead? He wished it were something so simple, so familiar. No, it was unlikely that a dinosaur would have wandered so far away from its native environment. More likely it was an alien species, one of the makers of the *Dragonstar*, stirring from some secret place in the control-section.

Mishima did not know what to make of such a thought. It had long been an accepted theory that the crew of the *Dragonstar* had abandoned the ship eons ago. Now, thinking that some of them might have remained on board was oddly terrifying to him.

And that should not be so. Hadn't the alien designers of the vessel left elaborate dioramas and teaching machines to explain the purpose of the "seed ship"? Such thoughtfulness spoke of a benign intelligence, did it not?

Perhaps. But the *Dragonstar* had recently turned upon its guests—unleashing the radiation which drove some of the Saurians mad, then sealing off the interior and jumping off into hyperspace. Didn't sound very benign, did it?

Cavoli and Visigoth walked ahead of him, the other two Warriors behind him. The strong odor of the Saurians reminded him of graduate school summers when he worked as a masseur at the beef salon in Kobe. His job had been to feed the steers Kirin beer and give their flanks a tenderizing massage twice a day. He wished he was back in Kobe at this very moment. The Earth seemed so far away, so alien, as to be nothing more than a place in a fairy tale.

Mishima shook his head slowly. What a bad dream this all had become. . . . He wanted to see what was ahead, and yet he didn't. Why had he tagged along? His presence would be a hindrance if there was trouble, and he should have admitted it to himself before volunteering.

Suddenly, the Saurian General stopped, tilting his head to the side, listening. He hissed and barked out a short message which his translator—now on loudspeaker mode—processed as quickly as possible: "It comes closer."

"Hey!" said Cavoli. "I hear it, too!"

Mishima moved past the Saurian General and concentrated. Yes, there it was—a rhythmic cadence which suggested a steady gait. Something walking toward them wearing hard-soled boots, which tapped out a telegraphic message of its journey.

For another moment, the group stood in silence listening to the steady *tap-tap-tap* of the footsteps. Whatever it was, it was moving briskly and with confidence. There was a steady, machine-like aspect to the sound.

"Hey, what're we gonna do here?" asked Cavoli. "We can't be all bunched up on this walkway—it's too crowded!"

Mishima looked over the low railing. The gangway was suspended over the outer hull plates at a height of less than two meters. If everyone climbed over, they might gain an element of surprise. He offered his idea to the others, and before he realized it, Cavoli and the Saurians were heaving themselves over the side of the catwalk. He followed their example and hunkered down in the shadows next to a support beam.

From his position, he still had a good line-of-sight angle on the walkway. He would see what was coming before it had a chance to spot him—unless it possessed sensory powers he hadn't counted on. . . .

The *tap-tap-tap* of its relentless approach was much louder now. It walked with a boldness which suggested that it didn't care if it was heard or discovered. And that meant it was either very stupid or very confident.

"Jeez, it sounds like it's gettin' pretty close," said Cavoli.

"Don't do anything unless I give the word," said Mishima, feeling suddenly silly and inappropriate in the role of leader.

Visigoth passed along the command to his two charges, and the entire group remained huddled in waiting. The *tap-tap-tap* grew absurdly loud. Mishima looked up into the dwindling void of the gangway and saw a dim spidery shadow take form on the outer bulkhead. Whatever was coming toward them had just passed one of the amber auxiliary lamps.

"Get ready," said Mishima.

Cavoli raised his weapon. The Saurians seemed to be coiling up like snakes ready to spring.

The approaching shadow suddenly took form and substance. Emerging from the darkness and ambling along as though it were out for a walk in the park, the thing strolled past the men and lizards who waited in ambush.

A robot!

Mishima was both shocked and relieved to see the mechanical construct walk briskly past them. Looking like a four-legged daddy longlegs, the robot scissored along the gangway at a smooth pace. It sported two multijointed arms but with no hands, claws, or other recognizable ends. Standing up, Mishima clapped his hands, but the robot walked on, ignoring the sound.

"Where's it going?" asked Cavoli.

"I don't know," said Mishima. "In the general direction of the others, it seems."

Visigoth asked if they were planning to "kill" the metal creature, and Mishima told him they would follow it for a while, and only kill it if necessary.

The small group climbed back over the railing and trailed the walking robot. At first they remained cautious, hanging back, stalking the machine like a predator, but as they moved along, it became obvious that their tactics were unnecessary. Mishima could see that the machine was rather single-minded in its purpose (whatever that might be), and that reacting to living organisms was not part of its programmed repertoire. Eventually the small party edged its way closer, until they were within several meters of the machine. Still, it ignored them.

He radioed back to Becky, reporting what they had discovered, and prepared them for the machine's arrival if it indeed walked that far along the gangway. Mishima secretly hoped for a comment or possibly a line or two of advice from Colonel Kemp, but the ex-leader remained silent until the radio link was broken.

"I feel kind of silly," said Cavoli, "just followin' this tin can. . . ."

"I know," said Mishima. "But I would like to observe it just a little while longer."

Mishima felt foolish himself, but followed a hunch that he should not act rashly. He kept wondering why the aliens would have built such an odd-looking device. And why have it walk on long, spindly legs? A wheeled or treaded device seemed more practical, he thought.

His questions were answered as the robot approached a bank of machinery lining the inner bulkhead. Nimbly it climbed over the railing and up the face of the machinery like a mechanical fly. Of course! thought Mishima. Wheels would not give it access to the machinery.

Access for what?

For repairs, of course. Mishima watched as his suppositions were verified. The robot paused as it hunched over an unidentifiable device. A panel opened in its body and it slipped one of its arms into the cavity. When the arm reappeared, there was a small tool-like appendage on the end of the forearm. Mishima nodded as he watched the robot begin to dismantle a piece of the larger machine. Using various tool-arm ends, the robot performed some sort of maintenance on the machinery.

Mishima explained what was going on to the others, then radioed back to Becky. Everyone agreed that the repair robots were most likely harmless, but that some caution should be exercised when encountering them.

"We're right here watching the robot," he said in a calm, modulated voice, no longer edged with the suggestion of panic. "Why don't you get the group moving and we will meet you right here?"

"All right," said Becky. "We're heading out now."

She signed off and Mishima listened to the idiot hum of the open channel for a moment before switching it off.

He should have realized sooner that they had chanced on some kind of maintenance mechanism. It had long been realized that the *Dragonstar* was a self-sufficient, self-repairing entity, but it was also true that no one had ever actually *seen* how any of the maintenance was effected. It was as if little elves slipped out of the woodwork when everyone was asleep and fixed everything, and nobody had ever been able to catch the elves at work.

Until now, that is. . . .

"All right," he said, addressing the others. "Let's relax for a minute or two, till the others catch up."

"You mean we're not going to mix it up a little with the tin can?" asked Cavoli.

Mishima could not discern whether or not the trooper was joking, but he smiled, anyway. "No, I don't think it will be necessary," he said. "But keep an eye on it when the rest of them show up. Just in case."

"No problem, boss," said Cavoli, grinning. "If it makes a funny move, I'll turn it into spare parts."

Mishima nodded. He wasn't sure he actually liked this fellow Cavoli, but he seemed like the type who would be good to have in your corner if things got sticky.

The group passed the next ten minutes watching the maintenance robot. It was an incredibly agile, delicately appointed machine. Mishima was fascinated as he watched it scramble nimbly about the rack of alien devices. It was quick and facile as it changed tool bits on its spider-like limbs, making adjustments and replacements. When its tasks were completed it climbed down from the bulkhead and mounted the gangway, heading back toward the control end of the vessel.

"Okay, watch it now," said Mishima as the robot approached his group.

Everyone spread out, forming a gauntlet of bodies through which the walking machine could pass. The robot paused, as though sensing the presence of the possible obstacles, then proceeded to move carefully between them. Cavoli and the Saurians kept their weapons trained on the robot but it ignored them totally. As it cleared the corridor of their bodies, it picked up its brisk walking pace, and Mishima had an idea.

Radioing Becky, he spoke quickly. "Becky, listen, the robot's heading back in the direction it came—back toward the control end of the ship. I think it might be a good idea for us to stay on its heels. It might lead us to something interesting."

There was a slight pause, then:

"No problem," she said. "Phineas says we can catch up at double time. You guys keep up with our friend. . . ."

Mishima closed the channel and got his group moving. Walking with brisk, long-legged strides, they were able to keep pace with the robot. Checking one of his directional instruments, Mishima was able to calculate their position along the length of the vessel, and after several more minutes had passed, he estimated that they were drawing very close to the point where the control-section of the *Dragonstar* would be located. He wondered if his theory would be correct—if there would be free access between the inner and outer hulls to the business end of the ship. . . .

There came a sound of footfalls behind him; he knew it was Becky and Kemp and the others half-jogging to catch up. Greetings were exchanged and the others looked ahead to admire the newest surprise to be found on the giant ship.

"So that's our native guide, eh?" said Kemp as he fell into step at Mishima's shoulder.

"Yes, I just checked our position and we are approaching the point where the flat end of the cylinder wall sealed off the interior."

"How much farther?" asked Becky.

Mishima shrugged. "Any moment now."

Kemp shined his lamp ahead on the gangway, past the spindly figure of the maintenance robot, who still ambled heedlessly ahead of the group. "Can't see much, but it looks clear. . . ."

"That's what I'm hoping for." Mishima grinned at the Colonel, who had made no attempts to flaunt his experience or in any way influence the group. In fact, Kemp had tacitly helped Takamura make some critical decisions when things had gotten sticky. It seemed as though he was constantly reassessing Kemp. Mishima had always respected the man for his many accomplishments in service to the IASA, but had never trusted the egomaniacal streak in his personality. Perhaps Kemp's encounter with the *Dragonstar* had been more than just a humbling experience. Maybe it had been a real object lesson regarding the vicissitudes of life.

Kemp seemed to be changing, growing less authoritarian and less full of self-importance. Mishima wondered if Becky had noticed any differences in her former lover. And he also wondered why he would even ponder such a thing.

The group followed the maintenance robot for another thirty minutes—until it stopped and climbed a ladder which led to a platform about three meters above the gangway. Above the platform lay an access hatch, which presumably opened up into the interior. Mishima gathered his crew together as they watched the robot climb toward the platform.

"Where's it going now?" asked Kate Ennis, who had been walking silently alongside Colonel Kemp.

"The control-section," said Mishima. "We're definitely far enough along to be underneath it."

"You're sure?" asked Becky.

"Positive."

"There's a hatch above the platform," said Kemp, playing the beam of his torch over the closed access.

Nimbly the robot attained the platform, then stretched out one of its spider-arms to touch a control panel adjacent to the hatch.

"It's goin' up!" cried Cavoli. "C'mon!"

Mishima nodded. "Go on! Don't let it get through and seal us off!"

Cavoli and Krolczyk bounded up the ladder with surprising quickness. Cavoli reached the platform just as the robot had begun to lift itself through the hatch. Getting as close to the machine as possible, the trooper mimicked its climbing movements as it passed through the hatch. Simultaneously Krolczyk levered his rifle through the opening so that the hatch could not swing shut without meeting some resistance. As the robot cleared the aperture, disappearing into the shadows of the interior, Cavoli bolted upward and passed through, standing quickly and holding the hatch open manually. Krolczyk joined him in the opening and signaled to the others. It was a smooth, impressive display of training and gymnastics which Mishima could only envy.

"Nice work!" he said, not trying to conceal his admiration. "Hold on till we can get through."

His heart started thudding in his chest as he ascended the ladder, hoping that his hunches had been correct. Mishima climbed up slowly and was pulled up through the hatch by Krolczyk when he gained the platform. Looking around, he recognized the sleek, polished corridors of the control-section. He exhaled with a rush of breath and felt himself smiling broadly.

"We did it! This is it!" he yelled down to the others.

As the rest of the team passed through the hatch, Mishima fought to keep his excitement under control. A warm current of satisfaction gushed through him. They had achieved the first objective of his plan.

"Do you recognize any of this?" asked Kemp.

"Not really," he said. "But you have to understand that most of the control-section my group explored looked pretty much the same, pretty much like this."

"Should I contact the Council?" asked Becky, already keying in the hailing signal.

Mishima nodded and placed the receiver to his ear. Nothing but static. He winced, tapped the headset.

"What's wrong?" asked Becky.

"I don't know. I'm not getting through," said Mishima. "It's probably the shielding . . . I hadn't even thought about that."

"What shielding?" asked Kemp.

"The wall which separates this end of the ship from the open Preserve is lined with alloyed shielding. We never did figure out why. But without booster amps, we had trouble with radio-com."

"Didn't we prepare for that?" asked Kemp.

Mishima shrugged. "What can I tell you . . . ? I had forgotten about that problem until just now."

"So we can't reach the Council?" asked Kate. She was standing off to the side, near the group of Saurians, who had huddled about their leader, eyeing the empty, seemingly endless corridor with great suspicion.

Mishima shook his head. "I'm afraid not."

"That's no good," said Becky in a remonstrative, almost motherly tone. "You should have remembered, Mishima. . . ."

Kemp smiled. "Hey, we all make mistakes. That's why they still put erasers on pencils. . . ."

"You should be an authority on mistakes," said Becky.

"All right, that's enough," said Mishima, shocked at how quickly Rebecca had lashed out at her former lover. If there was still that kind of feeling involved, he wondered what kind of emotional potentialities still sparked between them.

"It's all right, Doc," said the Colonel, grinning. "She's right, you know."

"Perhaps," he said, "But this isn't the time or place to be filling out performance-rating charts."

"That's right, Mishima," said Becky. "But what are we going to do now?"

"Obviously someone is going to have to go back and report to the Council."

"Sounds reasonable," said Kemp. "I could go back."

Mishima's expression must have belied his surprise. Kemp explained himself further: "It looks pretty tame around here, and if you do get a chance to tinker with the controls, I'm not going to be much help. I can at least use my bureaucratic skills to file a complete and accurate report with the Council."

Mishima nodded. He had to admire Kemp's humble acceptance of an errand boy's job. "All right," he said. "Sounds good to me."

"Okay, then," said Kemp. "I'll see you all back at the ranch. . . ."

"Wait a second," said Kate Ennis. "I think I'd like to go back, too."

"Really?" asked Becky, her eyes flashing slyly from Kemp to Kate and back to the Colonel.

"Yes," said Kate. "Like Phineas says, there's no sign of trouble, and I don't think Dr. Takamura's going to need the Saurians back here. And if the Warriors aren't needed, neither am I, right?"

Mishima listened carefully to what the journalist was saying. It was certainly true that as long as they had no fights on their hands, the Saurian Warriors would be next to useless in the control-section. Besides, Mishima had never learned to feel at ease around the foul-smelling creatures. He could never fully trust them. Why not send them back with Kemp and Ms. Ennis? It sounded like a good idea.

"I tend to agree with you, Kate," he said after a pause.

"Good," said the journalist. "I kind of felt like a fifth wheel around here, anyway. . . ."

Mishima smiled, but inwardly he felt that Kate believed what she was saying. Apparently she did not realize how much he would have valued her experience in dealing with the Saurians if there had been any real trouble. He listened as she explained the change of plans to Visigoth, who appeared pleased to pass the new instructions along to his four charges. The Warriors seemed to be a bit claustrophobic, and the confining geometry of the hive-like corridors must have been making them anxious.

"Be careful," said Mishima. "If all goes well, we'll make our way back through the Temple entrance, and we'll be seeing you soon."

Good-byes and good-lucks were exchanged, and he watched them descend through the hatch and climb back down to the gangway.

That was when the ship was racked by another series of shipquakes and the groaning sounds of metal in protest.

CHAPTER 13

GOD, she was glad to be getting out of this damned tunnel!

The thought passed through Kate's mind like a welcome breeze. She had never been comfortable in confined areas, and combined with the acrid body odors of humans and Saurians alike, Kate had been fighting back waves of nausea and dizziness for the last hour or so. Not that she would have ever wanted to admit this to Phineas or the others, but it was true just the same.

Phineas . . . He was the only thing about the whole ordeal that was making it worthwhile. But the gravity of their situation and her growing paranoia of being confined had not allowed her to think much about him.

She didn't even care about the ship-quakes, she just wanted to get off the gangway and out of the tunnel. It had taken her and Phineas almost ten minutes to calm the Saurians after the hatch had closed over their heads and the platform pitched and shook like a yacht's poop deck in high chop. Phineas had tried explaining to Visigoth the stress on the *Dragonstar*'s bulkheads, the molecular bonding problems, but the Warrior leader must have failed math in school because he hadn't listened very well.

The lizards had been snorting and hissing and lashing out with their vestigial tails, and Kate was afraid for a moment that they might lose control. Thankfully Phineas had been able to influence Visigoth enough to control his underlings, to get them to climb down to the gangway and begin the journey out of the tunnel.

Now that they had been on the metal walkway for more than twenty minutes, the Saurians had settled down and had set a long-striding pace, which she didn't mind keeping.

"At this rate, we'll be out of here in no time," said Phineas, fighting to keep his breathing under control.

"They don't have to hurry on my account," she lied.

94

"Bullshit!" Phineas chuckled but didn't look over at her. "You can't wait another second to get out of here."

"What?"

"You might think you're fooling me, Kate . . . but you're not."

"I'm not?" Even to herself, her voice sounded relieved, now that she needn't keep up that stupid front that everything was just fine. She grinned and looked over at him as they walked. His eyes were bright, his jaw firm and full of strength, and his hair fell about his forehead in a most roguish fashion. He even had good teeth.

"I recognize claustrophobia when I see it," he said. "You see plenty of it when you spend a lot of time in space vehicles."

Her relief was being replaced by embarrassment. "I'm sorry, Phineas. I guess I'm just not cut out to be much of an adventurer."

"Don't be ridiculous. You're doing fine!"

Kate wondered if he was sincere, or if he just felt sorry for her. Looking straight ahead, over the broad, muscular shoulders of the Saurians, she saw the pumping machinery which fed the underground stream. Beyond this lay the entrance to the Mesozoic Preserve.

Seeing this, the Saurians broke into a trot, not afraid to display their anxiety in leaving the tunnel. For once, Kate felt in perfect synch with them. The gangway sloped up to the cave mouth entrance, giving way to a rock floor. Kate and Phineas followed the Saurians out onto the riverbank. She felt as if a heavy, wet cloak had been lifted from her head and shoulders.

The Saurian Warriors had spread out and were sniffing the air, eyeing their immediate surroundings with suspicion.

"Tell them not to wander off just yet," said Phineas. "I want to radio the Council and tell them what's been happening."

Kate nodded and conferred with Visigoth, who passed along the instructions to the others. As Phineas reported back to the Council, Kate watched their reptilian companions form a rough circle around their position. She had seen the Warriors in fighting situations; they were scary to watch. The clamor of battle and the scent of spilled blood drove them into a frenzy which could only be stilled by death. They were good types to have on your side, no doubt about that.

Phineas flipped off his LS helmet radio, walked over to her side. He gestured upward at the hazy sky, through which the illuminating rod at the zero-G central axis could barely be seen. "Our timing was a little off," he said.

"What do you mean?"

"It's going to be dark soon."

"We're only about an hour from the gate," she said. "We should make it."

Phineas sighed. "Maybe. But it would be cutting it close."

"What's our alternative—could they send out the ornithopter to pick us up?"

Phineas shook his head. "It's not airworthy yet. And the OTV's not big enough to carry all of us."

"What're you saying, that maybe we should hole up in the cave till morning?" Kate shook her head. "I don't know, Phineas, I don't know if I could take it."

"You might have to. It might be a hell of a lot safer than getting caught in the forest after dark."

"If we hurry, we can make it," she said. "Please. . . ." She hated herself for using the "helpless female" voice, but she knew it still worked on a lot of men. Besides, the thought of being stuck in that cave all night with five Saurian Warriors made her shiver.

She and Phineas alone—that would be a different story!

He exhaled slowly, checked his chronometer. "Let's see what old 'Goth has to say about our chances."

"You're going to take *his* word for it?"

Phineas grinned. "Why not? He *lives* here, doesn't he?"

"He also has an allosaurus hide stretched across his helmet. He's probably itching for a fight."

Phineas looked at her, still grinning. "Well, Kate dear, if that's the case, you don't have to worry about him voting to stay out in the cave all night, do you?"

He was right, and she felt foolish again. God, she was sounding like a silly, flighty ass! Maybe she should just shut up and let the others decide. . . .

Just as Phineas had figured, Visigoth saw no problem in trekking back to the Barrier Gate by nightfall. She felt good to be heading back to the security of the Enclave, and whatever dangers might await them in the forest did not seem very threatening when tempered with the knowledge that they were going "home."

Forming a single-file column with Visigoth and his charges in the lead, the group moved across the grazing plain. Kate followed the Saurians and Phineas followed her, looking back every so often to protect their rear. To cover their ass, as he had so aptly phrased it.

It was easygoing while they remained out in the open terrain of the plateau, but as the land dipped down and merged with the edges of a dense prehistoric forest, Kate sensed a change in the air, like a gathering storm. As if foreshadowing the coming twilight, the green shadows of the forest enveloped them, making distant objects dimmer and less distinct. Colors of blossoms and buds seemed more saturated, more dream-like. The sounds of their footsteps became muffled and were swallowed up by the dense foliage. The first cries of the night predators ripped through the thickets of conifers and protofirs off to their right.

Clouds of insects buzzed above their heads, and countless small, scurrying things thrashed their way through the underbrush. Unseen creatures hustled by her feet, seeking safety from another night of feeding and death. Kate tried to keep her mind off such things by concentrating on the passing scenery. She told herself that she was experiencing the Earth just as it had been more than 120 million years ago. It was like going on a time machine, like living out your craziest dreams.

It was not a dream, but she knew it could easily become a nightmare.

A high-pitched scream exploded from the dense flora to their left. The poor creature sounded close enough to be in her hip pocket and she couldn't stop herself from jumping back. Phineas moved up to steady her shoulder. The Saurians had become more agitated in their movements, turning back and forth as they pushed through the forest, looking as though they were performing some kind of ritual dance.

Something was happening out there. Something was coming near them, she could feel it.

"Take it easy," he said, holding his heavy assault rifle ready.

"What was it?"

"You're asking *me*? How should I know?" Phineas shrugged and indicated that she keep up with the Saurians. "But I've got to tell you that it's just about feeding time at the zoo, so you'd better start expecting things like that."

"I know that, Phineas. It's just that *knowing* about something and then really *experiencing* it are two different things."

He chuckled. "You're telling me!"

They trudged forward in silence, and again the forest seemed to be swallowing up their every sound. The humidity and tropic heat sapped her energy, weighted her down. Visigoth paused several times to sniff the air, to bark out brief orders to the others. The Warriors were clearly expecting trouble.

Another scream, this time impossibly close to their column, strangled off in midcry, gurgling into silence.

"Christ-on-a-crutch that was close!" said Phineas.

Visigoth had halted the column and signaled one of his Warriors to take the point of the column. Kate watched the red-shirted Saurian disappear beyond the fronds of giant primordial palms. The grizzly General motioned them to move forward, and just as the column began moving, the vanguard Saurian broke free of the dense foliage, hissing and barking excitedly. His voice was loud enough to activate Kate's translator, and the device picked up something about a "nest."

She mentioned this to Phineas, and he reacted instantly.

"Goddammit, wait!" he cried as he pushed past her toward Visigoth and the other Warriors. The Saurians had gathered together and were pushing forward into the underbrush.

For a moment, Kate felt totally alone, as though they were all deserting her. Seeing Phineas's back to her made her feel suddenly vulnerable. She ran forward to join them.

"Phineas, wait! What's the matter?"

She followed him as he pushed through a barrier of sapling cycads. Ahead she could see that the Saurians and Phineas had crashed their way into a small clearing. There was a semicircle of man-sized boulders surrounding a clawed-out pit, and the surrounding plant life looked as if it had been recently savaged by an indifferent terra-forming machine.

The Saurians bounded toward the pit as Phineas cried out, trying to halt them. Kate moved forward, looking over Phineas's shoulder to see what was in the pit.

"Goth, stop!" Phineas was screaming. "Wait! No!"

The Saurian leader paused at the rim of the pit, his weapon raised over the still-glistening bodies of the four newly hatched creatures. Visigoth appeared surprised that he should not dispatch them.

"Oh my God, Phineas, what *are* they?"

Kate regarded the hatchlings quickly. They were bipedal carnosaurs—no doubt about that. Balanced expertly on their hind legs, the creatures eyed their audience warily. Their large heads appeared to be almost half their body mass, and their young, snapping jaws were already filled with rows of sharp teeth. With round, flat eyes glaring, they stood defiantly amid the cracked, leathery wreckage of their eggs. Although their tan-and-yellow-striped hides were still shining from the mucus of their eggs, the hatchlings were already as tall as a five-year-old child.

Visigoth grunted, still keeping his crossbow aimed at one of the babies, still staring at Kemp.

"Phineas—" she began again.

"I don't know for sure what they are, but I think they're little T. rexes. . . ."

"Oh God. . . ."

"Visigoth," Phineas was saying, "leave it alone . . . the mother's got to be somewhere close!"

Before the Saurian General responded, one of the other Warriors fired his crossbow, sending a squave into the panting belly of the closest hatchling. The squave's jaws started churning on impact, burrowing into the baby rex with incredible speed. The baby screeched out a piercing death-cry so intense it hurt Kate's ears.

The next instant, chaos took charge. The other Warriors unleashed their bows, and all four hatchlings were struck down. What had been a warm nest was now a slaughtering pit. The babies fought against the squaves which chewed through their soft parts and the nest was a thrashing tangle of blood-smeared bodies. The sounds of the abattoir rose up and mingled with the strong coppery scent of death.

Kate stood transfixed by the execution-style killings, unable to move. It was all so graphic, so horrible, her mind refused to process what she was seeing, refused to react. Suddenly Phineas was grabbing her upper arm, yanking her roughly away from the edge of the pit.

"C'mon, we've got to get out of here now!"

The Saurians were jumping up and down, shrieking and hissing in the joy of their kill. Kate looked away from them and saw the terror in Phineas's eyes.

"C'mon, Kate . . . now!"

His voice was consumed by the sound of thunder. It was a roaring so terrible that Kate felt paralyzed by its low-frequency vibrations. And she could feel the pain and the outrage in the cry of the beast. It was the tortured cry of a mother who senses the worst has happened . . . who *knows* she has lost her babies.

Behind them, the forest seemed to explode.

The hot, heavy air had been shattered like a sheet of glass by the cry of the female tyrannosaurus, and now the stand of ginkgoes and palms beyond the nest also blew apart in a fury of advancing flesh. Looking up, Kate saw the mother slash through the trees like a berserk construction crane. Thrashing its giant, turret-like head from side to side, the female strode forward, straddling the nest between its impossibly thick legs.

Visigoth and the other Warriors had broken ranks at first sight of the female, and, still half-shocked, Kate felt herself being pulled along by Phineas. Heedlessly they crashed through the underbrush, but looking back, Kate caught a photographic glimpse of the mother, bending her immense bulk low over the nest, using her snout to nudge the now-limp bodies of her young. In that instant of recognition, Kate swore she could see true suffering and pain in the eyes of the beast.

It was a terrible image she would always remember.

And suddenly the rex was pulling herself up to her full height of almost ten meters, her broad chest heaving as her lung bellowed out a cry of frustration and revenge. Her jaws snapped open and shut, as torrents of saliva ran like rain from her mouth. Then she paused to pick up the scent of the killers.

Blind panic flashed like lunatic neon right behind Kate's eyes. Her thoughts were fragmented, her movements automatic and unplanned. We're going to die, she thought. It was the single cogent notion in her head. Phineas continued pulling her along as they crashed and thudded madly through the forest. She could not sustain the breakneck pace. Her legs were like rubber and there was a fiery pain in her right side.

Behind them, the forest was being ripped apart, the sound of its destruction chasing them down.

"It's a hell of a fix they've put us in now," said Phineas. "Goddamned lizards!"

"Where are they?" she asked.

"Who the hell knows!"

The tyrannosaur bellowed again, and Kate looked back over her shoulder. The shadowed bulk of the great beast loomed over them like a tall building—a building that moved and with incredible agility. It seemed that it could cover the distance separating them in several more long, bounding strides.

Up ahead, another clearing revealed itself, and as they entered it, Kate saw what had become of the Saurian Warriors. Two of

them had climbed into the spreading limbs of cycad trees while
Visigoth and the two others had fanned out on the opposite side
of the clearing. All of them had their crossbows aimed at the
region behind and above Kate and Phineas.

"Hurry up!" he said. "If I can get past the clearing in time, I
can get set up for a couple of shots."

She ran as hard as she could. While her body was crying out
that it could take no more punishment, her mind kicked in the
override controls and pushed things a little further. A blowtorch
burned through the right side of her waist and her lungs heaved
without rhythm. Her eyes blurred and burned from the salty
sweat which leaked into their corners, but she kept her legs moving. Phineas had never let go his grip, and the vise-like pinch of
his hand was a comforting, inspiring kind of pain.

She was going to make it, dammit . . . !

The undergrowth of the forest beyond the clearing became a
haven, a goal to reach and be finally safe. She kept in sight, and
tried not to think of the eating machine at her heels.

But she looked back instinctively in time to see the carnosaur
emerge from the trees. The creature paused for an instant, tilting
her great head and studying the field as a gamester might survey a
playing board.

That pause was all Phineas needed. He tugged her along and
together they flung themselves headfirst into the brush. The
Saurian Warriors also used that freeze-frame instant to launch
their feeble attack. Screaming out in unison, all five launched
their bows. Three of the squaves struck the thick, crusty hide of
the rex's hind legs. The impact was not enough to penetrate the
calloused flesh and the squaves fell harmlessly to the loamy soil.
But the remaining two entered the softer, more vulnerable flesh
of the rex's underbelly, instantly chewing and gnawing and rend-
ing their way into the body cavity.

The rex was quick to react, screaming in pain and renewed
anger. With a quick dip of her head, her heavy, shovel-like jaws
plucked away one of the squaves with amazing delicacy. And
then, with a move like a karate kick-fighter, the beast leaped into
the air and used her left hind leg to scrape across her belly, dis-
lodging and killing the remaining squave.

If Kate had not seen the dance-like maneuver, she wouldn't
have believed it possible. The female tyrannosaur was quick
beyond all imagining.

While the Saurian Warriors were still reloading their bows, the rex dropped her head and charged them. Phineas took aim with the heavy assault rifle, unleashing a clip of explosive bullets in a blur. But the beast was too quick for his first salvo, having already moved inside the range of his aim. In an eye-flash, her great jaws descended and snapped up the nearest Warrior. There was a glimpse of his legs, a jerk of her head, and the saurian was a small lump working its way down her throat. Ignoring her quick meal, the rex crashed forward into the nearest cycad tree. The concussion of her great body shook loose the two Saurian bowmen, and they dropped from the branches like pieces of ripe fruit.

In an instant she lashed out with one of her massive hind claws and raked the nearest felled Warrior into a smear of red pulp. It happened so fast Kate wasn't sure what she had seen until the image burned in her mind like the retinal print of strobe. The second Warrior leaped up and raced headlong between the rex's legs, jamming his pike upward into the soft, genital region. It appeared to be a practiced maneuver, and the carnosaur bellowed in pain.

Visigoth and the other remaining Saurian launched new squaves into the rex's underbelly, then charged out of the bush with pikes raised. She reacted by back-stepping with a nimble half-jump and a dip of her head. The Saurian between her legs, suddenly exposed, looked up in time to see her heavy jaws envelop him and close with the finality of a bank vault's door.

Phineas had aimed his rifle at the beast but had not yet fired a shot.

"What're you waiting for!" Kate screamed, hanging on his shoulder.

"They're in the way! Damned lizards!"

But this proved to be only a temporary problem. After seeing the third of his small platoon wiped out, Visigoth barked out the order to retreat. Miraculously he and his single Warrior were able to dodge the next vicious swipe of the rex and duck into the edge of the forest, running as fast as they could.

Phineas seized the moment and opened up with the Heckler & Koch. Its ratcheting report was a counterpoint to the constant bellow of the rex. The first volley of explosive slugs ripped into her nearest hind leg, shredding it into a bright pink mist right down to the giant gleaming bone. The beast shrieked in agony and she spun toward the fury of her newest attacker. Her eyes were wide and yellow, glazed with madness and exquisite pain. Tilting her head to the side, she bent down to examine her slayers.

As Phineas slammed home another clip into the chamber, Kate could feel the wash of the beast's breath, a dank wind smelling of blood and decay. The nightmare head dropped lower still as the rex staggered forward, crippled by the first magazine of ammo, but still driven to its instinctive task of killing and eating.

"Get back!" Phineas was crying as he unleashed the second clip.

The slugs stitched a solid line up the rex's neck, into her open maw, and into the granite-hard skull. The C-4 explosive bullets opened up the beast like a coroner's blade; they shattered the bones in the skull and jellied the brain.

Abruptly the rex straightened up, became rigid, then convulsed violently as its nervous system short-circuited. Kate felt Phineas tugging on her arm, but she was transfixed by the sight of the monstrous killer as it began a brief, obscene dance of death. Throwing back her head, the beast's jaws sagged open as blood and spume frothed up her throat. She turned in one great circle, thrashing her tail and pistoning her hind legs in one final paroxysm, before pitching forward as though in slow motion.

"Look out!" Phineas was screaming, as though from a great distance, even though she knew he was right beside her.

Kate felt herself being pulled backward with a snap of her neck. Looking up, she saw the body of the rex covering the whole of the sky. As she moved, the beast's falling trajectory seemed to be following her, slowly descending to crush her like a bug.

There came the sound of snapping limbs and branches and the thunderous *whump* of impact. Something scraped her shoulder, hard enough to throw her to the ground. Her head hit something hard, and that's when the darkness came.

When she opened her eyes, there was a bright light to her left. A dull, throbbing pain seemed to be capering behind her right eye. There was nothing but darkness beyond the glare of the single lamp.

Until Phineas Kemp leaned forward, the orange glow of the bulb illuminated half of his face. He smiled and slowly lifted her to a sitting position, steadying her against his chest. She felt dizzy, disoriented, but the firm strength of his embrace was reviving her quickly. The pain began to subside.

"Well, I think you're going to make it, lady. . . ."

"What happened?"

"When mom took a tumble, what was left of her head missed you by a couple of centimeters. Just caught your jumpsuit and pulled you down. You hit your head on a tree trunk or something. You've been out cold."

"Where are we? Are we safe?" Kate looked around, but could not yet focus on the dim shadows beyond the single pool of light from his lamp.

"We're back in the cave. . . ."

"What?" Her heart jumped as she realized they were still out in the Preserve, and it was definitely dark now.

"Take it easy. Nothing's going to bother us in here."

"But why? How . . . ?"

Phineas smiled, gave her a comforting squeeze on the arm. "When the tyrannosaurus went down, her carcass started attracting scavengers immediately. We had to get out of there before the place was overrun. . . ."

"Oh God" was all she could whisper.

"So I picked you up and carried you back here. It was the closest, and definitely the safest."

"You carried me?"

"We would've never made it to the gate," he continued. "I radioed the Council, told them what happened. They're going to send the OTV out in the morning."

"What about Visigoth?"

Phineas shrugged. "Last I saw, he was beating cheeks into the forest. He hadn't gotten back to Hakkarh when I was on the horn. . . ."

"I hope he makes it," she said. "Did you see the way they stood up to the rex?"

Phineas nodded, grinned. "Yeah, those guys are either very brave or very crazy."

"Like you," she said.

"Huh?"

"Very brave to save me like you did. . . ." Kate smiled and sat up straight. She touched the edge of his jaw. "Or very crazy to think you'd be safe spending the night in a cave . . . with *me*."

Phineas swallowed, but said nothing. He seemed a bit shocked by her forwardness, but not displeased.

"You mean I'm *not* safe?" he asked finally.

Kate began unbuttoning the top of her jumpsuit.

"That depends," she said, "upon what you mean by 'safe,' doesn't it?"

CHAPTER 14

PHINEAS sat in the back deck of the terrain vehicle with Kate. In the front of the cab sat Mikaela Lindstrom with James Barkham at the controls. Barkham, knowing the exact location of the cave entrance, had volunteered to come after them. Each time Phineas looked up at Mikaela, he saw a special light burning in her eyes. It was the light of *knowledge*, of certainty.

When the OTV had pulled up to the cave that morning, and Mikaela first opened the bubble to regard the bedraggled pair after a night in the wild, Phineas knew that Mikaela had *known* immediately.

It was as though he had been wearing a cheap sign around his neck, or maybe even stuck to his forehead, which proclaimed: I gave Kate a good pranging last night!

He wasn't sure what she was feeling, or how she planned to deal with it. Outwardly her face revealed no emotions whatsoever. She had asked a raft of concerned questions when they first boarded the vehicle, and had seemed curious to see the tyrannosaur's nest, even though it had been picked fairly clean by scavengers by the time Phineas directed them past it. Yes, outwardly Mikaela was acting as though nothing had happened, as though nothing were different.

Only her eyes betrayed her.

She probably thought he was feeling quite good about the whole thing, but on that score she would be wrong. Just when Phineas thought that he might be starting to truly understand the dynamics of his relationships with women, Kate Ennis managed to foul things up again.

Here he was, finally realizing that not only was it possible to have women as close friends but it was desirable as well. In fact, he had considered Kate a close friend, and had been feeling good about the way he had adjusted to that kind of bond between them. Then he has to go and save her silly life, and they get to play marooned-on-a-desert-island for the night, and everything goes flying down the crapper.

Last night, after they'd made love, he felt like he was drunk on a heady aphrodisiac. He couldn't think of anything but green-eyed Kate. Long-legged Kate. The Kate who wanted him all for herself. And then after they'd fallen asleep in each other's arms, he didn't have to think about it, either. And it hadn't been difficult to avoid the implications of the whole thing when she woke him up this morning for round two. . . .

Afterward, when they dressed and waited for the OTV, he tried to talk to her about it, to analyze what had happened and what it all meant, but she kept shutting him down. Kate hadn't wanted to face it, to talk about what had taken place. "Not now, Phineas," she had said. "Not yet. I have to sort things out."

She had to sort things out? Christ, what about *me*!

And what about Mikaela? Would she confront him? Maybe. Would he tell her the truth? He wouldn't want to lie to her, but what the hell *would* he do?

Rely on spontaneity, he decided.

Dammit! This was crazy. Here they all were in the middle of a prime fix, hurtling through hyperspace to an unknown location, and all he could think about was how to manage the women in his life. . . .

It was truly insane.

Barkham had been talking, but Phineas hadn't been listening. Suddenly he was aware that he was being addressed directly, and he looked up at the driver.

". . . the farm, eh, Colonel?"

"I'm sorry, Jim, what was that again?" He cleared his throat.

"I was just asking you if after seeing Visigoth running off into the night, you probably figured he'd bought the farm . . . you know, gotten his ticket punched?"

Phineas grinned. "Oh yeah, right. He put up a hell of a fight with just those silly weapons they carry, though."

Barkham chuckled, brandishing his super-white teeth. "Yeah, I'll tell you, he caused quite a stir among his caste-mates when he came strolling up to the gate this morning!"

"He's a tough son of a bitch. I'm glad he made it."

"He wanted to come back out and get you. Says you saved his life," said Mikaela. Her voice was even and as natural as could be.

"I'm flattered," said Phineas.

Mikaela smiled. "I'm sure it feels good to be a hero again," she said without looking back.

Phineas said nothing. He gazed out at the passing landscape, daring not to look at either Mikaela or Kate, who had been very quiet during the entire trip. Phineas thought that was a very coy way to handle things. He found her silence worse than the imaginary sign hanging around his neck.

Immediately upon returning to the Enclave, Phineas and Kate met with the Council and went through a thorough debriefing of the mission. Bob Jakes was pleased with its success, and announced that his people would try to locate Takamura with radio-sensors, despite the heavy shielding separating the Preserve from the control-section.

The Council decided to call a general assembly of all the survivors so that an announcement could be made about Takamura's efforts. Phineas didn't think it was such fantastic news, but he agreed with the Council's Chair, Joy Davison, who believed that the news would be a good morale booster.

Joy had been correct. After the assembly was recessed, a spontaneous party broke out under the large tent. Everyone was in a festive mood, and you could just sense the subtle suggestions of renewed hope running through them.

Someone had handed Phineas a cup of wine and he was sipping it slowly. Mikaela stood by his side, watching one of the engineers strum on a guitar. Others, including Kate, were dancing and clapping their hands as he sang a popular song.

"It's good to see this," she said. "Usually there is an undercurrent of despair, of resignation."

"Hope springs eternal, isn't that what they say?"

Mikaela turned and faced him, saying nothing. It was the first time they had been able to speak privately since he'd returned.

He smiled, put his arms around her. Her eyes were focused tightly on his. "You haven't told me how glad you are to see me . . . or that you were worried about me . . . or that you love me."

"Neither have you," she said.

"Hey, this is the first chance we've had to talk. Give me a break!" He smiled and tried to appear nonchalant, but he thought he sounded like a bad actor reciting lines.

"So talk," she said. There was not the hint of a smile on her pretty Scandinavian face. Her blue eyes stared at him with frosted clarity.

"I love you, Mikaela," he said, meaning it, but feeling a hollow sensation in his gut.

"*Do* you?"

"What the hell is that supposed to mean?" He knew what was coming, and decided that maybe a good offense would be the best defense.

"Oh, I don't know . . . maybe I should not have said it."

Mikaela did a half-turn away from him, looked back, then out to where Kate Ennis was dancing with the others. She made sure he noticed.

Phineas smiled. "I don't believe it—my enlightened, rational scientist from Sweden is jealous!"

"Does it really surprise you?" She moved closer to him.

"No, I suppose not," he said. "I guess we're all a bit jealous when you come right down to it."

"What happened out there, Phineas?"

He looked at her, and found that he had to look away. A bad sign, that.

"Do you mean did we get it on? Isn't that what you mean to ask?"

"Phineas, you don't have to get so testy."

"Oh, I don't? Well, thanks for your permission, madame."

"It doesn't really matter—" she began.

"But you still want to know, don't you?"

He could feel his blood getting up. They hadn't had a good fight in weeks, and he found he was in the mood for a skirmish. He still didn't know if he would cop to doing it or not.

"Phineas, it's not like that," said Mikaela. "It's just that a woman *knows* when another woman is after their man. And I know Kate Ennis wouldn't let an opportunity like last night go by without making her play."

He smiled. "And yet, you say it doesn't matter. Now, what the hell does *that* mean?"

"I mean realistically, rationally, sex is no big deal, is it? Two people, getting together, that's all." Mikaela looked into his eyes again. She was easing up, softening. "*We* have more than just sex, don't we?"

"Of course we do."

"Well, that's what I mean when I say it doesn't matter. It

really doesn't. I feel secure in the knowledge that we have a multidimensional relationship."

"We do indeed," he said, hoping that she had decided to drop the whole issue.

"But," she said, "just to satisfy my curiosity, I *still* want to know what happened last night!"

"You will never cease to amaze me, Mikaela." She had him disarmed now, and he was confused. He had no conception of how she might react if he told her the truth.

"You're stalling," she said.

Phineas exhaled slowly. "All right, I'll tell you exactly what happened."

"You will?" She seemed surprised.

"Yes, of course. Why not?"

"Go on."

"Well, it was about ten minutes getting back to the cave entrance, and it was getting dark by then. Kate was still out like a light, and—"

"Phineas, I don't want a minute-to-minute accounting. I *know* she woke up and batted those big green eyes at you. . . . I want to know what you *did* about it!"

He shook his head, grinned.

"Well, if you must know, I—"

He never completed the sentence. A ship-quake was coming on, but more violent than anything yet experienced. A sound like rolling thunder across a vast plain hammered the air. It ran on as though it would be endless, and the hull shook violently. Nearby Saurian buildings resonated from the monstrous vibrations which rippled through the great ship's hull. Phineas remembered Takamura's analysis and feared that the whole vessel might be breaking up.

The merriment of an instant before vanished, and people started running in all directions. There were cries of panic punctuated by voices of reason and calm, trying to keep order to things. Taking Mikaela's hand, Phineas pulled her out toward the open space of the market boulevard where there was less chance of something falling on them. He found himself seeking out Kate in the churning crowd, but she had disappeared in the rush of human traffic.

"What's happening?" yelled Mikaela above the din.

"Not sure! It's different from the other quakes."

"Let's go to Jakes's tent," she said.

"If it's still there. . . ."

They ran into the open boulevard and headed for the large vendor's tent where Bob Jakes had sequestered all the surviving lab equipment. The tent served as a kind of clearing house for all the various sciences represented and a headquarters for any kind of instrument analysis needed. Just as they reached the entrance, the vibrations ceased, the terrible sounds diminished to nothing.

The sudden stillness seemed as freaky as the chaos had been. Phineas was merely grateful that the gigantic hull had not split like a bean pod, spilling them all out into the null-space of the universe ripped inside out. Just what they needed. . . .

"Is it over?" asked Mikaela, hanging on his arm.

"I think so."

"What was it?"

"That's what we came here for," said Phineas. "Let's see what Bob can tell us."

A tactical trooper cleared them for entrance into the area (probably because of Mikaela's position on the Ruling Council, he thought later), and they joined a crowd of other science types who had gathered around one of Bob Jakes's workbenches. The chief physicist stood in the center of the pack, nervously cleaning his twentieth-century spectacles with the hem of his lab coat. He nodded as he saw Mikaela and Phineas approach and join the others.

"We've just gotten some data off the scanners," he said in a voice full of choked emotion. "We've jumped back into real space."

CHAPTER 15

CAVOLI AND KROLCZYK had been wisecracking as they walked along ahead of Mishima and Rebecca Thalberg. They were either trying to relieve tension or perhaps dispel the growing boredom of the expedition. Whatever their reasons, their coarse humor was starting to bug Takamura.

It did not seem to be bothering Becky, however. Sometimes she had laughed, and had even joined in on the banter once or twice.

Maybe he was just starting to get edgy.

They had been walking through what seemed like an endless system of corridors. There were levels upon levels of the control-section, laid out in an orderly grid-like fashion, so that the whole end of the cylindrical ship resembled an immense hive. Using the instruments he and Becky had brought along, they had plotted out the most direct route to the access to the Temple of Hakkarh. Mishima estimated they should reach that point within several hours.

"You've been awfully quiet for a while," said Becky in a half-whisper so that the two troopers in the van could not eavesdrop. "Something wrong?"

He sighed, glanced at her. There was something about her dark liquid-brown eyes and thick brown hair that excited him. Just looking at her recalled the sweet smell of her hair when he had buried his face in its scented depths. The memory of her aggressive, yet submissive, lovemaking stirred him, and he felt a warm glow in his groin. He could almost experience it all over again.

"Mishima, I said is there something wrong?" Becky interrupted his pleasant fantasy and tugged his sleeve.

"Oh no! I'm sorry," he said, feeling his cheeks flush. "I was just daydreaming."

"For a while there, you looked like you were upset about something, then you had a funny little grin on your face. Must have been *some* daydream!" She smiled.

He nodded. "I guess I'm just getting impatient," he said. "Walking through this place is like being in a maze! It's taking longer than I'd thought."

Becky shrugged. "We're making good time. And besides, none of us have anything better to do, right?"

"I suppose so. . . ."

The two tactical troopers paused as they reached an intersection of passageways.

"Which way, Doc?" asked Krolczyk. He was tall and rangy and sported a gold earring in his left ear. He had a sharp wit and feral eyes. Mishima thought he would've done very well aboard an eighteenth-century frigate.

Becky checked the hand-held map-scanner, tilted her head to the right.

"Take a right," said Mishima.

"You got it," said Krolczyk, leading the way.

Mishima had noticed that he and Cavoli had long since dispensed with creeping down the corridors with their rifles leveled at the hip. The control-section was as quiet as a pathology lab. They had not even seen another maintenance robot.

"Good thing you got them instruments," said Cavoli. "We'd be lost as shit otherwise."

Krolczyk grunted as he walked ahead. "I feel like a rat in a maze. . . ."

"Well," said Mishima, "it will—"

Another ship-quake suddenly braced the vessel with a series of severe shocks. An ominous sound like rolling thunder echoed and reverberated down the hallways. It rambled along the passageways like a beast in search of prey. The vibrations in the hull were so great they were all thrown off their feet.

"Jesus!" cried Cavoli. "What happened?"

"Everybody okay?" Krolczyk was trying to get to his knees as another series of groans and the cry of shrieking metal passed through the hull.

And then it was abruptly over.

The silence which followed seemed all the more intense in

contrast to what he had just experienced. Eerie. Mishima felt a chill race down his spine.

"That wasn't like the other ones," said Mishima, getting to his feet.

"I know," said Becky. "It sounded different, somehow."

"Oh, it was *definitely* different," he said. "Something is placing additional stress on the hull. The engines, perhaps. . . ."

"What do you think it means?" Becky looked up at him with a concerned expression.

"Just a guess, but it could mean that we are breaking out of hyperspace. . . . I don't know, I could be completely off base."

"What're we doin', Doc? Everything okay?" Cavoli moved back to assist Becky to her feet and gather up her splayed-out packs of electronic gear.

"I think so," said Mishima. "Let's try to get back to the Temple entrance ASAP."

"You want us to double-time it?"

He shook his head. "To tell you the truth, I doubt if I could keep up with you. Let's just keep up a brisk walking pace, all right?"

"Brisk," said Krolczyk, smiling. "Okay, you got it." He turned and started walking with long, quick strides.

Mishima and Becky fell in behind the two troopers and walked without speaking for a few minutes. Suddenly her radio crackled and popped. Static laced the words of Bob Jakes, but at least he was coming through.

"This is Council HQ, do you copy this, Becky?"

"I can just barely hear you, Dr. Jakes," she said as she halted and hunched down over the portable transceiver.

"We are using a jury-rigged amplifier to boost our signal," said Jakes. "Reception is lousy, but acceptable. Are you folks okay in there?"

"Affirmative," said Mishima. "Did you get anything on your gear from all that noise? What happened just now?"

There was a pause as some fine tuning was applied to the transmission. Jakes cleared his throat and spoke in a voice which was degrees cleaner. "We had a feeling you might not know. . . . That's why we tried to raise you. . . . We broke through!" The radio crackled for an instant. "We're out of hyperspace!"

The words were scratchy and barely intelligible, but they hit Mishima like a karate kick to the solar plexus. *The ship was back in normal space*. Rationally he was pleased that the transition had been made safely, but emotionally he felt cheated. His dreams of taking over the controls and successfully bringing the ship back into normal space-time had been shattered.

"That's fantastic!" he said automatically. Becky and the others added their own comments simultaneously.

Actually, Mishima thought, it had been a silly dream. An adolescent power-fantasy, a Tom Swift fairy tale notion. In a way, perhaps it was better this way. Now he could concentrate on getting back to the Temple entrance, opening it, and at least providing the researchers access to the alien artifact once again. At least his little foray would serve some good cause. . . .

"Dr. Takamura, are you there?" Jakes's voice danced among the bursts of static.

"Yes, right here! Listen, do you have any idea where we are?"

Jakes chuckled. "Good question! It's one we're all asking. The scope-cam on the hull made the FTL jumps intact. We appear to be heading for an orbit around a red giant. You should see the size of the star. Incredible. . . ."

"With the telescope camera still working, you might be able to get some data to help dope out our location," said Mishima. He didn't know that much about astrophysics, but with the help of one of the DEC units, they might be able to extrapolate their location in the galaxy.

If, that is, the *Dragonstar* was *still in* the galaxy.

"We're way ahead of you on that one," said Jakes. "We're working out some preliminary mappings now. It's going to take a little time, but we might come up with some answers sooner or later."

"Beautiful," he said. "I figure we're less than two hours from the Temple entrance. Plan to meet us there when we spring the locks on that place."

"Sounds good, Doctor," said Jakes as another burst of static encrusted his words. "We will keep in touch till then."

"One more thing," said Mishima. "You said we're closing on a red giant . . . do you have any readings on it?"

Jakes chuckled again. "Nothing yet. We're working on it. All we have is what we can see of it."

"And how does it *look*?" he asked.

"Like a big, hazy tomato," said Jakes. "Seriously, though, I gotta tell you: This star looks very unstable."

CHAPTER 16

PHINEAS KEMP LISTENED to the entire radio conversation with Dr. Takamura and had to stifle a little grin. He could not help but wonder if Takamura felt as if his thunder had been stolen. It looked as if the *Dragonstar* had been able to get itself out of hyperspace *without* the help of the Good Doctor, thank-you-very-much-have-a-nice-life-and-all-that-jazz.

And there was Takamura roaming the endless halls of the ship's control-section, his "important mission" reduced to nothing more than serving as a glorified doorman—assuming he would be able to open that door from the Hakkarh Temple. If that was a bust, the scientists would feel doubly foolish and defeated.

Phineas felt sorry for Takamura, especially since Becky had been present to witness his disappointment. It was always worse for a man to suffer defeat or humiliation in the presence of a woman he desired or loved or needed.

Now, there was a perfectly chauvinistic notion, he thought sardonically. Not that he cared one way or the other. Because he honestly believed it to be true—in fact, he *knew* it was true because he'd experienced it himself. One of the most difficult things he'd ever had to do was look Mikaela in the eye after everybody had voted him out of power. Oh sure, she'd been comforting and understanding, but it had still hurt like hell. And hadn't he felt like a perfect fool?

But the game wasn't over until it was *over*, and he felt that his chance for vindication would come—sooner or later—and he would show the whole bunch of them that they needed him, after all.

Someone cleared his throat and the area became very quiet. The absence of sound gently tugged Phineas from his inner

116

thoughts. He regarded Mikaela at his side, then focused his attention on Dr. Robert Jakes.

After Jakes signed off the radio, he turned and stared silently at the small assemblage of science types and research assistants. The IASA had empowered him, as Project Director of the team of scientists, to study the *Dragonstar*, and Jakes had been aboard the alien vessel almost from the beginning. Even though the women had suffered through differences of opinion several times in the past, Phineas had always liked Bob Jakes. He was a perceptive, no-bullshit kind of guy, and his habit of wearing spectacles when surgery or perma-lenses would correct his eyesight indicated his individualistic nature.

"All right, people . . . we have some work to do," Jakes said. "Tom, I want the scope-cam mapping data processed ASAP. Jorge and Nikita, I want your people to finish the computer model on that star out there—I want the best projections possible. I'm also going to need a few people stationed up by the Temple entrance to assist Takamura when he gets there, if he needs it. He'll be expecting some kind of welcoming party, too, I'd guess."

As Jakes spoke, various factions of the assembled group nodded and split off to work on the assigned tasks. Jakes spoke slowly, but with the tone of gentle authority which was universally respected. He doled out some smaller jobs among the remaining people until only Phineas and Mikaela stood by his desk.

"Is there anything we can do?" asked Phineas.

Jakes grinned. "You can sit down and have a cup of coffee with me for starters. How's that?"

They pulled up chairs and sat down while Jakes poured off three mugs of black liquid.

"So we've jumped out of the frying pan and into the fire, eh?" asked Phineas.

Jakes shrugged. "Maybe. We're spiraling in toward this star," he said, leaning back over his desk to tap a flat-screen display, which pictured a large scarlet sphere. It did look like a hazy tomato.

"Into the heart of the sun?" Mikaela spoke softly.

"No. It appears that the ship is setting itself up for a tangential rendezvous with the orbital path of the star's sixth planet."

"What's the rendezvous ETA?" asked Phineas.

"At present velocity, the stellar orbital insertion is about two hours away. Then about another hour before we could achieve a stable orbit around the sixth planet itself." Jakes pulled off his glasses and cleaned them with the edge of his lab coat.

"Sounds like this little lost dog has finally found its way home," said Phineas. He felt a chill race down his back at the thought of confronting the builders of this vessel.

Jakes nodded. "Yes, it does sound like that, doesn't it?"

"And you have no idea where we *are* yet?" Phineas sipped from the steaming mug carefully. Jakes favored a strong blend of coffee.

"Not really. The idea is to feed the positions of the sky-map into our biggest computer, and by using known star positions in the galaxy as a referent, calculate where we are right now. The problem is creating the program which can perform this kind of analysis."

Phineas nodded. "You mean you want the computer to try to recognize constellations and known stars from *this* vantage point, even though they will most likely look totally different?"

"Basically, yes."

"God, who's going to write *that* program?"

Jakes grinned. "We're hoping that one of the smaller portables will do the job for us."

Mikaela shook her head. "Computers writing programs for other computers—it's incredible, isn't it?"

"Been going on for a long time, Mikaela. It just gets more complicated. That's the way it's always been with our jobs, right?" Jakes cleared his throat. "I'm also trying to get some readings on the effects of that hyperspace jump on the outer hull. Following up on what Takamura discovered."

"You mean we might have sustained some damage in returning to normal space?" asked Mikaela.

"Too early to tell," said Jakes. "It's just that I want to cover all the bases on this thing."

She nodded and forced herself to smile. Phineas could see that she was feeling uncomfortable as the newest realities of their plight were made evident.

"And what about that star?" Phineas glanced at the flat-screen monitor. "Is it really ready to blow?"

"I like to keep you on your toes, Phineas."

Again Jakes shrugged. "But you never can tell about these things. In terms of a star's lifetime, 'ready to blow' can mean anytime within the next fifty thousand years . . . or it can mean tonight. Odds are though it won't go anytime soon."

"And you don't recognize this star from any of the catalogues?" asked Mikaela.

"We don't have a top astronomer on board, and that would help. All we can go on is the data bases included in the basic program-bundle," said Jakes. "But then, you have to realize, there are millions of stars far away from us—at the opposite end of our galaxy, for example—which have yet to be catalogued. This one could easily be one of them."

Phineas nodded, sipped his coffee. No one spoke for a moment, and the atmosphere among the trio became heavy and full of ominous anticipation. It was like sitting out on a front porch, waiting for a mean summer storm to pounce on you.

"Then how did you know so quickly that this star was unstable?" asked Phineas. "How did you pick up on it so fast?"

"Some things you just can't miss, and this star has all the classic, easily identifiable symptoms. Remember when Betelgeuse supernovaed back in '16?"

"Of course, I was on the Uranus mission. It was the brightest thing in space."

"*Easily* the brightest. Back on Earth, I can remember you could see it up in the sky during broad daylight," said Jakes. "Well, they learned a lot from that explosion. Betelgeuse had expelled ring-like clouds of nitrogen gas, and possessed a heavy iron core which ultimately caused the outer shells of burning gases to collapse, then the shock wave and the explosion."

"And this star looks like Betelgeuse?" asked Mikaela.

Jakes harrumphed. "It could be its brother. Betelgeuse was about twenty times as massive as Sol. The star out there is about the same size as Betelgeuse, and it ejected a nitrogen clump quite some time ago—more than sixty thousand years—so it is very near the end."

"How can you tell how long ago?" asked Mikaela.

"By noting the distance the nitrogen is from the star and measuring its outward velocity," said Jakes. "That part's pretty simple, really, and you don't have to be a hotshot astrophysicist to figure it out."

"I'll take your word for it," said Mikaela.

"Thanks," said Jakes, smiling. "Because I've just about exhausted everything I know about astronomy. I've been sounding good up till now, but anything beyond this, and I'll be doing it with mirrors!"

Phineas had been thinking about all the facts Jakes had been reciting. Some of the things didn't make sense. "You know, this is sounding crazier and crazier all the time," he said.

"Yes . . . ?" said Jakes.

"Well, think about it—if that star is as unstable as it appears, why would the ship want to park right up under its nose?"

"I've been thinking about that, too," said Mikaela. "And I don't like the conclusions I'm coming up with."

Jakes nodded. "I think we're *all* thinking the same kinds of things. . . ."

"You mean we're providing taxi service to a bunch of aliens who've decided it's time for a little planetary exodus?" Phineas looked from Jakes to Mikaela as he sought confirmation.

"I'd say that's got to be a possibility," said Jakes.

Phineas felt his blood pounding behind his ears. The very idea that there might be some kind of confrontation with alien beings was getting his adrenaline pumping. Getting up from his chair, he began pacing within the confined space of Jakes's desk and the rows of lab benches.

"I know this isn't really my place to be suggesting policy, since I'm not part of the Council," he said, looking at Mikaela and then Jakes, "but *both* of you sit upon that lofty dais, and maybe you can convene an emergency session and make a few suggestions in my absence. . . ."

Mikaela smiled. "And you were disclaiming all rumors to being the power behind the throne!"

"I'm serious. If what Bob says is correct, and our initial instincts as to *why* this ship is heading for a planet encircling a dying star, then I think we might be in for a scrap."

"Of course, they might be friendlies," said Jakes.

"And I *might* live to see one hundred twenty," said Phineas. "But I'm sure as hell not counting on it."

"So you're saying we should prepare for the worst?" asked Mikaela.

"Damn straight! We've only got about three hours before we achieve a planetary orbit. Christ knows what's in store for us after that. . . ."

"He's right, Dr. Lindstrom," said Jakes. "Even armed and ready, we're most likely going to be at a sad disadvantage. But if they come in here and catch us with our drawers around our ankles, we won't have a chance."

Phineas grinned. He couldn't have phrased it better himself, and it pleased him to know that he had the support of a man like

Jakes when it looked like showdown time was fast approaching.

Mikaela considered their words for a moment, then stood up. "You're right. Let's get in touch with Joy Davison and Dennis Patrick. We're going to need a *plan* very quickly."

Mikaela moved to the radio console on Jakes's desk and began calling the two available members of the Council. Phineas continued pacing, looking out at the activity going on all around him. The ragtag collection of scientists were doing their best to quantify what was happening all around them, and then, with luck, maybe explain it correctly.

He wondered how he could best help out in the present situation. He wasn't really much on military strategy or tactics—old Coopersmith had had a real knack for that sort of thing—but there weren't that many among the survivors who *were* qualified. Maybe the best thing to do was get together with the best tactical heads available and come up with a basic defensive alignment. Probably the hardest part of the whole operation would be explaining it to the Saurians—especially Visigoth and his bunch.

Well, at least they had Thesaurus in their corner, and Kate seemed to get along with him fairly well.

Kate.

He hadn't had much time to think about her since all the excitement started, but she had definitely become a factor in his life. Even though he tried to prevent it, she had gotten to him, slipping under his armor almost effortlessly. It surprised him that he could even be concerned with such things when there was a good possibility that they all faced major problems, but such was the power men and women exerted over one another. He feared it would never change.

But for now, he would have to change gears and try to think about how a basic plan of defense, or at least readiness, might be activated.

With the Council involved it was probably going to be attempted by some idiot-committee.

Running things by committee had never turned him on. In fact, Phineas had always loathed that kind of crap. With committees you always had all the members falling all over each other to get under the spotlight when something went right, and of course doing a lot of ducking and finger-pointing when things went wrong.

He would rather make decisions on his own and then stand up for the heat or the praise.

Which is exactly what he had always done, and the reason he was currently dethroned. . . .

Well, that was okay, he thought. What goes around, comes around, and if he had learned anything during his imprisonment aboard the *Dragonstar*, it was surely patience—and maybe a little humility.

For the time being, he would be happy to just take up a weapon, like everybody else, and do his part. And he wouldn't go volunteering for any of their committees, either.

Just as Mikaela was finishing up on the radio, one of Jakes's assistants dropped some tyvek fax-sheets on his desk, taking a moment or two to point out a few figures, nodding his head several times as Jakes questioned him. The assistant moved off, Mikaela switched off the radio, and just like that the trio was regarding each other again.

"Davison and Patrick are coming here, Dr. Jakes, if that's okay, and we will have an ad hoc emergency session of the Council."

"Fine," said Jakes.

"In that case," said Phineas, "I'll just ad hoc myself out of here."

"Where are you going?" asked Mikaela, a bit surprised at him.

"I don't know. Maybe I'll go back and oil my guns. We're going to be needing them, I have a feeling."

"Don't you want to listen to the meeting?" she asked.

"Not really. And I don't want to get named to any committees, either. Just assign me somewhere, and you can count on me to be there."

Mikaela shrugged. "Any preferences?"

"I guess I could go up to the Temple and wait for Takamura to get through. The entrance up there is also a likely place any *other* visitors might want to come through," said Phineas. "Speaking of Takamura, somebody should radio him our latest plans."

"We will," said Mikaela. "Be careful, Phineas. I'll join you as soon as I can."

"All right. Have a nice meeting, folks, but I'd advise you to keep things short and sweet."

He turned to go when Jakes stopped him with a word.

"Wait," said the Chief Research Project Director.

"What's up?" said Phineas, turning back to see that Jakes had picked up the fax-sheet recently delivered to him.

"I think you have a right to know this, Phineas," said Jakes. "I

just got back some preliminary data on the amount of stress the
ship sustained when jumping out of hyperspace."

"Yes . . . ?" said Phineas, feeling a cold fist tightening at the
base of his stomach.

Jakes sighed and plopped the sheets to his desktop. "The
numbers say this can wouldn't survive another FTL jump."

"What?" said Mikaela, her voice on the edge of an emotional
abyss. Her normally radiant features seemed suddenly slack and
wan.

"You mean we're . . . we're *stuck* here?" asked Phineas. "No
matter *what* happens?"

"It looks that way," said Jakes. "Unless . . ."

"Unless *what*?" asked Mikaela.

"Unless the ship is programmed to automatically take us back.
But if that happens," said Jakes, "it might fold up like a cheap
accordion."

CHAPTER 17

KATE FOUND HIM SITTING in the Temple of the Philosophers. He was alone, facing the metallic panel that had once been a sliding partition which opened into the alien control-section of the *Dragonstar*. She approached him carefully, so that he would not hear and turn until the last possible instant.

Centuries ago, when the Saurians, with their pre-electrical technology, had selected the flat end of the giant cylindrical ship as the site for their Temple, perhaps a precognitive notion led them to actually enclose the hatch within the walls of their edifice. Or maybe the Saurian Priests had discovered the secret of gaining access to the control-section, and never revealed that hidden knowledge.

Kate did not know, but she found it remarkable, and certainly beyond coincidence, that the Saurians had selected this particular site for their most important of all buildings.

But seriously now, she had not come up there to contemplate the architecture or the history of the place, had she?

Kate smiled at the thought and closed the distance between herself and her prey.

"Hello, Kate," he said without turning around.

How the hell did he know it was her? She asked him that very question and he turned, and allowed himself to smile.

"Don't take this the wrong way," said Phineas, "but I guess you could say I've been expecting you."

"Really?"

"Yes. That, and I recognized the sound of your footsteps. You have a short, precise way of walking. I remember taking notice of it when we were on the gangway."

He grinned as he sat cradling his weapon. As he neared forty years old, he still looked young and healthy. There was no grey

124

in his sandy-colored hair, and few lines around the corners of his blue eyes. Surprisingly the stress of the past few months had not aged him as she had seen it ravage some men. He must be tough, as advertised, but he certainly could be gentle when he wanted to be.

"Phineas, I know you haven't been avoiding me, but I thought we should talk."

"I have, though," he said. "I *have* been avoiding you. It's just that the recent turn of events has made it easier for me to appear busy."

"All right," said Kate. "Let's take it from there. Why, then? You don't have to, you know? Are you afraid I might try to make things difficult for you?"

He shrugged. "I really don't know, Kate. Mikaela seems convinced, though . . ."

"That I might try to cause trouble? Or that I took you to bed the other night?"

He smiled. "Well, *both*, I guess."

"She's only half-right, you know."

"If you say so."

His matter-of-fact attitude irritated her.

"Phineas, don't be so constipated! I'm trying to talk seriously with you."

"Oh, I know you are," he said. "It's just that I'm not sure what I want to say to you, Kate. You've got me damned confused right now."

"Really?" she said, masking her surprise and excitement at what he could have meant by the word "confused."

"Yes," he continued. "I'm not going to stand here and tell you that I didn't like what happened last night. I enjoyed the hell out of it! But up until then, I had considered you a good friend. I was just starting to get comfortable thinking of a woman as a friend— instead of some kind of . . . of *adversary*."

"*That's* how you see most women?" What was he talking about?

"Well, maybe that's not the right word," he said. "But, Jesus, Kate, I always feel like I'm a player in a big game when I'm dealing with women. But with you it had been different. . . ."

". . . until I seduced you?"

"If that's what you did . . . then yes, until then."

"Well, why does that have to change everything?" It was a

loaded question, she knew. A bit unfair, perhaps, but she was interested in his reply.

He stood up, started pacing about the area in front of the sealed door to the control-section. "I don't know why it changes things—it just *does*, that's all."

"Phineas, that's no answer."

"It's the best one I've got. It's just the way I *feel*. How else can I describe it?" He paused and the way he looked at her made him appear like a small boy. Helpless and confused. "And to make things worse, you're probably going to tell me that you're falling in love with me. . . ."

The nerve of him! Kate was instantly angered and shocked by his glib pronouncement. How could he say something like that so *easily*, so smugly! And then suddenly she found herself analyzing her anger and her indignation, and she knew what he was saying was true.

And wasn't that why she was feeling so outraged? Because the truth had a way of hurting like nothing else could? And hadn't she been intending to tell him how she felt about him and that she really didn't care how he felt about her or Mikaela or any other woman in his life? She had just wanted to get her feelings out in the open. Isn't that what she'd been thinking before he stole her thunder?

Oh yes. It certainly had.

"What's the matter?" he said without malice or satire. "Did I say the wrong thing?"

She could say nothing, and only stared at him.

"I'm sorry, Kate, if I sounded presumptuous, but I could just feel that you were going to say something like that."

"I was," she said. "In fact, I *am*. I *do* think I'm falling in love with you, Phineas."

"Oh, Jesus. . . ."

And she told him everything. How long the feelings had been brewing . . . How it felt to watch him with that little tight-assed blonde, Lindstrom . . . How she had been wanting him ever since almost the first night they had met and started planning the documentary about the *Dragonstar*. She explained how it didn't matter how he felt about her, and that it just felt better getting her feelings out in the open.

"It might feel better for you," he said when she finished, "but what about *me*?"

"I would think you'd feel good, flattered and all that."

"I think I'm beyond that sort of thing now," said Phineas. "No, it's more like I feel *obligated* to love you in return. Isn't that silly?"

She wasn't sure if "silly" was the right word. "Absurd" seemed more appropriate.

"You see, Kate, I'm not sure how I feel about *anybody*, anymore. Sometimes I even think I still care for Becky! Can you imagine that?"

"Yes," she said softly. "I think I can." She could feel the pain of being so honest oozing out of him, and she felt sorry for him. It was an incredible thing to see him so vulnerable, especially when he seemed so strong and competent all the time.

"You can?" He sounded surprised.

"Yes. We can't always explain why we feel a certain way. I just wanted you to know what it's been like for me, knowing you." She paused, moved closer to him. "I'm scared, Phineas. I try to keep myself busy so I won't think about the pickle we're all in, but sometimes I just can't keep it away. Sometimes I think we're all going to die out here, and there's no sense worrying about anything. We're just finished, that's all. But if that is true, then I wanted you to at least know how I felt about you . . . before it's all over."

"We've got a long way to go before it's over, Kate."

"You might believe that. I'm not so sure. We're headed toward a planet now, and I think that's the place where everything works itself out. . . ."

"I'm not giving up hope until there *is* no hope," he said.

"I wish I could feel that strongly about the whole mess we're in. But I can't. And there's a rumor that the hull's not strong enough to make a return jump, even if we could get back. It might be true. You were there when Dr. Takamura ran those tests. . . ."

She wanted him to confirm or deny the rumors, but they were both distracted from their conversation.

There was a sound at the entrance to the Temple behind them, and she turned to see Mikaela Lindstrom enter the structure along with several other men and women carrying weapons. There were six Saurians also included in the group. Thesaurus and another Priest, plus four Warriors.

Mikaela Lindstrom walked over to Phineas silently, with no

readable expression on her face. Thesaurus approached, but seemed to sense a need for privacy among the humans, and hung back, waiting to be invited closer. The other humans and Saurians spread themselves out at various guardposts within the Temple.

"We've just attained a stable orbit around the planet," said Lindstrom, making a point of speaking only to Phineas.

"What's it like down there?" he asked. "They been able to get a good look at the planet's surface?"

"There isn't much to see," said the paleontologist. "One major landmass surrounded by ocean. The terrain is fairly well destroyed by the heat and radiation from the red super-giant."

"You mean it's a dead world?" Phineas sounded disappointed. "You mean we got here too late?"

"Too late for what?" asked Kate.

Lindstrom looked at her, but said nothing. Kate could feel the cold aura of jealousy enveloping her like a prison.

"I don't know," said Phineas. "I had a feeling we'd been brought here for a reason."

"I, too, have had such feelings," came the translated words of Thesaurus.

Phineas looked up and gestured the Saurian Priest to join the small group. The old Saurian reached out and touched Phineas's shoulder.

"He wants to be here, in the Temple," said Lindstrom. "In case there are any new developments."

Phineas nodded. "It looks like things are going to be pretty dull."

"Perhaps not," said Thesaurus. "I have entertained a very strong notion—almost a precognition—that we have come to this place to meet our destiny."

Phineas grinned and looked at the Saurian. "The way things have been going, I'm not sure I want you to be right or wrong."

"Colonel Kemp?" a voice crackled in the headset radio of his LS helmet.

"Kemp here."

"Dr. Jakes wants to inform all the sentry positions," said the voice on the radio. "We've just detected activity on the planet's surface."

"What kind of activity?"

"Not sure yet, but it looks like three vehicles have been launched."

Kate was standing right next to Phineas, and it was impossible not to hear the message. There was a lump in her throat and she couldn't have spoken if she'd wanted to.

But she didn't have to ask if the vehicles were headed their way. . . .

CHAPTER 18

"SO WHAT ARE WE GOING TO DO?" asked Rebecca Thalberg at the meeting, her fragrant primeval tea ignored in front of her.

The other members of the committee sat without contributions, their feelings showing in their eyes. Mishima read them easily; they reflected his own emotions.

Ships belonging to an intelligent alien life were apparently on their way to dock with *Artifact One*. The first contact between mankind and a more advanced (at least technologically) race of intelligent aliens. But more important, it was the first contact between the IASA crew and the Makers of the *Dragonstar*.

Or at least their distant descendants; millions of years had passed. What had the Makers been; what had they evolved into? How would they deal with the captured prizes?

These were the questions in the eyes of his crew-mates—but there was also the unspoken fear that had been covered up by activity and the need to stay alive. The fear of the unknown.

After all, who could blame them? They were light-years away from the security of Earth, traveling along in a hostile environment to God-knows-where. Jakes's announcement that the frame of the *Dragonstar* could not withstand the arduous pressures of FTL was not exactly a welcome bit of knowledge. The implications had clearly sunk in quite well. Chances were exceedingly slim that they would ever return to Earth.

But beyond these fears, survival shone in these eyes like hard diamonds, and this perception eased Mishima's trepidations.

Still, there was this little matter of what to do.

"What is there to do? Wait. Prepare our spirits for this august meeting."

"Prepare our *spirits*!" blurted Phineas Kemp. "What kind of proper military action is that?"

Mishima had been watching Phineas lately, and had observed him as being under a peculiar pressure. Something to do with females, ah yes. Rats always acted erratically in pressured and enclosed circumstances. Also, he had not quite relinquished his fancied role as leader and decision-maker, despite his sorry past; orders and decisions and evaluations seemed to ejaculate from him like semen from a half-cocked male organ.

"This is hardly a typical military situation, Phineas," said Becky. Always eager to take a jab at her ex, Mishima was gratified to see. "We don't know yet that our visitors are hostile."

"Ah, but we don't know that they are *not*!" Phineas said. "We must take the proper precautions to defend ourselves."

"What's the use, Phineas?" said Mikaela Lindstrom. "They built this ship eons ago—God alone knows what weapons they have."

"No, Colonel Kemp is correct," said Mishima in a calm, assured voice. "My suggestion for spiritual readiness is inclusive of what he terms 'military' readiness. But then, are we not as militarily prepared now as we can ever be?"

Kemp looked at Mishima with a clear expression of pity. "Position, man. We've got to get ourselves in the proper positions!"

Mishima nodded. "Perhaps. But do you not think, Colonel Kemp, that a formal offensive position might induce the aliens to—how do you say it in your country?—shoot first and ask questions later?"

The laughter eased the tension in the gathering.

"Mishima's right, Phineas," said Becky. "There's no reason we can't just effect a nonthreatening observational attitude. That way we can watch the entry of the aliens without alarming them—and be in a suitable position to offer resistance should that be necessary—"

"Or possible," Dr. Jakes said, shaking his head. "I don't know—we're talking eons of years of superior technological development here. I say we just go with the flow, as it were."

"The Tao of the physicist!" Mishima said, grinning.

The others laughed again.

Kemp rolled his eyes. "We're on the verge of what could be the most important conflict between man and alien—and you guys are laughing! I'm glad we're not recording this for the documentary!"

Mishima studied Kemp a moment. There was no doubt that the man simply itched to take the reins of control and do something typically in the Western military tradition. But Mishima also sensed that this would be an extravagant mistake, and he had to diffuse not merely Kemp—but the Phineas Kemps in the rest of the committee.

"I agree partially with Dr. Jakes," he said in a soft but nonetheless strong voice. "But we must also speak to the proud resistance that lies within us all, the fire that shines so brightly, say, in Colonel Kemp. Our readiness shall be armed—not merely with weapons but in attitudes. Be sure that if aliens fire at us, we shall return that fire as long as we are able. Our dignity demands that."

"That's right," said Phineas Kemp, gratified. "If we go down, we go down fighting!"

There was a murmur of assent around the table, but those eyes still showed misgivings and fear.

Dr. Jakes examined his watch. "Well, if you've got something planned, you'd better tell us about it. There's less than an hour until those alien ships interact with us."

"Fine, that leaves us with sufficient time to mobilize," said Mishima calmly. "This is what I suggest."

Mishima's suggestions were so solid and sensible that they might as well have been orders.

They were simple. All he wanted was a small party—welcome wagons he called them, with a wry smile—at each of the three main hatches. Dr. Jakes projected that the aliens would choose the largest, so Mishima suggested that the principal leaders of the human and Saurian communities, including himself and Colonel Kemp, should station themselves at that post, with secondary representatives posted at the others, all the while in constant communication with one another. This way, he could keep an eye personally on Kemp. If the man was leading one of the other parties, God alone knew what he would do when the aliens trooped in. Phineas Kemp could not have gotten as far as he had in the IASA without a cool head, Mishima knew. But then, the Colonel had not exactly had the best of luck lately, had he?

So it was that within forty-five minutes of the suggestion and the agreement by the others of its efficacy, a party of twenty men and Saurians stood by the main hatchway, with several OTVs ringed about them, mostly to protect them from any roving dinosaur predators.

"And to think," said Phineas Kemp, "this is where it all

started." He looked over to Becky Thalberg, standing by Mishima.

"Yes," said Kate Ennis. "It's too bad there wasn't a civilized party waiting for *our* team."

Mishima sensed Becky flinching at that comment. This Kate Ennis certainly could fling the *faux pas*. He put a gentle hand on the small of Becky's back and rubbed it in what he hoped was a comforting way.

Becky spoke tensely. "Yes. I'm the only one left of that venture, it seems. Almost appropriate, I think, that I'm standing here now. . . ."

"What have you got for us there, Doctor?" Mishima asked Jakes, who sat nearby in the back of an OTV, behind a portable set of scanners. "What is the estimated time of arrival?"

Jakes hit a button and read off the numbers. "I have four point twenty-four minutes till docking—and apparently we were right . . . it's going to be this hatch."

"You're certain?"

"Yes."

"Fine." Mishima turned on his radio. "Delta Two and Delta Three. Come in."

The other greeting parties chimed in almost simultaneously.

"We have docking here at Delta One. Return to base."

"Affirmative!" the units responded.

"Well, we're the ones, then," said Kate Ennis.

"Yes," Colonel Phineas Kemp sighed. "As usual."

We're the ones, thought Kemp as he uneasily touched his side-arm. He looked around at the others, who stood tensely waiting. He looked at Mikaela Lindstrom and at Kate Ennis, both clearly tense but excited, and he thought about the aliens just about to arrive—and it seemed as though the problems that faced the three of them were very petty indeed. Was all this business with the three of them really just because of the pressure? Or was it a way to get away from the grim reality of being castaways here—like a fantasy soap opera in the middle of a swampy prison?

He looked at them both and then thought, No. For he still felt love for Mikaela, perhaps deeper than ever. And when he caught sight of Kate, her wide-eyed awe at all this, the way she wore her personality on her expressions . . . he knew that she touched him as well. No, it wasn't just an elaborate escape, his feelings. Feelings weren't that at all. . . . They were somehow tied quite intimately into everything. Just *how*, Phineas Kemp did not really know. But the fact that he had learned this much at least somehow pleased him, made him feel like a deeper person.

Nice thing to know, when you're staring possible eternity in the face, Phineas Kemp thought. Are *deeper* people any less dead?

No, definitely not. But perhaps they were very much more *alive*, even if only for a very short time.

"We have docking of interspatial vehicle," reported Jakes, not looking up from his readouts.

Two minutes of tense silence passed.

"We have alien boarding through lock," Jakes said tersely. "Communications procedure initiated."

Mishima Takamura's welcome wagon watched as the main door began to cycle open.

CHAPTER 19

WITHIN HIS COCOON, Timothy Linden dreamed.

He dreamed dreams of magenta and turquoise, of blood and starshine. There was the smell of an Arabian bazaar, the feel of classroom chalk dust, the taste of sex, and the roar of black holes.

Linden dreamed dreams undreamt by mankind, and yet they seemed all too familiar, as though his whole life had been lived in preparation for their birthing, and his whole essence a foreshadow.

Timothy Linden was unaware that the entirety of his skin had turned into a thick, rubbery hull to this ship of dreams he sailed, or that his colleagues had to loosen the bonds that strapped him to the table so that the leather would not cut into the fibrous hide. He was unaware of the caterpillar growth and mothy changes their devices had recorded beneath that grey-black-white exterior. He only knew the fantastic of his dreams, the breath of pulsing nebulae in his head.

Until the aliens arrived.

Something reached into him, and touched.

It swept through him, seeming to turn him inside out. Within the cocoon, he moved and he groaned and he shuddered at the touch. It was cold and alien, and yet it seemed to strike a chord at a depth of which he had not been aware.

Years, millennia, eons, epochs radiated outward around him, flung out into eternity like a web, at which he was the hub. Like a spider. And the flies that stuck to the web were civilizations: mere specks against the star-shot darkness.

His mind reached out to grasp at the meaning of his vision: his soul ached to catch the full resonance. . . .

But a wave of sudden agoraphobia gripped him.

The vision shuddered away like crumbling ice sculptures into mere cold. . . .

And Timothy Linden saw Marcus Jashad again.

Marcus Jashad wore the robes of the Mahdi.

He stood in the fields of the desert, with a blood-soaked scimitar in his hands. Dawn peered over the rim of the dunes, and Linden stared wide-eyed at the thousands of dead stretched out at the feet of this General of the Prophet.

"Timothy Linden!" cried Marcus Jashad. "My Hasan!"

"Leave me be, Jashad!" cried Timothy Linden. "Leave me be!"

"Behold, Hasan, the dead! They are the Unbelievers. They would not bow down before the Law of the Prophet of Allah, they would not take the Holy Koran with them to the stars! But Hasan! The Book is in your hand! And your spirit, yea, it soars through the Heavens themselves!"

A scarf was wrapped across the lower face of the Moslem terrorist, muffling his voice. Bloodshot eyes glared out from beneath heavy eyebrows and a death-pale forehead.

"Hasan, have you forgotten your Vows? Have you neglected your Sacred Training?"

"No, Jashad. I have not forgotten."

"The moment is ripe as the pomegranate upon the vine. Seize it! Take it! Bite it! And behold! With the touch of your scimitar, the Unbelievers in your midst shall fall into Hell, and the word of the Prophet shall be propagated among the New Chosen in the Heavens!"

And then a wind that smelled of rot swept across the dunes, and the robes of Marcus Jashad fluttered and the scarf around his head was unraveled . . .

. . . leaving a death's head with live and molten eyes grinning beneath the turban and the hood.

Timothy Linden awoke, screaming, from the vision.

He awoke, and he was immediately aware of a smothering constriction all around him, dry and irritating. With a moan, he pushed outward upon what bound him down. His hands and his arms struck out from the crust of the cocoon. His shoulders struggled against the straps. They seemed possessed of great, new strength, these shoulders, these muscles, and the straps snapped easily.

The cocoon crackled like dry corn husk as Linden slowly but surely broke his way out of it. He stepped down from the table, crunching the remnants of the dry exodermis. He paused a moment as things swam around him, and he recovered his equilibrium.

He was in the camp's sick bay, a large prefab "tent" manufactured of a highly porous material. As he scanned the room, his mind catalogued and comprehended the uses of every single machine, every bandage and hypodermic. Linden was instantly aware of the content of the air he breathed from the hydrogen to oxygen ratio to the trace of argon. He became aware of the radiation filtering through the top of the tent, through its door. He sensed . . .

He sensed a wide panorama of the five senses normally bestowed upon mankind. . . . And he was also aware of *other* senses he did not comprehend but instantly utilized nonetheless.

The information and sensory data bored into him on dozens of levels.

He gasped, and he fell to his knees. His brain felt as though it were on fire. Too much . . . Too much input! He groaned with the pain, and his sanity seemed to be bending, breaking into new patterns.

He sensed that his fellow humans were gone. They had left him here, deserted him. Terror and fear of desertion flooded him and he shivered there on the floor, naked.

After a time, he realized that his mind seemed to be either acclimating to the new sensations . . . or damping down the more unfamiliar ones. He felt a little better, felt more in control. Simply because the others were not in the camp did not necessarily mean they had deserted him. They could not have left the *Dragonstar*; surely. . . .

And as soon as the idea came into his head, he knew that they had not left the *Dragonstar*. No, he could still sense the presence of the other humans. . . . They were simply not here in the camp.

He went to a closet and dressed himself in the IASA uniform he found there. He found a backpack, and he stocked it with food he found in a refrigerator, certain medicines and equipment, and a canteen of water.

He went outside into the daylight. In a nearby tent, he found a rifle, a handgun, a knife, and ammunition, which he took.

When he left the tent, though, he heard something.

A group of Saurians was patrolling the camp, left behind by the humans. He did not see them; but he could sense them. Before he could run, they turned the corner, and they saw him.

They stopped, clearly stunned at this strange new creature before them.

Then, screaming, they raced toward him, instinctively intending to kill the intruder.

Timothy Linden did not have time to arm his weapons. He

had time only to draw out the knife he had taken before the Saurians—all five of them—were upon him, screaming and lashing at him with their own weapons.

He struck. A stab, a slash, a quick chop of his free arm; a kick, another slash.

The Saurians did not know what had hit them. Seconds after their attack, all five were on the ground, either dead or wounded horribly.

Timothy Linden stepped back, regarded his deadly handiwork calmly.

It is the gift of Death from Allah himself! the voice of Marcus Jashad crowed triumphantly. *Allah smiles again upon the cause of His Righteous Ones!*

The Gift of Allah, thought Linden. Coming awake inside of him. . . .

But why had the Saurians attacked him? Had they been instructed to do so by the others, if he escaped?

That must be it. . . .

But what should he do now?

And his mind reached out, questing. . . .

And it found the answer. . . . He felt the touch of the Alien Ones again, and knew the reason for his fear before.

Danger. There was terrible danger from them, he knew. He was not safe here in the camp, not safe from his fellow humans, not safe from the Saurians. . . .

And not safe from the aliens who were just now entering the ship.

This was why he had readied himself, not totally understanding the reason. This was why he had taken the guns and the knife and the supplies.

He had to prepare himself. . . .

He had to prepare himself in the wilderness. . . .

And there the Voice of Allah would come to him, and there he would come to understand why he had been chosen for this duty. . . .

And so Timothy Linden ran from the base camp into the primeval fields and forests, to hide and wait upon the whim of his Lord.

CHAPTER 20

A LOUD MECHANICAL HUMMING rose up from the hatchway, incongruent with the primeval sounds of the Mesozoic Preserve.

The airlock was in action on the hatchway.

The aliens had entered. The hatch on the space side had closed. The hatch on the interior was opening.

A great hiss sounded as the air pressure in the lock equalized.

Colonel Phineas Kemp felt as though his backbone had been connected to a voltage cable. Tingles of expectation shot through him. The creatures that emerged from that lock were their only hope of returning home. . . . But more than that, they were the race that had *made* this ship: an awe-inspiring thought if there ever was one.

"How long?" Mishima Takamura asked Dr. Robert Jakes.

"I make it about two minutes to emergence," said Jakes in a matter-of-fact professional voice that doubtless masked the suspense they all felt.

"And the translation computer?" inquired Takamura.

Ensign McDonald looked up from the blocks of speakers and other equipment rigged by a power-pak in an omni terrain vehicle. "Got the full complement here, sir. The aliens will, of course, have to cooperate. . . ."

"I suspect they'll know exactly what we're doing," said Takamura.

"On the other hand," Becky Thalberg pointed out, "if they're so terribly advanced, they're bound to have translation equipment of their own that will analyze our language."

"My experience has always dictated to be prepared for all circumstances," Dr. Jakes said, looking up from the lights and quivering needles on his own equipment.

139

"And so say I," said Kemp, hefting up his rifle to prove his point.

"Colonel Kemp, I appreciate the need for your form of preparation," said Takamura. "But could you please put the rifle to one side? I suspect the boarding aliens will be sufficiently intelligent to immediately recognize a weapon and may well take exception to it pointing at them."

Kemp stifled his immediate response to Takamura. Instead of telling the man what he thought of him, he brought the weapon down, marched the ten meters to the nearest OTV and slipped the rifle behind the vehicle. He stepped a meter away and held up his bare hands. "There you go, Takamura. No weapon, but it will be close enough so as to be available."

Takamura nodded, the tension showing in his face as he redirected his attention to the hatch.

Which was opening.

"Oh dear God, I don't think I can take this," said Kate Ennis. "I'm going to have to sit down for this one."

She went and sat in the driver's seat of the OTV which Kemp had placed his rifle behind.

"Well, Phineas," said Becky Thalberg, "this is what we've been waiting for. Too bad Amos Hagar didn't survive for this moment."

"Maybe his ghost is still lingering somewhere about," suggested Kate Ennis.

"I don't know. With my luck, he'd get eaten by *these* aliens," Kemp grumped.

"Quiet!" said Takamura. "Something's coming out!"

"No," said Mikaela Lindstrom. "It's just some kind of . . ." She stepped closer. "Some kind of light!"

"Don't go any farther!" said Takamura.

"Yes," concurred Jakes. "I'm getting an odd radiation reading here. Nothing harmful . . . but still, damned different from what I was expecting."

A dome of purplish-red radiance grew from the opened square hatchway like a holograph of a soap bubble being blown from a pipe. It grew to a height of a good twenty-five meters, then abruptly stopped. Lightning-like spurts of electricity crackled on its periphery. The smell of ozone spread out to the human observers, like the forefront of a thunderstorm.

"What the hell is going on?" Jakes said, staring in astonishment at his readings, then looking at the parade of rainbow colors beginning to march across the light-sphere.

"I guess we just have to sit tight and find out," said Takamura. Nonetheless, Kemp noticed his jaw clenching as he loosed the snap on his gun holster.

Kemp took two steps closer to his rifle, then turned and shaded his eyes from the sparkling illumination pouring off the light-sphere.

Previously clear, the bubble faded into translucence as its colors darkened and a light-shot mist began to creep through its interior like thick tentacles from below. This mist began to fold in on itself, roiling like the future within a fortune-teller's crystal ball.

And then forms began to float up from the hatchway, assuming a patterned position within the sphere. The flashes of sparks on the periphery and the occasional stabs of light from below illuminated patches of the form. Riveted grey metallic swaths. Spider-like articulated legs. An occasional glimpse of black scales, pale veinous flesh.

"It's some sort of force-field, that bubble," Dr. Jakes said after the first wave of awe had washed over the welcoming party. "Looks impenetrable by normal means, but conducive to sound." He looked over to McDonald, who was clearly shaken by the sight before him. "Try a standard message, Jim."

McDonald nodded. He brought a transmitter to his mouth. Flicked a switch. Began to speak.

His words were amplified and broadcast over the speakers, as well as via various radio bands.

"Greetings. We welcome you. We are of the planet Earth. We mean you no harm. We wish to speak to you. We wish to communicate."

There was no answer from the sphere. The smoky stuff within merely thickened, obscuring the floating figures within.

"Greetings," continued McDonald. "We welcome you. We mean no harm. We are natives of the planet Earth. We have been stranded upon this space vessel. We need your help. Who are you?"

No response.

"Maybe they're recording the language for translation purposes," Takamura suggested. "Repeat the messages, and then keep on talking. Continue with the procedure we discussed before."

McDonald nodded and obeyed.

When he was finished, he took out the large drawings that had been prepared. Drawings of the Milky Way Galaxy, the Sol system of planets. Of Earth, of human beings, lettered with the representative English names.

McDonald flashed these posters to the impassive and mysterious aliens.

There was no vocal response.

But halfway into the cards, a side of the bubble began to bulge.

"Look!" said Becky. "Something is breaking out of it!"

Something indeed, noted Kemp. A smaller bubble broke loose from the first. Humming and flashing with sparks, it seemed to carry one of the inhabitants of the sphere. Then another bubble separated from the main sphere, and another; until three separate force-field-enclosed aliens hovered in front of them. Hovered oddly humming, the black fog within the shells roiling, obscuring the creatures themselves.

Then the humming changed frequency. It slid up, then down, then up, in a definite pattern.

"You getting that, McDonald?" said Takamura. "I think they're trying to communicate."

"Yes, sir," said McDonald. "Analysis processes engaged."

"Shit," said Kemp. "That doesn't sound like communication to me. That sounds like some sort of—"

Before he could finish the sentence, a blinding star of light flashed in the middle of the central sphere.

"Weapon!" screamed Kemp.

Even as he said the word, a beam of intense energy flowed from the generating sphere to McDonald's equipment.

The translation computer was blasted to bits, and McDonald was thrown aside like a rubber doll.

Another beam, less intense, streamed from the bubble-alien to the left, enveloping Takamura in a momentary dazzle, then winking out.

Takamura crumpled to the ground.

"So much for a friendly first contact!" said Kemp. He leaped for his rifle in the back of the OTV. Becky Thalberg joined him there for cover.

Immediately the three bubble-aliens commenced moving, firing beams at the IASA members and the Saurians alike, striking them down as they had struck down Mishima Takamura.

Kemp aimed, and fired off a round of his rifle directly into one of the aliens, with absolutely no effect.

No way he could deal with the things this way, he thought.

"C'mon, Becky," he said. "Get into the OTV. We're getting out of here!"

Becky flashed him a frightened look, then without arguing, she leaped into the back of the machine. Kate Ennis was already at the controls, her arms instinctively covering her head. Kemp jumped in the passenger seat, immediately punching up the bubble top. As it came down over their heads, he turned to Kate.

"Okay, I've seen you drive these things before. Let's get out of here!"

Kate shot one look at Kemp, then looked out onto the clearing, where the aliens were picking off the IASA members one by one. Mikaela Lindstrom had just fallen; and Kemp groaned with the sight.

"Are they killing them?" Kate asked, voice on the edge of hysteria, as she started the OTV.

"No, looks like some kind of stun-beam," said Kemp. "All the same, I don't want it getting me. Do you?"

"No," she said, and swung the wheel, and then engaged the vehicle at maximum acceleration. "Where to?" she asked.

"To the main camp near the Saurian boundary. At the controls of this ship. . . . We'll be able to regroup there with the others, and maybe put up some resistance. We don't want any alien race thinking we're a bunch of wimps, do we? They'll have no respect for us." He noticed Becky looking out the back. "Well, are they following us?"

"No," said Becky.

But that was all she said.

Kemp looked behind himself after making sure that Kate had the OTV well in hand. The scene there was one of total chaos, the aliens striking down the few remaining team members. Apparently none of the others had been able to reach their vehicles; no other OTVs were following this one's example.

"Looks as though they're letting us go," said Becky. "They're not even attempting to come after us."

"Probably they figure they'll get us eventually," said Kate Ennis, wide-eyed. "I mean, how far can we go?"

"Well, we can go just far enough to put up a decent fight," said Kemp, the image of Mikaela falling still in his mind.

"You're right about the stunning," said Becky. "Look . . . they're carrying the fallen into that bubble."

Kemp looked. Sure enough, the bodies of his comrades were

rising ... held suspended by some sort of force.... Then, escorted by the alien-bubbles, they were swallowed up by the force-bubble.

"Specimens," Kemp muttered as Kate turned past a grouping of rocks and the view was obscured. "They're taking them as specimens, the bastards."

"Seems as though you were right, Phineas," said Becky. "But then, maybe we're only delaying the inevitable."

"Don't be so fatalistic, Becky," Kemp said, turning his attention back to the way ahead and to Kate Ennis's driving. "We'll figure something out."

"At least we can hope that the others weren't harmed," Kate said.

"I shouldn't have let that idiot Takamura *do* this kind of thing," Kemp fumed.

"Phineas, you can't blame Mishima," Becky said from the back. "And you can't blame yourself. In this particular case, it was all of our decisions.... There was simply no way we could be sure what was going to happen."

"What *did* happen was a chance we had to take," Kate agreed. "For all we knew, the aliens would be cute little bunny rabbits, coming to bring us Easter eggs!"

"Absolutely, Phineas."

"No time for Monday-morning quarterbacking now," Kemp said decisively. "We get back to camp, we dig in there, and then we wait for the aliens to come and get us."

"Maybe they'll be a little more polite this time," Kate said.

"Yeah," said Kemp. "Maybe they'll say 'please' before they use their stun-beams."

"Is it a possibility we can use radios to contact them, talk to them, reason with them?" offered Becky.

"I don't know," said Kemp. "We're going to have to think about this one. Think about this one real hard."

They all thought about it in silence as the scenery rolled past. The all-too-familiar primeval forests, the plains, the rocks, and the occasional herd of herbivorous dinosaurs grazing placidly, unaware that their Creators had just barged into their happy behemoth lives.

Kemp took a moment to supply Ennis with directions back to the base.

Then he asked, "Would you like me to drive?"

"Hell no. I can do that. I want you, Phineas Kemp, to remember that you're a top-notch leader. I want you to figure out how we're going to deal with this incredible mess." Her knuckles were white upon the steering wheel, and though she had never looked more beautiful, their time together was the last thing on Phineas Kemp's mind. In fact, it was almost a relief. Yes, he *was* terribly upset about Mikaela—but nonetheless, he reveled in the fact that, with Takamura out as well, he was at the head of the situation. When they reorganized, Phineas Kemp would be in charge again, and since he functioned best in a crisis, since he was totally *alive* at such times, he knew he would be able to deal with the problem.

And if he couldn't ... well, it was better going out feeling fully alive and in command than to check out in disgrace and demoted.

This would be the redemption of Colonel Phineas Kemp.

He just *knew* it.

As the OTV roared ahead, Kemp thought.

After a time, he spoke.

"Okay, this is it," he said with a decisive edge to his deep and resonant voice. "We get back, we regroup. We arm ourselves and we get the Saurians in order, tell them what is going on. You can take care of that, can't you, Kate? You've become somewhat the Saurian expert."

"Sure. And they love to fight. They'll be very excited, I'm sure," Kate said tartly, not sounding at all excited about the prospect.

"Fight those things we saw come out of the hatch?" Becky said in disbelief. "You've got to be kidding me! It was child's play for them to deal with capturing almost all of our party! Imagine if they really meant business."

"Defense on our part, stubbornness," said Kemp, "can only be construed as a sign of intelligent and resourceful beings. Perhaps a little concerted force on our part will make them want to *try* to communicate with us. . . . Something they refused to do a little while ago. Respect for the opponent goes a long way in establishing treaties."

"Treaties! Those things can squash us like cockroaches!" Becky said, exasperated. "Why should they settle for a treaty?"

"Very simple. We're desperate, right? We'll use a little military tactic that Marcus Jashad himself might have devised. We shall continue to attempt to communicate with the beings via the radios back at the camp. And we shall promise them that if they get too close to us, we'll blow the whole *Dragonstar*. Apparently they very much want the ship itself, and its inhabitants. This will at least make them attempt to communicate, parlay."

Becky was stunned and said nothing.

"Are you serious?" Kate demanded. "How could we possibly threaten to blow the *Dragonstar* up? I mean, can we?"

"For all intents and purposes, yes—it should be easy enough to rig up a bomb to blow a hole through the control-section big enough to depressurize the whole interior before there was any chance of repair."

"You're crazy!" said Becky.

"Drastic times call for drastic measures," Kemp said assertively. "You have any alternative plans?"

"Can't we just say we've rigged up a bomb, and not actually do it?" Kate said.

"Look, if the aliens are as technically capable as they seem to be, I'm sure they'd be able to sniff out a bluff, pronto. Now, I'm not saying that I would ever actually set this bomb off. . . . Just rig it. Hopefully the aliens will know little human psychology, and they will assume we're in a totally irrational state. All I'm after is a chance to talk with them, and so far they haven't bothered to try. We're just forcing them to."

"Whew," said Becky. "For a moment I thought you really had gone nuts, Phineas."

"We have to make the aliens believe I'm just that," Kemp said.

"And then, though, what are we going to actually *say* to the aliens?" asked Kate.

"Good question. Give us back our crew members or we'll blow this ship up? Then give us a ticket on the next starbus to Earth?" Becky demanded.

"Communication is of primary importance. As soon as they understand who we are and what we need, there's a chance. But without communications, there's no hope at all. That's what we're playing a gambit here for."

"But this might blow up in our faces, if the actual bomb doesn't," Becky objected. "I mean, the aliens are going to think they're dealing with the equivalent of terrorists! And they might deal harshly."

"No. Once we've *communicated*—and I cannot emphasize that word enough—we can simply tell them that it was all a trick to force them into talking. Whether they appreciate the joke and the strategy or not, we're still talking . . . and there's the chance of talking our way out of this situation. Otherwise, we're absolutely nowhere."

Becky gestured a surrender. "I guess you're right. I certainly can't think of a better plan. I suppose I just don't like this bomb business. At all."

"That's simple enough. We'll try to communicate via radio first, with no threat. If we get a reasonable response, there will be no threat. If we get no response, however, we shall prepare the explosive device." Kemp seemed very pleased with his compromise.

"That's an excellent idea," Kate said. "You really haven't lost it, have you, Phineas?"

Kemp smiled grimly. "Let's hope not, Kate. If I have, then we're all lost."

They drove on, negotiating a hilly area.

After consulting the directional readout for navigation, Kemp directed Kate Ennis to take a turn around a very large boulder.

Only a few more miles, he noted. A few more miles, a few more minutes, and we can start getting this thing together, start hauling our nuts out of the fire.

"Oh my God!" yelled Kate as she completed a turn.

Standing directly in their paths was a triceratops.

Frantically Kate Ennis hauled on the wheel, and the OTV skimmed over two large rocks.

"Watch out!" Kemp cried.

The wheel was wrenched from the woman's hand as the triceratops instinctively charged, striking the side of the boulder hard.

The last thing Kemp heard was Becky's scream, and then he was thrown into darkness.

CHAPTER 21

"MISHIMA!" called a voice. "Mishima Takamura!"

The man felt as though he were being summoned from the depths of the dead. Bits and pieces of his consciousness seemed to materialize from nowhere and to collect into a face. A woman's face, blurry.

"Becky?" he mumbled. His firstborn thoughts were for Becky, naked and offguard.

Imaginary brunette changed to blonde the moment before the woman spoke, and he knew it wasn't Rebecca Thalberg. "Mishima. It's Mikaela. Mikaela Lindstrom." The soft lines of her face flowed into recognizable form, and the bright blue of her eyes stared down at him sympathetically.

His awareness instantly snapped to his attention. He sat up and he looked around. "Where are we?" he asked immediately, though the question was more rhetorical than anything else. They were clearly in some sort of room, and clearly there were other inhabitants. Mishima focused and recognized them: Dr. Robert Jakes, James Barkham, and the Saurian known as Thesaurus.

They all seemed as perplexed as he was and they all looked as though they'd just regained consciousness as well.

"I don't know," said Dr. Jakes. "We could be on the alien ship, we could be on a planet. There's no telling how long we've been out."

The room was rectangular, about ten meters long, four high, and six deep. The walls were a beige alloy of some sort, as were the ceiling and the floor. There was no sign of a door.

Fully one half of the room was occupied by the couch-like expanse that they lay or sat on. It was a dark grey, with patches of white and black, and it was covered in an oddly pliant fabric.

"What . . . what happened?" Mishima said, rubbing his head.

"That's right. You were one of the first the things took out. Well, they stunned us all," said Barkham. "And they hauled us away. Seems obvious enough." He sat morosely in a corner, as though awaiting execution.

"No, you are not correct." Thesaurus said through his digital translator device. "I saw a vehicle depart. Someone escaped."

"As though that will do them any good," said Mikaela. "They'll get caught as well, soon enough."

"Well, we weren't killed. There's a plus," said Jakes. "And they've allowed us company. They probably don't know what to make of us yet. They want to study us."

"I don't understand," said Mishima. "Why didn't they even try to communicate?"

Barkham shrugged. "I don't know. Maybe their policy is to stun first and ask questions later. It's difficult to say when you're dealing with aliens. And of course that's not exactly something that we do every day, now is it?"

Mishima shook his head to relieve himself of his grogginess. The last-remembered images shot through his head: the floating alien-bubbles, the streams of energy, the feeling of being hit by a very large truck. "So I guess we'll just have to sit and wait for their next move."

"No, actually I rather fancied a jog around the park first!" Barkham said sarcastically.

"Hey, there's no reason for anger," Mikaela said, hopping off the couch and pacing. "I mean, we're still alive and we're absolutely unharmed. Just shaken up a bit. Doubtless we'll find out what's going on soon enough. Let's take Thesaurus's example. He's taking all this very well. And no wonder . . . he's run into aliens before. Haven't you, Thesaurus?"

"I live and I continue to learn," said Thesaurus. "I am open to the new and the wonderful. I am grateful for every new experience before I must expire. And, I confess," said the lizard-man, "I am very eager indeed to speak to the Makers of my home."

"You see! We should all take it this philosophically!" said Mikaela. "We are privileged!"

"Privileged?" Barkham said. "To get bashed on the head and dragged into an alien spaceship? Yeah, maybe I'm in a bad mood and maybe I should get a little more positive. . . . But I refuse to agree that I'm privileged!"

Takamura got off the couch and stretched. He then began exercising out the tightness in his muscles. "I suspect that we can argue all we like, and we shall still remain in the same situation. We may as well be stoical about it. That is, while we examine the walls for any possible exit!" He grinned.

Dr. Jakes had to laugh. "And why not? First thing rats do when they get put in a new cage is to try to find a way out."

It was a short search, and they found nothing, but Mishima felt better that they had at least examined their environment thoroughly.

He settled back on the huge couch in a comfortable position. "So much for that. I wonder if we're going to be fed and watered."

No sooner had he spoken than a portion of the central couch slid back and a small table elevated. On the table were five bowls of brownish gruel and five cups of clear water.

"Ask and ye shall receive," said Mikaela, crawling over to the table. She examined one of the bowls and stuck a finger in it, tasting it.

"Tastes like oatmeal, but less flavor," she said, making a face.

"Next time I'll be more specific," said Mishima.

Mikaela volunteered to be the first to eat and drink. She did so, with no ill effects. Mishima found the food to be as tasteless as Mikaela had indicated. But it was surprisingly filling and doubtlessly nutritious. Even Thesaurus had no trouble getting it down.

"Looks like our needs were specifically analyzed and met," said Dr. Jakes.

"Which means we're being more than watched," Mikaela said. "God alone knows what kind of devices they've got tuned in on us!"

"Not a pleasant thought at all," said Barkham, though the food seemed to have cheered him up a little. "I would think, though, that if they're going to be offering us our food, there should at least be some kind of sanitary facilities!"

No sooner had he spoken than a door in the side of the room opened. They all blinked.

Dr. Jakes, who was closest, examined what lay beyond the new door. He came back with a bemused look on his face. "It's a toilet. A toilet and a sink, and towels!"

"How thoughtful," said Mikaela. "They've even provided us with a modicum of privacy!"

Mishima sprang up from the couch, addressing the walls.

"Thank you!" he said. "Thank you very much. We truly appreciate your hospitality!"

The others looked at him as though he were crazy.

"Well, clearly they can understand what we're saying," said Mishima.

"All right," said Barkham. "Why don't you ask them where the hell we are!"

Mishima turned and addressed the walls again. "Is there any way that you'd be willing to communicate with us? We'd like to know where we are now, and what you intend on doing with us."

There was a moment of silence.

And then the whole wall by the couch came alive with colors.

The change was so abrupt that Mishima recoiled with shock. He noticed that the others had responded in just the same way, as though a sudden wave of fire had washed through the metal side of the room attempting to engulf them. But the three-dimensional quality of the colors retreated into flat images, utilizing light and shadow to illustrate depth.

There was a sun, burning in the night. . . .

It was a hazy reddish star, an occasional solar flare licking out into the darkness toward its planets. This full image of a sun dissolved into a representational view of the same star, much smaller now and surrounded by planets . . . and by something else. Another slow dissolve took the view from this system to an all-too-familiar object, drifting against a starscape:

The *Dragonstar*.

"It's showing us the star system we're in," said Mikaela, the first to recover use of her tongue. "It's saying, 'This is where you are'!"

"Obviously," said Barkham. "But what good does that do for us?"

"Shhh." said Dr. Jakes. "I'm concentrating."

The image of the *Dragonstar* faded away, to be replaced by the image of a huge grey planet—a planet without the usual features of continents and seas or clouds. Its entirety consisted of the geometric panorama of buildings of incredible heights, and fields of metal. Crystal sparkled in the sun on the day side, and on the night, strange colored lights burned.

"The central planet of the First Race," Barkham muttered, disobeying his own request. But no one seemed to mind—they were too busy staring at this incredible sight with awe.

As they watched, the images began to change faster, flashing down onto the surface of the metal planet and then *within.*

The viewers gasped. It was all too much to take in. Alien image piled upon alien image, and it felt to Mishima Takamura that his brain was overloading with the implications all these sights presented.

There were views of cities with unimaginably odd denizens roaming the streets. There were glimpses into alien biomes with the most fantastic of plants. And there was the sequence in which the wall showed corridor after corridor descending deep into the heart of this world, walls undulating with flashing lights and alien circuitry. And all through these wandered a most unlikely bestiary of aliens. Tall aliens and small aliens. Aliens with a multitude of limbs and aliens with none. Aliens with myriad eyes and aliens flowing through byways like wobbling piles of protoplasm.

"I don't understand," said Dr. Jakes.

"What's wrong?" Takamura demanded, unable to tear his eyes away from these views which affected him almost as strongly as mystical visions of the divine might.

"I see what Jakes is getting at," said Mikaela. "Where are the descendants of the dinosaurs?"

"Huh?" said Barkham, and Thesaurus's reptilian eyes tore away from the wall screen to stare at Lindstrom.

"So far we don't see anything much like Thesaurus out there," said Mikaela. "We had assumed that the seeders would have created life after their own images."

"Surely that doesn't mean anything," said Takamura. "There seems to be such a variety of alien life. There could be reasons for that we can't possibly understand right now."

"Perhaps if we simply watch," said Dr. Jakes, "the images themselves will explain."

"That's apparently what we're supposed to do," said Takamura.

The images continued, showing a dizzying number of views of alien vistas until Takamura had to close his eyes for a time to relieve his brain. When he opened them again, however, the wall had faded once more to black.

Then a galaxy appeared in the center of the screen.

The Milky Way.

Then their home galaxy faded away and another galaxy, nonspiral, took its place.

Another faded in and out.

And another.

"It would appear that we're being shown the range of this civilization's spread. Which would explain the number of aliens down on this planet. . . . This must be the central hub," said Dr. Jakes.

"Yes," said Takamura. "The capital. . . ."

"And they've brought us here. They've brought the *Dragonstar* back," said Mikaela Lindstrom. "And they're taking the time to actually show us where we are and who they are. . . ."

"I don't know," said Barkham. "It doesn't follow their modus operandi. I mean, they knock us out—"

"But they didn't kill us," said Takamura. "They dealt with us as possibly dangerous creatures. Without doing harm to us, they neutralized any possibility of a threat to them."

The wall went dark again.

Takamura wondered what was next. They all stared at the wall, waiting in suspense for the next step of the communication process.

Then the wall faded, and an image of a creature's head loomed. Its eyes were liquid sparkles of intelligence. It seemed to be staring straight into Takamura's soul.

It opened its mouth to speak, and Takamura shivered with the importance of this moment . . . the first verbal communication between the Creators and representatives of their children.

"Greetings," said a hissy alien voice, pronunciation totally off. "And fuck you all!"

CHAPTER 22

PHINEAS KEMP RAGED against the dark.

Somewhere deep in his being, he struggled up and out of the enfolding unconsciousness, as though he were at the bottom of some terribly deep well, with only a glimmer of light above him. It would be so easy to just give up, drift back to the bottom, and lie there in the warm sludge. But something called at him, something terribly urgent, and Kemp swam upward toward the light.

And broke through to the surface, gasping.

The light was blinding.

And he ached all over.

The scene settled in all around him, black and white resolving into harsh color: he lay in the wrecked OTV. He tasted blood in his mouth, felt warm liquid trickling down his face. He craned his neck and saw Becky Thalberg lying behind him in the canted car, unconscious and breathing shallowly.

He looked around and saw that Kate Ennis had either been thrown from the car or had managed to pull herself out of the wreck and was now kneeling in the dirt light meters from the OTV, groaning.

Nearby, three dinosaurs milled.

Triceratopses.

The triceratopses that had wrecked them.

They seemed a bit confused. Two were nibbling at clumps of vegetation growing from between some rocks. The other looked dazed. They were big things, with tough hides and a crown of three horns apiece upon their ugly heads. They were herbivorous. Kemp knew . . . but they could be awfully mean if riled. . . . And with the things that had been happening lately to the dinosaurs, there was no telling how the beasts would react to humans walking among them.

Kemp struggled to a sitting position. The top of the OTV had been smashed like an eggshell, but its ends still served as shelter from a possible attack by the triceratopses. It would be best to stay awhile inside.

"Kate!" he called. "Kate, are you okay?"

Kate groaned and did not respond. She seemed totally out of it, in some different world. The only thing Kemp's words seemed to do for her was to make her stand up, wobbly. She turned slightly and Kemp could see two rivulets of blood running down her forehead. She did not seem to see him. She opened her mouth and turned again.

"Rick?" she said. "Rick?"

Who was Rick? Kemp wondered. But then Kate started to walk, away from the OTV, toward the triceratopses.

"Kate!" cried Kemp. "No! Don't! Come back!"

"Rick?" cried Kate, clearly out of her head beneath the hot Illuminator. "Rick!"

She was walking directly toward the dazed triceratops.

And the triceratops grunted, its eyes focusing on the advancing woman.

"Kate!" Kemp cried. "Get away from it! Get away!"

The triceratops snorted. It pawed the ground. The other two looked up from their snacks.

Kemp fumbled for his rifle.

The dazed triceratops started running toward Kate Ennis, who did not seem to notice it at all.

It lowered its horns as it picked up speed.

"Kate!" cried Kemp helplessly. "Run! Get away!"

The pounding of the creature's feet upon the ground finally caused a little awareness to come into Kate Ennis's eyes. She looked up and Kemp saw that she could see the triceratops advancing upon her at a rapid clip. She screamed, and she turned to run. . . .

But she was too late.

The horn of the triceratops caught her squarely in the back, skewering her through, emerging from between her breasts red with her blood. The scream was ripped from her mouth as the triceratops tossed her up five yards in the air.

Her body hit the ground with a sickening *thwap*.

The maddened dinosaur commenced to trample her until her body was an unrecognizable splatter of blood and flesh and bone upon the harsh ground.

It sniffed the remains of the woman, then moved off to nibble on something edible. The others, after looking up in dull interest, returned to their own feeding.

Kemp stared on with horror, holding the gun he had not had time to use, not able to believe the awful violence he had just witnessed, not able to accept his loss.

Kate, he thought. Oh God, Kate!

Emotion choked his chest, and he had to turn away to prevent burning tears from coursing down his cheek. He had cared for her, in a curious way, in a manner he had never cared for another woman. . . . She was so effervescent, so *alive*. . . . And now she was . . . gone.

A groan from Becky Thalberg behind him returned him to the present reality, and his concern for her and his own instinct for survival turned him enough away from his grief that he was able to function.

"Becky," he said, turning around and touching her. "Becky, you're okay."

He saw her eyes flicker on. "What happened?"

"We had an accident," he said. "Kate . . . Kate Ennis is dead."

That brought her around. "Dead?"

"Don't look. It's not pleasant. The triceratops got her . . . the one we swerved to avoid. We have to get out of here, Becky. Grab our supplies and get out. The base can't be too far away, and we've got to reach it."

Becky didn't say anything. She seemed too intent on keeping herself conscious. Methodically she extricated herself from the back of the OTV while Kemp gathered their supplies. Carefully they got out of the OTV—wrecked beyond hope of use, Kemp noted—and took refuge from the triceratops behind it.

"Oh God," Becky said finally, glimpsing the remains of Kate Ennis. "Phineas, this is just too much. . . . I . . . I don't think I can take it."

"Shhh," whispered Kemp. "Not so loud. We don't want to attract the same attention from those creatures that they gave to Kate. Now listen—this is what we've got to do."

He pointed to the top of the large boulder, which was attached to a ridge leading around to the other side of an outcropping of rocks. "If we get up there, we'll be able to sneak off without the big bastards noticing. Feel up to a quick run?"

Becky seemed to be having difficulty breathing. "I don't know, Phineas. Something's wrong."

Kemp could see nothing physically wrong with her, and there seemed no sign of internal bleeding. From the way she was breathing, though, he could tell that her troubles were more psychological than physical. She was having what appeared to be a prime anxiety attack, and Kemp really couldn't blame her. After all she'd been through before—stuck in the Great Mesozoic Outback again. But they couldn't afford the time it would take for her to get better. They had to get away from these triceratopses.

"Dammit, Becky," he said. "You did just fine with Coopersmith. Don't I inspire you to survive?"

"You asshole," said Becky, her eyes flashing. "I can do just fine, thank you!"

"There you go! That's the spirit! Now climb those rocks and I'll cover you!"

She swallowed hard, still angry. But she glanced up at the boulder, squinting in the light from the sky, and she nodded her head.

Kemp put a gun in her hand. "And when you get up there, you cover me, right?"

"I'll think about it."

She ran.

The triceratopses did not seem to notice at first.

But when Becky almost lost her footing, she dislodged a shower of rocks which rolled down, causing noise that seemed to be of avalanche proportion. She kept moving up the edge, and she pulled herself to the top of the boulder.

However, the triceratops that had killed Kate Ennis started with the slide of rocks, twisting its tank-like head around, tiny eyes red and dangerous.

"Oh shit," said Kemp, raising his rifle.

The triceratops wasted no time as it saw the flash of movement behind the OTV, the splinter of light reflected from the metal of the rifle. It lowered its array of horns, snorted hard, and charged with a roar. Its tiny brain did not seem to be able to detach Kemp from the OTV. It headed for that first.

Kemp fired off a round, succeeding only in gouging off a chip of the creature's bony crown. The 'tops struck the OTV, its bloody center horn piercing the cracked top bubble. With a shake of its sinewy head, the OTV was steam-shoveled out of the beast's way.

The path was clear to Kemp.

Kemp aimed more carefully this time, firing directly into the triceratops's eye. It exploded, and the creature honked and screamed with pain.

But after only a short pause, it kept on coming.

Kemp turned and started to run up the way that Becky had run. Peripherally he noted that she had reached the top of the boulder and was peering down on the drama below.

"Becky!" he screamed. "I said, cover me!"

Becky seemed to be still stunned, but she recovered quickly enough, shooting down at the triceratops.

It roared with pain.

Kemp knew that he'd need both hands to scrabble up the incline and he didn't have time to sling his rifle around his shoulder. As much as he hated doing it, he had to: he hurled it behind him. The rifle struck the 'tops in its beak-like maw. Instinctively the thing grabbed it and snapped it in half with its mouth. Then it lunged up the slope toward Kemp.

The ground seemed to shake, and Kemp could swear he felt the creature's breath at the back of his neck.

From somewhere Kemp called on hidden reserves, and somehow his feet kept their purchase as he scrambled up the hill.

Then, with a terrible roar of frustration, the triceratops lost its footing. One limb went out from the other and the thing tumbled down the incline to land in a great heap at the bottom, struggling to right itself.

Breathing harshly from the exertion, Kemp flopped over the edge of the ridge, then crawled up toward where Becky kneeled, just as exhausted as he.

They breathed in silence for a moment, relishing those breaths.

Then Kemp said, "Come on. Time to march. No time to lose, we've got to get back to the camp, dinosaurs or no dinosaurs."

Becky Thalberg nodded grimly, too exhausted emotionally and physically to object.

They struck out for the base.

They marched for some time in silence.

After a short rest and two pulls from the canteen of water, however, once they were on their way again, they found that they were able to talk.

"I . . . I just feel terrible about Kate, Phineas," said Becky. "I know I was always very sarcastic about her, and on some levels I guess I was sort of jealous of her. But I did like her." She paused for thought. "Well, I didn't want her *dead*. I know you were fond of her."

Kemp marched onward stolidly for a few moments, then answered. "We've none of us any kind of guarantee on life in this place, Becky. That could have been you back there, it could have been me. I really don't think we have the luxury to feel grief. . . . We're too close to our own coming to grief for that, I think."

"Phineas, I've never heard you talk like that," said Becky, wiping away a sheen of sweat from her forehead. "It's not like you at all."

"I guess you can take this kind of thing only so long as a Mr. Positive," Kemp answered.

"You're not feeling grief, then?"

"I think I'm too numb for that, Becky. Maybe you'd better ask me tomorrow. If there is a tomorrow."

"You're still marching hard, Phineas. You haven't given up," she said, looking out at the stretch of primeval field ahead of them. "I wouldn't listen to yourself if I were you. I think you'd better just listen to the old Phineas Kemp. The one that nothing can stop when he gets a goal in mind."

"Oh. You mean the asshole?" Kemp muttered cynically.

"Phineas, I'd rather have a lovable asshole around than a dead cynic."

"Oh, I didn't know you cared so much, Becky."

"Oh, I do, Phineas. Now I want to thank you for snapping me out of it back there. I suppose it was a low method, but it worked."

"Something beneath Mr. Coopersmith?"

"No. Ian would have done the same thing if it was necessary for survival. Apologies are much easier than burial prayers."

"Well, then, I suppose I should apologize, shouldn't I?" Kemp took a deep breath and looked out at the curving landscape ahead of them. "Ian Coopersmith was quite a man, Becky. Despite my obvious jealousy—which I admit to—I always respected the man. Perhaps even envied him. I'm sorry about all the things I've said against him. And I can certainly understand why you loved him—and love him even now, I suppose."

Becky was taken aback by his words, Kemp could see.

Then her eyes hardened a bit. "Phineas. Is this a ploy?"

"What are you talking about?"

"You're just getting into my good graces, aren't you? This isn't Colonel Phineas T. Kemp I'm listening to. It's some other person."

"You think I'm trying to make time with you? Get on your good side for romantic purposes?" Kemp shook his head with disbelief. "Woman, you've got a defense system to rival a battleship! I'm telling you the truth!"

She softened. "I'm sorry, Phineas. I guess... well, I guess I have gotten defensive. Thanks for those words. I do appreciate them. I suppose I do still love Ian Coopersmith, yes. But Ian would tell me to keep on, to survive.... I can almost hear him now...." She looked at Kemp in a funny way. "And to think, Phineas, here we are. Isn't it ironic? Before, Ian and I were stranded out here. Now it's you and I."

"But you and Coopersmith, you survived, didn't you? It must have seemed very dark... very dark indeed, those days."

"Well, yes, and I certainly couldn't have made it without Ian," said Becky. "But I'll tell you something, Phineas, something I've never admitted to you. I don't think that either Ian or I could have survived if we didn't know that you were still out there, somewhere, working like an asshole maniac as you usually work, to rescue us."

Kemp raised his eyebrows. "Really?"

"Gospel, Phineas."

"I'm touched."

"The problem now, though, is that there's no Phineas T. Kemp out there, trying to get us out. Just a bunch of mad aliens."

Kemp mused on this awhile as they walked.

"I never knew you looked at me that way, Becky," he said finally.

"I suppose, for my sins, it's one of the reasons I loved you the way I did," she said, staring straight ahead as she spoke. "For all your deadheadedness, Phineas, I suppose I loved those qualities in you. In many ways, they are what moved Western civilization to where it is now. Pluck, pragmatism, plus an unhealthy amount of ambition. You may be an asshole at times, I guess, but that's just *you*. And I think you've grown." She shrugged. "Oh well, it all seems so unimportant now, up against all of this." She gestured out to the expanse of wildness.

"It is important," said Kemp. "It's helpful, Becky. Thank you. It means a lot to me lately. I guess... I guess I've been very confused about where I stand with the opposite sex. I guess I've *always* been confused."

"Oh, you mean you and Mikaela. . . . And Kate, right?"

"That's right. I mean, it seems silly in the middle of the struggle to survive, but I was honestly getting confused."

"Do you think it could possibly have something to do with some weird kind of instincts coming into play in the situation we're in?" suggested Becky. "Kate *was* after you, you know. . . . You could smell the scent she was giving off. Could be an ancient survival mechanism in her, the need for the security of a Protecting Male." She chuckled. "And you, Phineas Kemp, sure try to manufacture that particular pheromone."

"I don't succeed?"

"Clearly you succeeded with Kate. But it's all unconscious . . . . I'm not saying you tried to do it on purpose, Phineas. I'm just saying that there are interpersonal dynamics that have been occurring in our group that could be just as scientifically fascinating in their own way as the *Dragonstar* itself."

Kemp snorted derisively. "Sounds more interesting to a bunch of soap opera viewers, maybe."

"Hey, Phineas, you've been selling soap for years. Didn't you know that?"

"What?"

"And who do you think was sponsoring your wonderful worldwide broadcast, the glorious *Day of the Dragonstar*? The United Fund for Overblown Egos?"

Kemp smiled. "Okay, *touché.* I was just busy trying to deflate the old ego. As though reality hasn't done plenty to help me out lately!"

They continued marching along, talking occasionally in this bantering manner to keep their spirits up.

"I'm getting déjà vu," said Becky. "This is just the way that Ian and I talked when we were stranded in here. Of course, you don't have a charming British accent."

"Nor his kind of wit, I suppose. I guess I never sat around much thinking up jokes."

"How far do you estimate the base is, Phineas?"

"A few klicks, Becky. I don't know if we're going to make it by darkfall."

"We'll have to try, won't we?"

Kemp smiled. "That's the spirit . . . old girl!"

Becky laughed.

They were approaching another series of hills, bordered by outcroppings of rocks.

Kemp looked around, his brow furrowing with thought. "Isn't this the place where Doc Jakes was getting those odd radiation readings?" he said to himself more than to Becky. "Yes . . . and this was the place where that strange thing happened to Lieutenant Linden. . . ."

"The guy with the cocoon. . . . We've quite forgotten all about him. . . . Just too much to take, Phineas. Overload time."

They walked past some large rocks, meaning to skirt them and then strike out toward the base in the direction that Kemp judged to be correct.

Suddenly a voice called out from the rocks.

"Poor Colonel Kemp," it said. It was a male voice . . . but it sounded deeper, garbled somehow. "I suppose you're trying to head back to the base camp. But you're going the wrong way."

Becky and Kemp stopped in their tracks.

"Who's that?" Kemp demanded, drawing out his gun.

Becky clicked off her safety.

"You're quite right, though," said the voice. "I've been listening to you, you know. This is the place where Dr. Jakes sent me."

Kemp blinked.

"Linden? Timothy Linden? Come out, man, and show yourself!"

"That's right, Colonel Kemp. Timothy Linden."

"But you were secured back at the camp," said Kemp.

"That's correct as well. I was able, fortunately, to break my bonds. But there is much to talk about, Colonel Kemp. Much indeed."

A figure stepped out from the rocks just twenty meters away.

Becky gasped. "You're not Timothy Linden!"

"That," said the creature, "is quite true. No, I am what Timothy Linden has become."

The creature walked toward them.

CHAPTER 23

THEY ALL STARED at the image of the face in the screen, stunned.

"*What* did it say?" Mikaela Lindstrom finally said.

"Just what you heard," said Barkham, grinning. "Well, the same to you, lizard face."

Barkham's description was not quite accurate. The huge face that swam before them could have once been reptilian, but there was enough change in bone structure and eyes and coloring—no snout, for instance—that the thing was far more alien-looking than reptilian.

"Greetings," said Mishima Takamura, stepping forward. "But I fear you have the wrong use of that particular word. The word 'fuck' has sexual and often violent and certainly aggressive connotations."

The creature seemed to think on this a moment.

"Ah," its voice came through the speakers again. "I confuse my own meaning. I wished you much fulfilling pleasure. Please excuse me."

Mikaela was very excited. "We're talking to it! We're actually communicating with a space-faring alien race!"

"An interesting form of first verbal contact," said Dr. Jakes with a bemused expression.

"A famous science fiction story had the first alien transmission of communications as a dirty joke," said Barkham. "I guess it all gets down to sex eventually from star to shining star."

"Thank you," said Takamura, taking on the role of group spokesperson. "We appreciate your efforts and your wishes. Why are you holding us prisoners, though?"

"Damned good question," echoed Barkham.

It took a moment for the alien to assimilate that. "We keep you in the room for your own safety . . . and ours. Time was needed to

163

analyze your thinking mechanisms and language sufficiently for adequate communication. Now we can communicate. We can explain much to each other."

"I am Mishima Takamura," said Mishima. He was about to introduce the other members of the group when the alien stopped him.

"Thank you, but we know all of your appellations," it said, its voice becoming more assured with the sounds of the new speech. "Let me introduce myself. I am Kii. I am of the Old Ones."

"You're one of the bubble-things that knocked us out?" Barkham wanted to know.

"No," said Kii. "Those were . . ." It paused, working its oddly shaped jaws as though looking for the right word. "Those were the Ones Who Enforce."

"Police. Cops," said Barkham.

"Or soldiers," suggested Mikaela.

"Neither and both . . . ," said Kii. "I understand your words. They are a war-like breed who enforce the status quo. But I am not totally familiar with everything. . . . You see, I have been asleep for oh, a very long time indeed. Asleep . . . And the signal from the vessel that brought you here . . . It has awakened me from my rest in the Cold World, on the edge of this system. All the conscious time since that signal, I have been discovering what has changed . . . and what has not changed . . . with my people."

"You must forgive us, but you've lost us, Kii," said Takamura.

"We have quite a few facts gleaned from what we've studied on the *Dragonstar* . . . the vessel that has brought us here," said Dr. Jakes. "But still there are huge gaps."

"But of course. However, your burning curiosity . . . I find that most satisfactory! Forgive me, but I am very excited. I am like a little one, with new toys!"

"Toys!" said Barkham. "Hey, we're intelligent beings. Beings with some heavy problems that *you* started!"

"Forgive my choice of words," said Kii. "But you will understand my excitement once you have heard my story."

"Well, we're listening," said Barkham. "Nothing much else to do!" He sat back down on the couch and propped his head against the wall. The others chose to remain standing.

"I must say," said Dr. Jakes. "You're being awfully cooperative for a member of a race that just knocked us on our noggins and stuck us in a cell." His tone was suspicious, and Mishima had to agree.

"Please, I can understand your problem," said Kii. "But you must believe me. I do not represent the others. I am merely in charge of interrogating you while the others take full command of the seed ship you call the *Dragonstar*."

"Interrogating...," said Mikaela. "But you're answering our questions."

"Oh, be assured that my interrogation has already been completed. This is why I am equipped with your language. Plus, I understand much about what has transpired. And please, I must explain to you these things so that I may invite your cooperation. And in order for my plan to work, I must have your conscious decision to help me."

"Help you do what?" said Barkham suspiciously.

"Change the course of intergalactic history," said Kii. "And perhaps save your lives in the bargain."

Barkham brightened. "I like the sound of the last one."

"Is there hope, then, that we can return to our home planet?" said Takamura.

"Please listen," said Kii. "There is hope, but you must listen, and you must trust me."

They all exchanged looks which said, "Nothing to lose!" and Barkham said, "Go right ahead, Kii."

"Thank you," said the alien. "You are a most curious race. You have many qualities I have never encountered before in all my journeys among the stars. And again, this excites me, because I am one of the scientists who created the ship that brought you here."

That stunned them all.

It was Dr. Jakes who was able to come up first with the obvious statement of fact. "But...but that would make you over a hundred million years old!"

"Not really. Yes, I was alive and functioning millions upon millions of years ago...but after the dispatch of the seed ships that were built, I and my brethren responsible for their construction entered a most extreme form of suspended animation... perhaps tantamount to one-way time-travel, in fact. We wanted to see what would be the result of our efforts.... And we, frankly, despaired of the civilization that we left behind...which is why we hoped to change it...."

"Please, could you start at the beginning?" said Dr. Jakes, fascinated.

"I of course do not have time to give you all the specifics, so I will boil it down to essentials. I am of a segment of my original race known as the Planners. We were the force of scientists behind the outward expansion of life in the universe. You see, after many ages of intelligent existence, there was the natural urge to spread throughout the galaxies via colonization. But myself and my brethren felt that colonization was a dead end. For the political segment of our race, known as the Movers, had such a tight grip on cultural and intellectual growth, there seemed no hope for the kind of growth necessary to break out of our metaphorical eggs. And in fact, all these millions of years since then have borne out our projections. The history of our race has seen a wide sweep through the galaxies, but there have been long epochs of stagnation as well! And all of this, despite the fact that we have developed to the very height of our evolutionary capabilities. This, you see, was at the heart of why we made the seed ships the way they were: with full knowledge of our own growth patterns, but with the possibilities for variations... variations that would lead a new race out of the dead end that we faced!"

"Which would explain the dioramas... the systems inside the ship," said Dr. Jakes. "It foresaw some of the development the *Dragonstar* planted on Earth... but clearly not all!"

"Yes. And after examination of your species, I can see that your race is exactly the sort of thing we were looking for!"

"The human race?" Mikaela said, astonished. "You've *got* to be kidding!"

"No, I do not jest. Perhaps you are far from perfect in your present form.... But your possibilities... ah, endless! But I digress, and I must hurry. Again, simplifying matters vastly, I should explain that for the majority of the creatures of the universe—of which you saw a representation via this screen—their way of life is quite satisfactory. And the Enforcers... also known as the Movers... keep it that way. This is why your race will doubtless cause them all great consternation.... And why I must save you."

"Sounds good to me!" said Barkham. "But what makes us so special, Kii? What's the magic ingredient?"

"Ah, a curious and unforeseen development in your brains

. . . something that you call your limbic systems. It gives you what you call . . ."

"Emotions!" said Mikaela. "Well, isn't that something!"

There was a tear in her eye as she looked around at the others, smiling.

CHAPTER 24

HE STILL LOOKED HUMAN . . . but just barely.

Humanoid, thought Kemp. That's a better word.

Oh sure, Timothy Linden still had four limbs: two arms, two legs. But they were longer now, jointed strangely.

And his face . . .

He had no ears, and his nose was a mere tiny bump above a slit of a mouth. He was bald now, and his whole head was more ellipsoid than before, his skull almost pointed. . . .

But the eyes . . .

The eyes were the most different: they were wide and large now, with no brows and huge black pupils that seemed to look into and through . . .

Everything.

"My God," said Becky. "What's happened to him?"

"Whatever's happened," said Kemp, "he can still point a gun. . . . Linden, what's your problem? Are you mad? We're your friends!"

Those huge orbs blinked, and Linden staggered a bit.

"Friends? If only you knew the truth, Colonel Kemp. But then, soon you will!"

"Now, Linden, we're not going to hurt you and we're dealing with a very serious situation. We've got to get back to base camp. Whatever's happened to you, you're still an intelligent creature and you've got to see reason."

Linden twitched a bit. "Reason? Reason! What does reason have to do with destiny! With revenge!"

"Linden, what are you talking about?" Becky said. "What revenge?"

"Colonel Kemp, do you remember a man named Marcus Jashad?" Linden spat, weaving unsteadily on his feet.

"Jashad. Damned right I do. The terrorist who tried to take over the *Dragonstar*. But what have you got to do with Jashad, Linden?"

"Jashad lives yet!" cried Linden. "Jashad lives in my soul. He shall be avenged, and the Word of the Prophet, the Way of Allah, shall be propagated among the stars!"

"You're crazy!" said Becky.

"No. Not crazy. You see, I was never truly with the IASA, you fools. I was a sleeper agent with the TWC, planted within the IASA for just this moment! And I have been activated, and lo, the sword of Allah shall strike down all of you unbelievers."

"Phineas, could this be the truth?"

"It's a possibility. But what's more important is that it looks as though Linden's on his last legs. He's fighting something. . . . I can sense it." He turned back to the transformed man. "If that's the case, Linden . . . why haven't you killed me?"

"I wanted . . . I wanted you to know . . . to know that . . . it is not I . . . not I who is your executioner. Not Timothy Linden . . . but the spirit of Marcus Jashad himself!"

"I find that very hard to believe," said Kemp, stalling for time. "No, maybe I don't. Jashad always was a coward. It's totally like him to gun down an enemy in cold blood. Typical of the camel dung the TWC has been producing this past century! Come on, Linden, maybe you were a sleeper agent, but you also grew up in our system, experienced it. Sure, maybe you were trained to obey the doctrines of the TWC. But you've a *choice* now, man. And haven't you looked in a mirror lately . . . ? You've changed!"

"It is . . . it is the will of Allah! He has visited me with new powers, new strength."

"Oh, come on, if Allah was so powerful, he would have protected your wonderful Marcus Jashad, right? No, Linden . . . it wasn't Allah. . . . It was some sort of radiation. . . . Accept it. Accept the truth and let us help you."

"Unbelievers! Deceivers! Devils!" cried Linden.

But his gun was dipping, and his eyes were closing.

"Deep inside, Linden," said Phineas Kemp, "you know it's not true. Not true at all!"

Deep inside, the creature that had been Timothy Linden was in turmoil.

Traitor, cried the voice of Marcus Jashad. Kill him! Kill the wretched infidel!

The voice raged within Linden like thunder over the desert. But even as it demanded action, Linden found it growing curiously remote.

Part of him wanted to kill these two enemies standing before him. But there was a much larger part of him now that was...

...different...

...so much different....

And then it began to settle upon him like a slowly drifting veil. A peace...

No! No! cried the warrior in the wilderness, his turban flowing about his skull-like face, his rifle raised like a lightning rod. Obey! Obey!

...a peace like the wind between the stars...a gentle understanding. It touched him quietly, and it pierced him through and through....

...and suddenly his very soul seemed to radiate out, to blend with the essence of the universe. And he became the universe, and it became him.

...and the lightning came down upon the madly ranting figure in the desert, and it struck him like living fire. The spirit of Marcus Jashad wailed, and was consumed in sun-bright light, and then his terrible voice was no more....

Timothy Linden dropped the gun.

He looked down upon the two standing below.

"Pardon me if I have frightened you," he said. "Thank you for bearing with me."

He then collapsed in a dead faint.

"What was that all about?" said Becky Thalberg.

"I *thought* something strange was going on," said Kemp as they walked toward the fallen Linden. "I sensed it...."

"Sensed it? That doesn't sound like the pragmatic Phineas Kemp."

"On the other hand, though, it was fairly obvious the guy was having some serious interior conflict," said Kemp, kneeling down by Linden. "I wonder if this 'sleeper agent' stuff was for real, or just a psychosis caused by the radiation."

"If we can keep him alive, we can ask him," said Becky, taking her canteen from her pack. She lifted the oddly shaped head and poured some water onto Linden's lips.

Linden spluttered, choked.

"He looks alive enough to me. Now, if we don't drown him . . ."

The giant eyes fluttered. They opened and they stared up at Becky and Kemp.

An odd smile came to the strange mouth.

"Thank you," said Timothy Linden. "Thank you for not attempting to kill me."

"What's happened to you?" Becky said. "Have you any idea?"

"Yes. Yes, I think I understand now. . . ."

"This 'sleeper agent ' stuff, Linden," Kemp barked. "Was that true?"

"As a matter of fact, Colonel Kemp, I'm afraid it was," said Linden, sitting up, calmly contemplating his environs. "But don't worry. That demon has been exorcised. And in that phase of my existence, neither I nor my partner, Alexandra Marshall, was able to effect any damage. . . . Unless you wish to count my withholding my discovery."

"Discovery? What discovery?" Kemp demanded.

"Look at me, Kemp. As you can see, I have been transformed. My transformation was not caused by an odd beam of radiation, but a specific dose in a specific place. And that place, and the knowledge gained from that place, I withheld from you, hoping to use it for my own gain, and for my purposes as a secret agent of the TWC."

"And if that's true, what's to make me believe that you've actually changed affiliations?" Kemp said suspiciously.

"I have changed, as my features have changed, Colonel Kemp. And if I had not, then you both would surely be dead now, is that not correct?"

"He's got a point there, Phineas."

"Too true. Well, then, Linden, what's happened to you? And I should let you know that we've been—"

"Invaded, yes. By the Movers of the Imperium. You were able to escape, but the others were captured and are now being held in the alien spacecraft."

"How did you know that?" Kemp said.

"Oh, I know a great deal now," said Linden, standing and brushing himself off calmly. "It is a part of my new nature. I seem to be able to just reach out"—he held a hand out and placed it upon Becky's head—"and touch knowledge and truth."

"The others . . . they haven't been harmed, then?"

"No. Far from it. Presently, in fact, they speak with a member of the alien race known as an Old One. His name is . . . yes, it is Kii."

Kemp was stunned. "I find it very hard to believe that you can do this. . . ."

"Believe what you like, but I quite assure you, Phineas Kemp, I speak the truth. And I know much."

"But how?" Becky said. "Has it something to do with this transformation you've been through? And exactly what *is* this transformation?"

"There's really no time for discussion," said Kemp. "We've got to get back to the base camp."

"That is ill advised at the moment," said Linden. "And in the long run, it will do you absolutely no good. You alone will not be able to stand against the Movers, Phineas Kemp."

"But we've got to *try*," insisted Kemp. "We can't just stand around with our thumbs up our asses!"

"No, there is no reason for that. But settle down and listen to me a moment. It is vital that you do so."

"Phineas, we really have nothing to lose," said Becky. "I mean, if he knows all these things . . . maybe he's our hope!"

"There's no harm in listening, I suppose," said Kemp, but he was still suspicious.

"No harm, I assure you. In fact, your destiny is involved," said Linden, his wide, unreadable eyes staring at Kemp.

"Actually I'd settle for a one-way ticket back to Earth," Kemp mumbled.

"That could be in the cards, Phineas Kemp. If you'll simply follow me and allow me to show you what I discovered myself, days ago. It is, quite simply, part of the key that will perhaps allow us all to return to Earth."

"I'm game," said Becky. "Lead on, Macduff, as Ian Coopersmith might say." She managed a glimmer of a smile.

"How do we know we can trust you?" Kemp insisted.

"What other choice do you have?" Linden stated frankly.

Kemp nodded. He was right.

"Okay. I'll come, if you'll explain what's happened to you and how you know what you know."

"Fine. This way, please." He gestured ahead of him. "I wish to show you the cave I found. . . . I was escaping a frightening dinosaur at the time. I found something most marvelous."

"That's right, the allosaur that you say killed Alexandra when you went out to check that radiation source for Jakes," Kemp said.

"Yes, and it was a fierce thing . . . a thing with two heads."

"This damned radiation . . . It's been the bane of my existence. What the hell is it, and what the hell is it doing?"

"Yes, it was the radiation that changed those dinosaurs . . . and also caused the Saurians to lose their senses and eat John Neville in the midst of your broadcast," said Becky. "With your new-found knowledge, can you explain the radiation, Linden?"

Linden was leading them around the rocks to a clearing. "Yes. Yes, I believe that I can. It's all involved with the very nature of the *Dragonstar*, you see."

"You mean, as a seed ship?" said Becky.

"Yes, and as a laboratory in action as well—an automatic system for the creation and *customizing*, if you will, of life."

"I don't understand."

"Come with me," said Linden. "Follow me into the cave, and I will show you."

"That's what we're doing, isn't it?" Kemp said.

"Just making sure!" The creature that had been Timothy Linden gave the weirdest smile that Kemp had ever seen.

The cave was a small and narrow one. They had to duck under the overhang to get inside.

"Hey, you got a flashlight?" said Kemp as Becky grabbed his hand.

Linden, up ahead, said, "That's not necessary."

"Not necessary!" said Becky. "I can't see a thing."

Linden did not respond.

They moved back toward the rear of the cave, and then Linden instructed them to halt. "Please do not be alarmed at what happens next. You will be perfectly safe."

No sooner had he said these words than the floor gave way beneath them. Kemp heard a cry of astonishment and was startled that it was his own.

They slid down a long chute and were deposited in a heap in the darkness.

Then the lights came on.

Kemp stared around in awe. They were in a rectangular chamber with silver sides from which protruded screens and dials and all manner of oddly shaped nozzles and extrusions . . . whose tips were now glowing all manner of colors.

"My God," said Kemp, drawing his gun. "This is some sort of trap!"

"Please," said Linden's voice. "As I said, do not be alarmed."

"Where are you?" said Becky, standing up and looking around.

A round hatchway opened, and Linden peered through. "Right here. Come through, if you like."

Kemp let go a sigh of relief. "It would seem as though the guy's on the up-and-up."

But the next room proved to be much the same: alien devices. Linden was examining them, mouth pursed thoughtfully.

"So are we going to get an explanation, or what?" Kemp said grumpily.

"Explanation. Oh yes, of course," said Linden. "So much easier, though, to show you some of the actual devices utilized. Now, where shall we begin?"

"How about with why you look the way you look?" said Becky.

"That will come in due course. Let's start at the beginning. Life on Earth as we know it was shaped by the seed ship we call the *Dragonstar*. However, so far, our scientists have been unable to determine exactly *how* that was achieved. First, let me tell you that there was never any 'crew' of the vessel. It was all automated."

"That would explain that robot . . . ," Becky said.

"And it would explain other things as well," Kemp agreed. "Like why we never found evidence of crew members in the so-called crew section." He looked at Linden. "But how do you know all of this?"

Linden touched his oddly shaped head. "I just learned myself. It's written in the Book of the Cosmos, as it were . . . and I can now read that Book. But let me explain further. The *Dragonstar* comes to the Sol system."

"Where it shapes the emerging life-forms growing in the oceans of Earth," said Becky.

"Precisely," said Linden. "Shapes them toward the reptilian norm . . . creates the dinosaurs, as it were. But we've not been able to determine exactly how. . . . Well, naturally they were shaped by the environment on Earth to a certain extent. But actual types and breeds of the creatures were created here, on this ship, through genetic splicing . . . but also through something else . . . radiation!"

"Creating mutations, of course. An important part of evolutionary development," said Becky.

"Yes, but that's not the whole story. Our scientists were unable to unravel all the secrets in the control parts of this vast ship. Believe me, most—like this section—were not even discovered. You see, there was a breakdown in the *Dragonstar* system millions and millions of years ago. . . . But the ship itself had time enough to adjust. It projected what would happen. It knew the patterns of life and intelligence that were growing within it and upon the Earth. It created the dioramas for the Saurians, and for us, when we attained sufficient technology to land upon the vessel and penetrate its defense. For such, perhaps, was written in the Cosmic Book. Even I, though, do not understand the full story. . . . Perhaps I will someday."

"Well, tell us what you *do* understand, goddammit!" Kemp said impatiently.

"Yes," said Linden, looking thoughtful. "Yes, of course. Now, you are well aware that the presence of humans upon the *Dragonstar* had activated much of the machinery."

"Right! Like the whole interstellar drive which has zipped us across the universe!" Kemp said.

"Not only that, but also the devices used for shaping lifeforms. But because of the millions of years of inactivity, many of these functions—mostly the radiation directors—malfunctioned."

"I see," said Becky, her face showing her sudden understanding. "That would explain all the bad effects . . . the carcinomas in the dinosaurs, the crazy spells in the Saurians. And the changes in the dinosaurs. . . . But I still don't understand the changes, Linden. . . . Which brings us around to you, doesn't it?"

"Yes, that's right. To me, and all the marvelous machinery you see around you." He looked at them both and a pregnant silence dropped between them. "Has either of you ever heard of a creature on Earth named the *axolotl*?"

Both Kemp and Thalberg shook their heads.

"It's a salamander. Mexican, I think. When scientists discovered it, they naturally took it out of its environment to test it. Experiment with it. And when they put it into a different environment—it changed."

"Changed?" Becky said.

"That's right. Apparently it was accidentally placed in an environment with different trace elements. The active one in this case was iodine. The creature turned into another creature . . . it became an adult. Its previous form had been a larval one . . . albeit a reproductive larval stage. The axolotl was a neotenous creature, you see."

"Neotenous?" said Kemp. "So? What does an amphibian have to do with anything?"

"I present this as an example of neoteny, Colonel Kemp. So that you'll understand. You see, many of the dinosaurs and probably the Saurians as well are neotenous. And I am living proof that human beings are as well."

Becky listened to this in stunned silence.

It began to sink in on Kemp as well.

"The radiation," said Becky. "It served the same function on you as the iodine on the axolotl. But what you're saying is . . . you're telling us that it's a natural stage of human growth!"

"Precisely! It was designed into our genetic development by the *Dragonstar*. Only it never occurred on Earth. . . . There never occurred the correct radiation dosage. The sort of dosage these machines are equipped to give. So you see there was always another secret aboard the *Dragonstar*. . . . The secret of where mankind has been headed all along: to a totally new and different stage of development. And I am privileged to be the first to undergo that change!"

CHAPTER 25

"EMOTIONS!" said Barkham disbelievingly, staring at the alien face in the screen. "Emotions!" he cried, growing red in the face. "How would emotions have anything to do with it!"

"Perhaps not the sort of emotion that you are presently expressing," said Kii. "Not totally, anyway. No, perhaps what I mean to say are the systems that seemed to have been coordinated by your mammalian background as opposed to your reptilian—or even your more recent neo-cortex development which gives you your intelligence."

Takamura said, "You mean, the development of the limbic system ... the mammalian part of us ...?"

"Yes," said Kii. "The complex part of your makeup that bonds your people not with instinct, but with something more ... something quite unique that you've developed between your intelligence and your R-complex."

"You mean, love, hope, charity, affection: like that?" Barkham said. "The stuff that makes us different from old Thesaurus here, right?"

"Precisely! It is unique in the universe. . . . And, from my analysis, I find it quite a new and wonderful dimension in life. It is just the sort of development that my fellow scientists and I dreamed about when we sent out the seed ships. . . . You are the culmination of that dream. The human race has developed what we've been looking for: the key for continuance of life in the universe!"

"I don't understand," said Mikaela.

"It's actually very simple," said Kii. "As I intimated before, civilization among the known peoples of the universe has reached a point where it remains static, just short of stagnation. This point is fiercely maintained by those in charge. Any hint of its deviation is cut short. . . . This is precisely why the *Dragonstar* was recalled. There was the possibility that the sort of life had developed which did not meet the status quo of the Enforcers, the Movers. It had to be checked and certified congruent with the political system that governs most of the known universe."

"So that was why the 'stun first and ask questions later' policy upon first contact was implemented?" said Dr. Jakes. "But why are they leaving you alone with us . . .?"

"The Enforcers awoke me specifically to deal with this case . . . not a very pleasant bunch, I'm afraid. They handled it all quite badly. But fortunately I was able to convince them that I was a thoroughly good citizen and could be quite trusted to deal with you in the proper way. Which of course was analysis, pure and simple—and if contact was necessary, then so be it."

"So you're completely in charge of this operation of analysis and contact?"

"Completely."

"Then," said Takamura, "do you mind if we ask your intentions?"

"I was just coming to that. My intentions, really, are quite simple. You and your fellow humans must be released. And you must be returned to your home planet, Earth. There you must work to unite your nations and work toward a civilization that can withstand the might of the Enforcers . . . who will surely like to snuff your kind out."

"But how can that be done?" Jakes said. "We've determined that the hull of the *Dragonstar* itself cannot withstand another insertion into hyperspace. That's got to stay here!"

"Yes, my analysis shows that is quite true," said Kii. "For that reason, and for others, this is why this ship we are presently on must be stolen."

"This ship . . ." said Takamura, "this ship has a hyperspace drive?"

"Oh yes indeed," said Kii. "It has also the majority of your fellow crew members, a goodly number of the Saurian race . . . and much of the technology that will equip you later to deal with the Enforcers. And it will also have me, Kii, because I certainly do not intend to linger and face the music. Besides, you will need a pilot to help you get back to Earth, won't you, and a friendly helper to prepare your planet for the coming vengeance of the Enforcers."

"Sounds pretty good to me!" said Barkham. "Whenever

you're ready to let us out of this pen, we're ready to go!"

"Just a moment," said Takamura. "You're telling us we're going to hijack this starship from creatures who have the power we saw displayed. It sounds rather difficult to me!"

"Yes . . . and a little too pat," Jakes added.

Kii gave an alien sound that must have been a sigh. "I can only request that you believe me. Do you actually have any other choice?"

Takamura looked at the others, who had the same surprised expressions.

No. Of course they didn't have any choice. They were at the mercy of this alien. They would have to believe him . . . and if he was correct, the proper window on the opportunity for escape was only the length of time that most of the Enforcers were out checking the *Dragonstar*.

"But what about Phineas Kemp and the others who are still in the *Dragonstar*?" said Mikaela.

"All possible efforts will be made to rescue your crew-mates," said Kii. "However, you must remember, there is more at stake than merely you or your crew-mates."

"More at stake. What do you mean?" demanded Barkham.

"I think he's talking about the Enforcers . . . the intimation of threat to Earth," said Dr. Jakes, wearing a thoughtful frown.

"That is correct. And there is no intimation involved. The threat is real. The Enforcers are now aware of the existence of Earth. They have its location, and they know that human beings are a potential threat to their political hold on the universe. Doubtless, if all is left as it exists, in a few decades an armada will be sent to Earth, part of the program of our exodus from a dying sun. That planet will be enslaved. If, however, we can escape this system in this ship, we can head back to Earth. And your people, through the efforts of myself . . . and others . . . will have a chance to oppose the Enforcers. . . ."

"Others?" said Takamura. "What others?"

"That is a matter that you will discover later. Right now it is necessary to take action. So, I must ask you . . . will you cooperate?"

"Yes," said Takamura, knowing that the others agreed with him. "Yes, we will do as you say."

"Excellent," said Kii. "Then listen carefully. This is what we must do."

CHAPTER 26

"COME ON, LINDEN," said Phineas Kemp. "Don't play coy with us. This is no time for withholding the facts. Tell us what you need to tell us . . . and then tell us what we need to do."

Kemp was feeling nervous. He had noticed an almost indiscernible change in the chamber's machines. A few rods and attachments seemed to have moved a bit; there was a definite taste of electrical charge in the air. The lighting seemed a bit more various, the shadows deepened a bit in corners. Kemp's hackles were up. He felt the need to get out of this place as soon as possible. Get on with business.

Becky, on the other hand, seemed totally fascinated with Timothy Linden—or rather, what he had become. She wanted to hear everything. "Phineas, Linden did say that all this would lead up to that soon enough. Don't be so impatient."

"So impatient! These aliens, these so-called Movers or Enforcers or whatever have got most of the others in captivity, and you're telling me to be patient?"

"You forget, don't you, that only Linden knows the way out of here?" Becky said. "We're rather a captive audience, aren't we?"

"Please, please!" said Linden. "You are not my prisoners! It was necessary to bring you down here . . . necessary for you, necessary for others, necessary for Earth, in fact!"

"Necessary for Earth! What are you talking about?" Phineas demanded.

"Has it ever occurred to you, Phineas Kemp, that the Movers are now bestowed with the evidence that another civilization is launching into space . . . a civilization that might be dangerous to *their* civilization? And now they also have the location of that civilization!"

"Dangerous? How could we be dangerous to such a highly developed bunch?" asked Becky.

"I have perceived that their civilization has stopped growing, ceased developing, and is kept in check by the Enforcers. The efforts of the earlier Old Ones—those who sent out these seed ships—are now seen as subversive to the status quo. The potential of human beings for transformation from their neotenous forms into something of a more cosmic nature will be viewed as hazardous to the welfare of their society's structure. . . . You see, although such occurrences are not uncommon in their own civilization—indeed, it is part of their life cycle—it is under strict political control."

"And you know all this, huh?" Kemp said suspiciously.

"As I told you, I simply have a new Awareness!"

"Well, then, goddammit, just what is this new Awareness telling us to do!"

"You shall be happy to know that the Old One I mentioned before has allied himself with our cause." Linden paused for a moment, his strange eyes unfocused, his tongue slightly protruded as though tasting the cosmic waves he was detecting. "Yes," he continued abruptly, "my premonition has proved correct. Even now, as we speak, the others are agreeing to a plan."

"A plan?" said Kemp. "What sort of plan?"

"A plan quite simply to hijack the Enforcers' starship and return to Earth," said Linden without emotion.

Kemp felt adrenaline rush into him. "That sounds like my kind of plan!"

"So then what we have to do is to get aboard the starship," said Becky. "Not get back to base camp."

"Then we'd better get to it," Kemp said. "Linden, can you help us get back?"

"Of course. That is my intention now. We must all get back to the alien starship."

"Well, then," said Kemp, "what are we waiting for?"

"There is just one more thing," said Linden.

"Yes. Well, man . . . or whatever you are. Spit it out!" said Kemp angrily. "Tell us, and then tell us how to get the hell out of this awful place."

"All in good time. In fact, I should think, from my Awareness, that there are faster ways to get to the alien starship than over a terrain covered with hostile creatures."

"A very good point," said Becky. "But what about the Enforcers themselves?"

"My Awareness tells me that they are now dispersed through the *Dragonstar*. Only one remains aboard the alien starship. And one stands guard by the hatchway. Now is the best time to go there."

"Then let's do it," said Kemp.

"A moment, please. If you'll just wait a moment, there is that one more thing I mentioned." Linden went to the wall. There he hit a switch.

A panel opened in one wall.

Across the chamber, another panel opened.

"You will understand all, soon enough," said Timothy Linden. "Soon enough."

He hit another button, and Phineas Kemp was blinded by the eruption of radiation.

CHAPTER 27

MISHIMA TAKAMURA watched the door open.

"The guy's really on the level,"said Barkham, looking over to the image of Kii.

Which was fading away.

"I will join you soon," Kii was saying. "In the meantime, you might need these."

A table rose up from the couch. Upon the table were their weapons.

"A gesture of goodwill." said Kii. And then the alien was gone.

"Well, hot shit," said Barkham, wasting no time in strapping on a handgun. "I'm actually starting to believe this guy!"

Takamura directed the others to take up arms as well. Only Thesaurus did not take one. "I am most troubled, my friend Takamura," said the alien. "I hear nothing in this about my people. There are too many of us to board this vessel. What is to happen to us?"

"Don't worry, Thesaurus. We'll make sure Kii provides for you," said Takamura.

Thesaurus looked bemused at this glib statement and Takamura couldn't blame him. Just what *would* happen to the Saurians? They'd have to stay aboard the *Dragonstar*, most of them, as Thesaurus said. But this was no time to consider them, Takamura knew instinctively. He had to consider his own species. Here was territory well away from the land of ethics.

After buckling on their weapons, they headed out to the corridor.

"This way!" ordered Takamura, noting the angle that Kii had described. He just hoped that Kii would realize that they would have a difficult time navigating these corridors. They were cer-

183

tainly not the sort of ship's corridors that Takamura was used to, namely the usual rectangular sort. No, these were manufactured from a different sense of functional geometry.

For one thing, they were huge, designed to accomodate larger creatures. The corridors twisted and turned in all directions; it was difficult to tell even now which was the way that Kii had indicated.

The party bumbled on for a ways. A few times Takamura felt more like a character in a slapstick comedy than the leader of a group responsible for the future safety of humankind. But finally, after a few minutes of this charade, they were confronted by a large creature lumbering toward them.

Kii.

His reptilian heritage could not be mistaken. It was in the way he looked, the way he moved. He was large and forbidding, but Takamura and the others were so used to dealing with the Saurians that this creature—clearly from the same genotype—was almost anticipated. Besides, the gleam of intelligence and benevolence in his large, liquid eyes belied any fierceness in his movements.

The creature wore a torque around his neck: a translator. In his scaly arms, it carried a curlicued stick, with a light pulsing at one end: a weapon.

It croak-snarled something, and the communication emerged from the device around his neck:

"Greetings, comrades. I see you are ready for our adventure! Come!" He gestured a claw-like set of digits toward a sweep of corridor angling off to the right. "The single Enforcer still aboard this vessel is situated in the cabin of the vessel. We must deal with him first, in the manner I prescribed, before we can hope to steal the ship."

"What about the others?" said Mikaela. "Our fellow crew members."

"They have been retained in their suspended-animation chambers. Only you have been awakened," explained Kii. "But come now, there is no time to waste!"

"Nice to know that clichés abound throughout the universe!" said Barkham as Kii turned around and prowled away down the corridor.

They had to double-time it to keep up.

"I'm confused," said Mikaela. "That, or I just wasn't listening when Kii outlined his plan. Just what is it?"

"Simple," said Takamura. "We provide a distraction after Kii opens the door. He comes in another way and zaps the guy."

"I *hope* it's simple," said Jakes. "But we just have to trust this thing."

"I just hope that he can take care of this so-called Enforcer so easily. . . . They seemed pretty tough to deal with outside."

"Oh, Kii assures us that he won't be wearing the bubble force-shield in the cabin," said Takamura. "No reason to."

"Yes, I don't suppose the thing will be expecting a crew of crazed Earthlings charging his battlements," said Barkham, joking to keep a tight rein on the fear that Takamura knew they were all feeling.

"Actually," said Dr. Jakes, "I suppose we should all feel complimented! I mean, creatures as advanced as these, afraid of human beings! Enough to want to travel all that way to wipe us out!"

"Complimented?" said Mikaela. "I'd hardly use that particular word, Dr. Jakes."

"How about 'persecuted,'" said Barkham. "Maybe they found out there were black people there."

"I suppose it is all related there," said Takamura. "After all, Kii did speak of status quo. Although he did point out that there were many varieties of races tolerated by the Enforcers."

"Yeah," said Barkham. "As long as they had the right color brain."

"It seems to be a tendency in the universe to discourage progress at a certain point in development," said Mikaela. "Creatures get smart enough to get afraid of the future."

"You mean like us?" said Dr. Jakes. "I must admit, I'm feeling a certain uneasiness."

"Well, what could possibly happen?" said Barkham. "We can only die horribly. Or be stranded in strange alien territory forever. What's to be afraid of?"

"We have to concentrate on what is important and forget our own petty fears," said Takamura. "We must remember that we are fighting now for our home planet. Fighting for all that we love."

"Easy for you to say," said Barkham. "For myself, I'm gonna be honest. I'm scared shitless."

"That's all right," said Dr. Jakes. "Somehow, Barkham, I think you're the sort that functions under any emotional condition. And I must say that I find myself encumbered with the same emotional problem as you."

Takamura said, "Yes. I think that we wouldn't be human if we didn't feel strong fear in this situation."

"Our wonderful and vaunted human emotions," said Mikaela. "But what was it that William Shakespeare said? A coward dies a thousand deaths, but the valiant only one."

"Well," said Barkham as the corridor widened out into a room that looked to be an antechamber to a larger area and the air took on a decided charged feeling, "here comes death number seven hundred and twenty-two."

The walls were filled with all manner of screens and oddly shaped patterns. Controls? wondered Takamura, surveying the painter's palette of colors. There'd be no time to find out, that was for sure.

Kii turned.

"This is the place," he said. "This is where you must be. I shall secrete myself and make ready. I wish you to cause a disturbance to attract the Enforcer's attention. He will come out of the control cabin and I will destroy him with my weapon."

"Disturbance?" said Barkham. "Disturbance? You *got* a disturbance!"

"Please, not yet!" said Kii. "Wait until I hide myself!"

"Gee," said Barkham as the big creature lumbered over to a dark corner. "Really highly advanced tactics, here."

Dr. Jakes shrugged. "I suppose some things will always stay the same!"

Kii disappeared within the darkness.

Takamura gave him a few moments to prepare himself, and then gave the orders: "All right. Let's have some good old-fashioned Earth-type ruckus!"

"And just be ready to stand out of the way of death rays and other assorted defensive equipment," Barkham commented, switching the safety off his gun.

They fired into the ceiling. Barkham let rip with a wail and then cried out, "Hey, bubble-brain! Let's have a look at your ugly face!"

"I don't think you have to insult it," said Mikaela.

"Why not?" said Barkham. "Might as well have some fun before it wipes us out."

"I love your positive attitude," said Takamura.

"Why doesn't it just check with its security system? Or robots or something," Barkham said. "Why is it going to be so stupid and waddle out here on its lonesome?"

"I don't know," said Takamura. "Perhaps it has something to do with its sense of honor."

"You're anthropomorphizing, surely," Dr. Jakes said. "Most likely, they generally don't have to deal with disturbances. It's simply not going to suspect that Kii's let us go. Or that there's any security problem."

Barkham shrugged. "Well, I'm not going to look a gift Enforcer in the mouth, that's for sure."

Then the control quarters door began to cycle open.

Something began to emerge. . . .

CHAPTER 28

THE RADIATION poured through him like soft sunlight upon a pleasant beach.

No pain, no bad feeling at all. Only a gentle tingle, the softest whisper of sensation penetrating deep into Kemp's body, his mind . . . and seemingly his soul.

Kemp stood stunned for what seemed like a very long time, but was actually only seconds. Beside him, Becky Thalberg seemed to have been immersed in pure bliss. She seemed to accept the touch of the radiation like a disciple accepts a divine ray from the eye of God himself. And in fact, it *was* pleasurable. . . . There was the feeling of calm, of unity with the nature of things, with the hint of a coming revelation, like a dawn just beginning to peek over the sill of night.

But it was unlike anything that Colonel Phineas Kemp had ever felt before. It seemed to challenge the very foundations of his existence, shake the very tenets of belief that he viewed existence from:

Don't struggle, it seemed to say in silent words. *Life is not struggle. It is growth and being. It is becoming. And you are its focal point.*

Phineas Kemp fought it.

"No!" he cried. "Goddammit, no!"

For a time he seemed to flicker in and out of existence.

And then he became aware of the creature whom Timothy Linden had become, standing in front of him, murmuring, "Don't fight it! Don't fight it, Phineas. You'll destroy yourself. You'll destroy what is good within you, and you'll destroy the hope of your people!"

The red fury filled him: the fury of his identity, his character. *I am me*, he screamed within himself. *I am Phineas Kemp!*

188

He stepped forward and began to throttle Linden with his bare hands.

Linden broke the grasp easily. He pushed Kemp back. Kemp stumbled against the wall from which the radiation emanated. And the tingle became almost a burning.

"No!" said Kemp, picking himself up and stepping forward, hands clamped against his head. "It's destroying me!"

"Not the real you, Kemp," said Linden. "The you of delusions. Your true self will blossom."

"Goddamn you to hell!" Kemp screamed as he dropped down onto his knees. "Goddamn—"

And then he fainted, and the light filled his entire mind to a brimming that blotted out all of him.

There was a time of darkness, curiously dappled and moiled with light and nothingness.

When he awoke, he was lying on his face upon the cold floor. His mouth seemed full of cotton, and a strange scent filled his nostrils: a smell like exotic flowers.

Reality gradually coalesced. There were no more beaming lights, and no more conflict within himself.

He felt very peaceful, but he was more than aware of the crisis that confronted him. Nonetheless, he seemed in perfect control. He knew what had to be done.

He arose.

Becky Thalberg was standing by Linden, who was examining a bank of controls, emblazoned with alien hieroglyphics. Linden pressed a few tabs, ran his hand over a long red plate, and then simply stared at the screen readouts.

Then he turned to Phineas Kemp.

"I thought perhaps there might be a little melodrama with you, Phineas Kemp. But you seem, in truth, to have handled it much better than I did."

"Of course," said Kemp in a low voice. "You did have problems, didn't you?"

"Yes. And only very recently resolved. But then, my particular instance of training and brainwashing was of a much more virulent nature. So how do you feel, Phineas?"

"I feel . . . I feel all right."

"Phineas Kemp is still alive, then?"

Kemp thought about this a moment. He looked at Becky Thalberg, who smiled at him knowingly.

"Yeah. Yeah, I guess the old guy is still kicking. Just a little wisened up, I suppose. Sorry about the pyrotechnics. It's just hard to let go . . . of certain things."

"It was more a matter of trust and surrender," said Becky. "Trust and surrender in something deeper. And you've always found it very difficult to acknowledge that there are deeper things in you, Phineas. You've always had to be in control."

Kemp thought about this. Although a part of him rebelled at the notion, the rest of him agreed that it was indeed so.

"Well, I'm far from in control now," he said. "Although I must say, I still don't appreciate the manner in which I was dunked into the baptismal fountain, so to speak." He glared at Timothy Linden.

"Oh, and I suppose you would have come down here gladly if I told you what was intended?" Linden looked at Kemp mildly.

Kemp thought about this. His first response was to scream at Linden. But then he checked himself.

No, Linden was right. There was no other choice that Linden had had. Still, though, it rankled. . . . But it was a very familiar sort of rankling.

A sweep of joy went through Kemp.

He still had his identity! He felt different, certainly, but he still recognized his grouchy old self!

Then suddenly he felt a moment of anxiety.

"Look what you've done. . . . Maybe you're right, and this will help us, and okay, I understand, it's for the good of all. I don't know exactly *how* . . . I just know. But what all this means, right, is that pretty soon Becky and I . . . we're going to be incapacitated. . . . Incapacitated like you were. And then we'll spin some sort of god-awful cocoons. . . ."

"Precisely," said Linden. "Which is why there's simply no time to waste. We have to get you back to the alien starship immediately."

Kemp nodded. "Sounds good to me."

CHAPTER 29

IT WAS BIG, it was nasty-looking, and there was no doubt in Takamura's mind that it was alien.

The Enforcer came through the door.

There was an obvious genotype relationship here with Kii. That there was a relationship with reptiles there could be no question. The Enforcer had a longer snout than Kii, though, larger and sharper teeth, and thicker-looking hide. Everything about it, from its claws to its feral eyes, spelled aggression and dominance. It even had a tail, which slithered along behind it.

In its long scaly arms was a rod-like weapon similar to what Kii carried.

"God," said Barkham loudly. "You *are* an ugly bastard! I see why you hide yourself in those force-bubbles! I would, too!"

The Enforcer fixed his eyes on the humans and it growled. It raised its weapon to fire.

"Shit!" said Barkham. "It's going to let us have it."

He leveled his own gun and fired a round.

The explosive bullet blew off a section of the Enforcer's shoulder, splattering the wall behind it with a curious shade of red blood. The Enforcer hissed and bellowed, and its flesh began to change colors, then moved over the wound in a rippling crawl, sealing off the spurt of blood.

The thing stepped back, its eyes filling with hate.

It brought up its weapon again, and Takamura, Jakes, and Barkham aimed and fired.

Holes thunked open in its chest.

The beast staggered back with shock, looking down at its wounds with dismay.

It was that moment that Kii chose to step out from his hiding place.

191

The alien ally aimed his own rod. Before the Enforcer could do a thing, Kii triggered the rod, and a bright burst of color blasted from its end, instantly connecting with the Enforcer.

The result was profound.

The alien simply seemed to explode in all directions, pieces of charred flesh banging against the walls, its singed blood bucketing onto the floor. Severed limbs spasmed for a moment, then shivered into stillness.

"Whew!" said Barkham. "Old Kii doesn't fuck around, does he?"

Kii lowered his energy rod and stepped toward the party.

"Please, now lower your weapons. The Enforcer has been dealt with."

"I'll say," said Barkham, uneasily eyeing the alien's remains as they stepped over the closest wave of gore toward Kii. "So what's next?"

"Next, doubtless, we must negotiate our way to the control-section," Dr. Jakes said. "And I must say, I can't wait to take a look at that."

Kii beckoned them onward, and they followed, stepping gingerly over what was left of the Enforcer through the cycled-open door.

Takamura took in a breath of awe.

The control room was like nothing he'd ever seen before: an expanse of crystal and gemlight and rinded in metal and color and streams of electricity and illuminated rods and screens with incomprehensible readouts. All within a bowl-like enclosure, clearly equipped for use in all kinds of gravities. There was the smell of power in this place.

And the ports, faceted like the eyes of a fly, were filled with stars!

"No way I'm going to be able to know what to do with this lot!" said Dr. Jakes, staring about him with amazement.

"This, in truth, is what I told you," said Kii. "I believe that I will be able to take care of controlling this craft and taking it and you back to your home planet."

"Pal," said Barkham, "if you can do that, I'll make sure that you'll be more than welcome in my neck of the woods. I'll even invite you for dinner."

"I should be more than glad to accept," said Kii, "but now I must deal with a few items."

Quickly the creature scanned the dazzling array of alien

equipment. Then it stepped forward and started diddling with them.

"I hope to God it really knows what it's doing," Barkham said.

"Considering how much it's gotten accomplished already, I can't see how we can do anything else but trust that it will!" said Mikaela. "My goodness, though, this is really quite some control room, though, no?"

"I feel so useless," said Jakes. "I truly hope that we can escape, if only so that Kii will be able to start explaining to me how all this works!"

"I think there are more important matters involved in the issue, Dr. Jakes," said Takamura, watching as Kii's claw-like digits worked over a series of convoluted key-like arrangements as though it were playing a musical instrument. The alien spoke a guttural language into a coil, and strange and subtle transmutations began to take place all along the contours of the controls. Colors washed across the expanse of crystal, seeming to describe all the moods of the spectrum.

And then, from the middle of all, a blister grew. The crystal in one part of the blister darkened, coalesced, then brightened into an image.

Takamura recognized the hatchway—then he saw the Mesozoic wilderness beyond it. The blister-screen was showing the inside of the *Dragonstar*!

"Yes," said Kii, "I believe all is under control. Now watch . . . the guard will doubtless come into view any moment."

They waited and they watched.

Within a matter of seconds, a large force-field ball drifted past the hatchway opening, momentarily blocking part of the scenery. A cascade of sparks crackled down its side: a miniature snap of lightning circumscribed its periphery.

And then it was gone.

"Your power rod sure isn't going to get to *that* thing," said Barkham.

"Yes," said Mikaela. "It's still wearing its force-field sphere."

"Kii, just how are those force-field screens generated?" asked Takamura.

"From a power-pak worn around the midsection of the user," Kii said, examining the blister-screen thoughtfully.

"So there's no other outside power?" said Barkham. "Then how long do they last . . . the power-paks, I mean."

"A very long time," said Kii.

"Hmm. Well, the question, then," said Barkham, "is how do you crack that particular nut?"

Kii said, "There is a good possibility which I took into account earlier."

"And that is?" Barkham demanded.

"I have access, of course, to other power-paks. I believe that if the circuitry of one can be changed, it might function as a canceling factor for others in the vicinity. Energy spheres within perhaps a seventy-five meter periphery would be nullified."

"Hey, that sounds just perfect," said Barkham. "Let's get to it, then."

"Yes. But one of us must be stationed here, equipped with vital essential information on how to maintain control of this room!" said Kii.

"Dr. Jakes is our engineer," said Takamura. "He's been heading a study of the mechanisms on the *Dragonstar*. He's the one who's best qualified."

"It all looks pretty baffling to me," said Jakes. "But I'm willing to give it a try."

"Excellent. Come here. This is the main device of control. We must adjust it according to your brain waves, or it will reject your attempts."

Jakes walked over to the control board that Kii indicated and they set to work.

"Here," said Kii. "This is the force-field bulb generator I described."

They had moved to another room. Dr. Jakes had remained in the control room, newly equipped with the necessary information to operate certain vital portions of the alien starship.

Kii was pointing to a rack of large ring devices, attached with bulbous fittings and seeming studded with jewels. Energy cells, Kii explained.

He took one from the rack, then carefully opened it up, exposing alien patterns of circuitry. With a small humming device he had procured from the control-section, he began to probe and prod at the interior of the device.

"I sure hope he knows what he's doing," said Barkham.

"He appears to," said Mikaela.

As usual, Thesaurus said nothing, merely watching everything with awe. The Saurian seemed to be absolutely dumbstruck with

Kii. He clearly recognized his relationship with the alien—and reacted to it by viewing Kii as a veritable god.

Takamura really couldn't blame him. Kii certainly did radiate a *presence*. Fortunately it was a good presence—a feeling of benevolence and trust.

"I just hope that we can do all this in time to save Becky, Kemp, and the others," said Mikaela.

"Well, it we can't, we can't. We're talking about all of Earth, here. Our whole race. If Becky and Phineas don't get to us in time, it's tough cookies for them. They'll have to stay."

Although Takamura felt chagrined at the way that Barkham had expressed it, he knew this was the truth. Once they disposed of the guard, they only had a short window on rescuing *anybody* out there.

After that, they'd have to take off and make their best effort at a run for it.

Kii's instrument hummed and spat. An occasional spark dropped onto the floor. He made grunting noises that Takamura fancied were noises of concentration.

Finally he closed a compartment and he looked up at his audience. "There. I believe that I have completed the job. Unfortunately there is no way to test it other than to actually use it against the guard."

"What? You mean just walk on out there and hit a button, and if it works, fine, and if not, then we're in trouble?"

"Yes," said Kii. He began to strap on the device. "Have you another idea?"

That stumped Barkham. He had no response.

"Very well," said Kii. "Now, Takamura, I perceive you as being the most reliable of your company, and the best shot. Here is my beamer rod." He handed Takamura the device which he had destroyed the Enforcer with. "You simply aim and press this tab," the alien instructed. "Once before you think you'll fire within the next few minutes. Twice to actually fire. The first pressing activates the power bulb."

Takamura nodded. "I take it that you wish me to fire it at the guard."

"Yes. When his force-bubble dissolves, he must be destroyed, or he will warn the others and they will return immediately—perhaps wrecking our plans."

"Can't have that," said Barkham. He pulled out his Magnum. "I'll give the guy a plug for good measure."

Mikaela Lindstrom reluctantly took out her weapon as well, and looked at Takamura. "I was just thinking. If Kii is so practical, why doesn't he just close up the hatch right away and rocket out of here? Leave the others behind. He has no particular emotional tie to any of them. . . . And it certainly would be safe for him."

"A good point," said Takamura, and he turned to pose the question.

"No need," said Kii. "My powers in English have improved. I understood what you said. . . ."

"So then why are you so concerned with the others in the ship?"

Kii said, "I have reasons to believe that your friends Phineas Kemp and Rebecca Thalberg have a great deal of importance to the future of your race. They must be rescued and brought aboard this ship and be taken with us to Earth. . . . At all costs. But let me explain . . ."

CHAPTER 30

"I'M NOT FEELING SO WELL," said Phineas Kemp.

Everything began to swim about him woozily. He had to stop in the passageway they were traversing.

Becky Thalberg, at his side, touched him with concern, then when she realized he might topple over, she grabbed hold of his arm. "Linden!" she called to the figure loping along ahead of them. "Wait! Phineas is ill."

Linden had found another passageway from the radiation chamber. A passageway that led downward. He had not told them where exactly they were going. He had just told them to follow: this was a much faster way to the alien ship, docked at the main hatch.

Linden returned to them. He touched Phineas and he nodded his head. "I was afraid of this. I saw the possibility, but I had hoped that it wouldn't happen so soon."

"I'd like to lie down for a while, if it's okay," said Phineas, feeling like his stomach was full of molten lead.

"His progression toward the cocoon stage has been accelerated. Perhaps he had already received a small dosage of the proper radiation before and was thus primed for the transformation. At any rate, it seems to be proceeding along on its natural course. Everything would be fine—if we weren't so far from the ship."

Kemp said, "Just leave me.... Leave me here. Go on. Get off this hellhole."

"No, Phineas Kemp," said Linden. "This is not in the cards."

"I can't...can't move," said Kemp. He felt paralyzed. His skin felt very coarse and odd, and a low fire seemed to be building within it.

"Of course you can, Phineas," said Becky. "Because you *have* to!"

"This is correct, Phineas Kemp. You must make the effort. We will assist you."

"No. I think I'm getting into this 'surrender' business," groaned Kemp. "I think I'll just lie here and surrender."

"That doesn't sound like the Phineas Kemp I know and love," said Becky.

"It's the new Kemp. Remember, I got zapped. I'm sick. Just let me die."

"He must be motivated!" Linden said, looking fretful for the very first time.

"No problem," said Becky. "You know, Phineas . . . if it were Ian Coopersmith in this situation . . . Well, I know that Ian wouldn't give up."

"Coopersmith!" growled Kemp. "That black bastard! I could beat him any day of the week."

With great effort, he got to his feet and started walking down the corridor on his own.

Still, Becky and Linden were soon on either side of him, assisting him.

Kemp kept on walking in a daze, somehow holding back the blurriness and pain about him.

"Where are we going?" asked Becky.

"The aliens who built this also built a transport system. Little cars running through pneumatic tubes," said Linden. "There's a station down here just a little way. If we can make it, we can use the car to travel to the station right by the hatch. From there, we can make it to the starship."

"Hopefully," said Becky. "How much longer does he have?"

"Have? Before what?"

"Before his skin starts structuring his cocoon?"

Linden looked at Kemp. "I'm afraid it will be in only a matter of hours."

CHAPTER 31

"YOU'VE GOT TO BE KIDDING ME," said James Barkham. "And how the hell do you know all this, anyway?"

"There are ways, my new ally, which you can have no conception of," said Kii.

The party was making its way through the alien starship toward its appointment with the alien. The hatchway was not too far away at this point, and Takamura could feel his adrenaline level beginning to rise again.

Still, all this was fascinating. . . . Imagine! Kemp and Thalberg touched with the same radiation that had done that strange business with Linden. And that it should turn Timothy Linden into a new creature. What was the term that Kii had used? Neotenous. Yes! Humans were neotenous! They had the potential to turn into something different, superior.

There was hope for the human race, despite everything.

But in order for that hope to go on, they had to get Kemp and Thalberg and Linden aboard this starship!

"Sounds like quite a bit of hogwash to me," said Barkham grumpily. "Colonel Kemp, neotenous? You make him sound like a pervert or something!"

"I'm sorry, I do not understand your meaning," said Kii.

"I think that, like all of us, Barkham has just been under a lot of pressure lately, and is not open to new concepts."

"Bullshit!" said Barkham. "I'm open to all kinds of concepts. I just can't see the Colonel fitted out in a cocoon, that's all. It gives me the goddamn creeps, that's what it does." In truth, Barkham looked quite a bit unsettled, thought Takamura. Perhaps more at the thought at it happening to him than to Kemp.

"I'm sure, Barkham, that it's not contagious," said Takamura.

Barkham chuckled, but he did not smile. "I'm just staying away from any goddamn radiation, that's all."

In truth, Takamura was more than a little upset himself.

Becky and Kemp. Together.

Thrown together by fate, it seemed.

It was just sinking in on Takamura: the implications. Somehow, he knew that Becky... Well, Becky would be lost to him forever now. No hope...

But to know that she would survive...

Survive and grow and be happy...

Well, that was the important thing, wasn't it? That was what mattered, that the loved one lived on....

Sure.

He somehow managed to kick the thoughts from his mind and proceed with the group, concentrating on the task ahead of him. After all, Kii had placed his trust in him. The energy rod seemed warm in his hand.

Kii wore his adjusted force-sphere generator around what served as his waist. The others held their own weapons ready.

Kii strode up to a panel of controls. "Are you ready, my new comrades?"

"Yes," was the general opinion.

"Very well. This must be done fast. We will travel through the airlock. As soon as we are through, whether or not I see the Enforcer, I shall press this device to start. Then, Takamura, you must be sure to deal with the Enforcer before he gets to deal with us."

"Ain't no way that bastard is going to get close with this baby," said Barkham, holding up his Magnum. "Power rod or no power rod. It looked to me as though Enforcers take Magnum bullets just about the same way as other creatures."

"Every little bit will help, I'm sure," said Mikaela. She turned to Kii. "Okay. I guess we're all about as ready as we'll ever be."

Kii hit the controls.

After the subdued lighting from within the alien ship, the light from the Mesozoic Illuminator was almost blinding as they reached the last hatchway door.

Takamura's eyes struggled to adjust.

Almost as soon as they neared the entrance onto the plain, the Enforcer hove into view. It seemed larger to Takamura, terribly impressive and frightening with its crackling energy and its sense of a coming thunderstorm.

And no sooner did it arrive than it seemed to see them: immediately it zoomed toward them, turning different colors as though in rage.

Kii fumbled at the device on his waist. His digits found the right controls, and there was a harsh keening sound, a staticky escape of power. Takamura felt his hair rising all over his body.

The force-field sphere stopped dead.

It changed colors, and the sparks stopped snapping.

Then it crashed down onto the ground.

The energy ball shuddered, became translucent, dissipated.

Standing before them was a naked Enforcer, all teeth and claws. Enraged, it charged at them.

"Shit," said Barkham, and he shot at the thing . . . and missed.

"Takamura!" said Kii. "Fire."

The bulb at the end of Takamura's energy rod was already pulsing: the weapon was primed. But Takamura had frozen for a moment at the sheer physical impact of the force-field sphere's presence. The raw memory of his previous run-in with the things bloomed in his mind, freezing his nerves a moment.

But Kii's cry and the sound of Barkham's shot thawed him rapidly. He pulled the weapon up, aimed, fired.

A stream of energy flew out with incredible force, smashing into the Enforcer and blowing it into a similar array of gory pieces as its previous victim.

"My God," said Barkham as the smoke from the remains dissipated. "That thing sure packs a wallop."

Mikaela shuddered. "I'll say. But I don't like it. . . . That blood is going to attract predators. It's not going to be safe here . . . not safe for very long at all."

"Yes, and we must wait for Kemp and Thalberg," said Takamura grimly as he lowered his weapon.

"I shall not await the meat-eaters," said Thesaurus. "I must go now. Go now, to be with my people!"

"What about the others . . . the ones who are still aboard the alien ship?" said Barkham.

"I trust them to your care," said Thesaurus. "Perhaps there will be a reunion sometime in the future. Now there is no time to release them."

"Yes, you're right," said Takamura. He held out a hand and Thesaurus shook it. "Farewell, good friend."

"Farewell," said Thesaurus. "And good luck."

Without further ado, the Saurian scampered off into the vegetation.

"What's to become of the Saurians?" fretted Mikaela.

"It will be all right with the Saurians," said Kii. "They are more to the Enforcers' tastes in the way of civilizations. They will be assimilated."

"Now, what's become of Kemp and Becky?" said Mikaela, looking as though they'd pop up from some part of the panorama at any moment.

"They shall have to get here very quickly," said Kii. "I fear that the guard Enforcer has been able to beam a message out to the others. They shall soon be on their way back."

"But that, surely, shall take them some time," said Takamura.

"They are very fast, these Enforcers," said Kii, shaking his large head as though sadly.

"Have you any idea at all where Kemp, Linden, and Thalberg are?" said Mikaela. "I mean, with your vaunted extra powers, and everything."

"I shall attempt to discern." Whereupon the creature closed his eyes.

Barkham said, "So we get to just sit around with our thumbs up our noses while we wait for the big critters . . . or worse, the whole gang of Enforcers . . . to get here?"

"I guess so," said Mikaela.

Suddenly Kii opened his eyes. "They are near. They are on their way. We must wait."

"Wonderful!" said James Barkham, clasping his gun firmly. "Meantime we'd best be ready for other visitors."

Takamura checked to make sure his power bulb was still pulsing.

It was.

CHAPTER 32

"PHINEAS. PHINEAS!" A voice came to him through the swaths of fog that seemed to be wrapped around his head. "Hang in there, Phineas. Don't go under! Hang on!"

It was Becky's voice. He recognized it.

"Becky?" he murmured, lying back in the oddly shaped seat. "Becky?"

"That's right, Phineas. It's me. Becky Thalberg. I'm here, and we're well under way. We'll be there soon. We'll be at the ship, and you'll be fine."

"Nice to hear," he said. "I think I'll take a nap in the meantime."

"No. Colonel Kemp!" said Linden, looking over at him from the controls of the tube-car. "If you lose consciousness, we will not be able to rouse you. And you are far too heavy to carry. You must remain mobile."

As promised, Linden had indeed led them to a pneumatic-tube station. And, as promised, there was a streamlined car waiting for them with ample room for them all. Kemp had slumped through the door, immediately collapsing on the first thing that resembled a chair. Becky attended to him while Linden scrutinized the control board. In less than a minute, he had somehow analyzed the operational systems with his new powers. A touch of the fingers, a wave of the arm, and a push to a pedal and they were on their way, sliding through the winding tube system with Linden monitoring their direction, making sure they would end up at the hatchway.

Linden's words did not do a great deal to encourage Kemp. He had always been a light sleeper, and it was seldom that he had difficulty jumping out of bed, alert and ready for action. Now, however, he was having severe problems. It felt as though a heavy weight rested on his whole body. A weight with invisible needles through which drugs were being pumped into every cell. Drugs that deadened him, made him very sleepy, sleepy. . . .

"Phineas!" said Becky sternly. "You keep those eyes open, do you hear me?"

"Hmmm? Open? Okay. Just let them rest a little, then I can keep them open."

She slapped him.

He barely felt it, but the simple shock of being slapped by a woman roused him a bit.

"Sorry, but I don't have any Aqua Velva," she said.

"Huh?"

"Your line is supposed to be 'Thanks, I needed that!' "

"Lines?"

"Forget it, Phineas. Just stay awake, all right?"

"Only a few more minutes to go, Colonel Kemp," said Timothy Lindon. "If you can just hang on, I'm sure we can shoot you up with something when we get there. From the medical supplies."

"How about a cup of coffee?" he said groggily. "I could really use a nice cup of black coffee."

"So could we all, Phineas," said Becky. "Look, why don't you just visualize it?"

"Visualize?"

"Yes. Pretend there's a nice, bracing, steaming cup of black coffee in front of you. Take it up in your hand—"

"Yes, yes, Becky. I've got it!" He found it very easy indeed to actually see the cup of coffee before him. Was this one of his new powers? There it was, in a white mug with the letters *IASA* printed on it: his favorite cup! He picked that mug up and he put it to his lips and he sipped.

"Euuch!" he said.

"What's wrong?"

"Becky, you never could make a decent cup of coffee!"

She laughed. "Nice to have a little touch of domesticity in the midst of drama and revelation, huh?"

Kemp chuckled and found his faculties returning to him somewhat. "Yeah. Domesticity. You give good domesticity, did I ever tell you that, Becky?"

"Well, I'm terribly flattered. . . ."

"And Ian Coopersmith never had to look at you in curlers, did he?"

Becky shook her head. "Yes, you're right. Out there in the middle of the Mesozoic Preserve . . . If Ian had gotten a good look at me in my curlers and night cream, he would have booted me right out of the tree to the carnivores. I'll have to give you that, Phineas."

"I can feel the lethargy coming on again," said Phineas Kemp, although he was feeling much more awake. "You've got to help me, Becky."

"What can I do?" said Becky.

"How about a kiss?"

She sighed and harrumphed. "How about another slap. Phineas, I thought Linden said you were supposed to be 'enlightened' now."

"Darling, you would make the Buddha himself horny!"

She laughed. "Well, I guess you do have a sense of humor . . . perhaps a little wit. Very crude, perhaps. . . ."

"So refine me!"

She shook her head. "Really, Phineas, I don't think this is the time or the place. . . ."

"You've got to keep me awake, right? This kind of talk always keeps me awake!"

"Don't you feel just a little bad about forgetting about Mikaela?"

"Christ, Becky, you think Mikaela is going to want to have sex with me when I look like *that*?" He pointed at Linden.

"Phineas, how do you even know that human beings kicked out of their neotenous phases are going to want to have sex, anyway?" said Becky sternly.

"Hey, Tim. What's the verdict on that?"

Linden did not even look up from the controls. "I have not yet had time to explore that phase of my being yet, Colonel Kemp. You shall have to wait. . . . But I have the feeling that, in your case, perhaps your sexual feelings will . . . mature."

Becky laughed.

"Oh, great. Ha, ha. Thanks." Kemp slumped back in his chair.

"But the main goal, right now, Phineas, is to survive," Becky reminded him. "There's much more at stake than sex."

"Yes. Yes, you don't have to remind me of that. I'm just trying to keep myself awake, Becky," Kemp said, a little peeved. "You really don't think I'm serious, do you?"

"Sometimes I don't know about you, Phineas."

"Yeah," said Kemp, massaging his eyes. "I know what you mean."

The cylinder whooshed its way to its destination, and Kemp fought to stay awake. He stood and stretched. He exercised. Still, he could feel the heavy blanket of sleep poised above him, ready to descend at any moment.

Finally the car jerked to a stop.

"According to my readings," said Linden, "this is the station corresponding to the main hatchway."

"Great," said Becky. "And are they still waiting for us?"

"Yes. I am positive that they are. Only we must hurry."

"I'm okay," said Phineas. "Lead on."

Linden opened the door and gestured them to follow.

They followed a corridor, each length lighting with their presence, then dimming with their departure.

Finally they entered a small room, with controls.

"It looks like an elevator!" said Becky Thalberg.

"Right," said Timothy Linden. "That's just what it is."

And he touched one of the controls.

CHAPTER 33

"Look!" said Mikaela Lindstrom. "Here they come!"

She was pointing, and Takamura followed the direction of her finger.

Coming through some vegetation, from the direction of an outcrop of rocks, were three figures.

One was Becky Thalberg, and Takamura's heart seemed to skip a beat as he saw that she had her arm around Phineas Kemp. But then he saw that it was not a gesture of affection: she was just helping him along.

The other figure, as it neared was more shocking.

But then Takamura remembered what Kii had said about Timothy Linden, and that explained this strange thing. It was the "adult" form of Linden.

This would take some getting used to. . . . Becky was going to become . . . become like *that*?

"Hey!" cried Barkham, waving at them. "Hey, over here!"

"I think they know where they're going," said Mikaela.

"Hold on a second," said Barkham. "Oh my God, look! The Enforcers! They're on their way back!"

Takamura's head snapped to the direction that Barkham was pointing. Sure enough, two force-field spheres were bobbling along at a good clip, just within view.

"How's that anti-force-field belt of yours holding up, Kii?" Takamura asked.

"It will be adequate. But your comrades must hurry, I fear." He pointed. "The life-fluid of the Enforcer has indeed attracted the attention of the predators in the area, as you predicted. Look."

A pack of allosaurs. Charging their way.

Takamura did not even have to think about his next action. He turned toward Becky and Phineas and Linden and he yelled, "Run! Run for your lives."

But they had seen the dinosaurs as well; they had indeed increased their paces.

The thirty seconds it took for them to reach the hatchway seemed to stretch out an eternity. Even as they stumbled into the hatch, Takamura cried out. "Kii! Hit the device."

The Enforcers were less then a hundred meters away.

Kii touched his button as Barkham fired into the group of dinosaurs coming their way, hoping to fend them off.

Barkham's shots had no effect, but Kii's device had a profound one: the force-field balls stopped as though they they had hit a wall. They sparked and turned an angry red.

Then they fizzled away.

The creatures inside tumbled to the ground, screeching horribly.

All this had not been lost upon the allosaurs. They halted, then dived toward what appeared to be easier prey.

The screams of the Enforcers were awful to hear as the dinosaurs tore them apart.

"Hurry," said Kii. "Go through the hatch. Get into the ship." He was taking off his belt.

The others obeyed instantly, but Takamura lingered. "What are you doing, Kii?" he demanded.

"I am activating this device so that it will affect any other arriving Enforcers. I will place it here, so." He put it down near the hatchway. "This will keep the scum spawn away, for a while, and it will give us time to separate the vessel. Now, comrade Takamura, I suggest that we—what is your phrase?—get the hell outa here."

Takamura nodded, then scrambled after Kii as the creature darted through the hatchway.

"What the hell is wrong?" Barkham demanded.

"You've got to be patient," said Takamura. "Kii has already told us, he's not exactly a licensed Star Pilot. He's going to have to wing this, so to speak. But first, he has to absorb whatever information he can."

"We've got to hurry," said Barkham, "before they somehow signal other starships to blast us!"

"I'm sure that Kii is more than aware of the situation," said

Jakes. "This is a damned complex system, let me tell you! I've been looking it over for a while."

The alien had connected himself to the control board with all manner of filaments and headgear. Kii seemed to be in some sort of trance now, his eyes closed, his body barely moving.

Kemp had been taken to a room to lie down; he was in bad shape. But Becky was here, and so was the strange new form of Timothy Linden.

"Yes," said Linden, surveying them all with his spooky eyes. "Yes, it must be soon.... And it will be soon. I sense that Kii has completed his grappling with the concepts and is even now engaging the operating mechanisms properly."

"How do you know all this shit?" Barkham demanded.

"I am different now," answered Linden.

"I'll say."

"It's what is happening to Phineas, Barkham," said Becky. "And it's what will happen to me. I'm afraid you're just going to have to adjust to it."

"Well, I don't have to like it, do I?"

"You must realize, James Barkham, that the transformation that I have undergone is something that could happen to you as well, with the proper dose of radiation. All of humanity is neotenous. All of us have the capability. It shall be, I hope, the great equalizer. It will bring us all together."

"And that's what's going to have to happen, from the sounds of it," said Takamura. "That is, if Kii is right, and the Enforcers are going to want to blow us all right out of the universe."

"Look, right now all I want is to blow this joint, if you know what I mean," said Barkham. He jabbed a forefinger at the concentrating Kii. "Can't you put a fire under that thing?"

"I'm sure, Barkham," said Jakes, "that Kii is in just as much a hurry as you are ... perhaps even more of a hurry. The Enforcers will just want to kill us. God knows what they'll want to do to Kii!"

"Are there any kind of screens here ... or instruments that can tell us what's going on out there?" asked Takamura.

"No. I'm afraid not. We're running blind." Jakes looked solemn.

"You mean, if there's a whole Enforcer armada out there after us, there's no way of knowing it?" Barkham said.

"That's right."

"I hardly think," said Mikaela, "that the Enforcers will have time to mount a countermeasure of that scope. I mean, they hardly expected this kind of thing to happen, did they?"

"We don't know . . ." said Barkham. "We don't know anything about what they expected, or their security measures, or how they like to torture prisoners or anything. . . . I know, however, that I'm going to feel a hell of a lot better when old Kii gets us safely onto the other side of hyperspace!"

"I think we all would, Jim," said Jakes. "But we have to accept that, as before, we are entirely in the hands of our new friend here."

"And how do we know we can trust him, anyway?" said Barkham, several drops of sweat on his brow. "I mean, this could all be some sort of setup!"

Timothy Linden answered this concern. "Please. I have special ways of knowing these things. Sensory awareness of things such as truth and destiny. I promise you, all my registrations upon this creature known as Kii inform me that he is telling the truth. I would stake my humanity on it!"

"Humanity!" said Barkham. "Fella, did anyone tell you that you're not looking particularly human lately?'"

"I am totally human, I assure you," said Linden.

"Wait a minute. . . . Didn't Kii say something about you being a TWC sleeper agent?"

"That's quite true. However, my transformation has freed me of that indoctrination. I am now fully equipped with my own free will."

"How do we know?" said Barkham. "How do we know that you're not just a part of the whole plot?"

"Plot?" said Becky Thalberg. "James, you really are getting much too paranoid. I think that this is a situation in which we're just going to have to cross our fingers and pray. If it will do any good, though, I can vouch for Linden. He's definitely on our side."

James Barkham slumped back into a chair-like thing. He wiped off the perspiration from his brow with the back of his sleeve. "Yeah. Maybe you're right. I guess I'm getting a little hyper over everything. Can't blame me, though, can you? Shit, this whole thing has been a pisser. Sorry, Linden. Hope my comments didn't bother you . . . 'bout you not being human."

"I can more than understand your feelings, James Barkham," said Linden. "With my background and my perceptions, I am

quite aware of the strange and convoluted courses of human feeling and thinking."

"Thanks, man," said Barkham. "I just sure hope that we get to
have the chance for a nice long philosophical discussion."

"That would be my pleasure," said Linden.

Suddenly a symphony of lights swelled up along the patterns
of the controls.

Sounds squealed, keened, whooped.

Kii stood up from his seat.

"The starting measures have been completed," he said.
"Please find a safe place. Prepare for takeoff."

Takamura and the others scrambled for seats.

As soon as they were seated, the contours of their chairs
changed. Like protoplasm, webbing strands grew across the
chairs, securing them in.

Kii sat back down, and the lights began an insane parade up
and down the floors and ceilings.

For a moment, Takamura thought he was losing his mind. He
felt as though he were being pulled inside out. He seemed to
merge with the room, the others, the universe.

Then everything seemed to explode into silence.

He was suddenly awake and aware. It was as though he had
emerged from a faint, the pieces of his consciousness collecting,
swarming up to a new whole.

A bit dazed, he looked around.

Kii was disengaged from his wires and controls. He was monitoring a sequence of lights. He looked up and around, noticing
the others had reemerged into consciousness.

"Ah! I trust you enjoyed your rest?" said Kii.

"Rest?" said Barkham, rubbing his head. "Cripes, how long
were we out?"

"Four point five of your time units," said Kii.

"Over four *hours*?" said Barkham. "It seemed like about four
seconds!"

"Yes," said Takamura. "That's the way it felt for me, too."

"You will be happy to know that we have successfully escaped
from the Enforcers' system."

"You mean, we've made it back to hyperspace?" said Barkham.

"That is correct."

"Whew. I never thought I'd be happy to get back here!" said
Barkham.

Jakes stepped up to Kii eagerly. "Perhaps now you will have time to tell me a little more of how all this works!" he said, his eyes filled with wonder.

"Of course. There will be plenty of time for that now. It will be some weeks before we return to your planet. There will be time for everything."

Takamura was suddenly aware that his arm were full of Becky Thalberg. "Oh, I'm so relieved to be back," she said.

His hopes pricked up a moment, but then she withdrew, and her face showed nothing for him but affection.

"How is Phineas?" asked Mikaela.

"I think he will be all right," said Becky. "But, to tell you the truth, I'm not feeling so well myself now. Any signs of anything growing on me yet?"

"No," said Takamura. "Not visibly, anyway."

"Well, it will be dermatology horror-show soon enough, I suppose. And I was always horrified with pimples!"

"I should go to Phineas," said Mikaela.

"I think he'd like that," said Becky.

One look at Mikaela told Takamura that she realized that Kemp would be lost to her, as Becky had been lost to him.

"I'm sorry to hear about Kate Ennis," said Mikaela.

"Yes. But it could have happened to any of us," said Becky.

"I'll go to Phineas and talk to him a moment," said Mikaela, after taking a breath of resolve. "But then, you must go to him. Becky. He will need you, I think. And you will need him."

Becky nodded. "Yes. Yes, I suppose you're right."

Mikaela got instructions from Kii, and then left.

"Well," said Takamura, "I suppose I should join Jakes. There is plenty I must learn from Kii."

He stepped forward, but his arm was caught by Becky.

"Mishima," she said.

"Yes, Becky?"

"I'm sorry it has to happen this way."

"One cannot argue with fate, Becky, can one?"

"No, I suppose not. I'm changing, Mishima. I'm changing . . . I can feel it. And I'm scared. Would you hold me?"

They embraced and she was warm and sweet and vibrant. A tear came to Takamura's eye.

"Thank you, Mishima," she said after a while.

"Thank you, Becky."

"I just want you to know . . . Want you to know that, in my

way, I've come to . . . to care for you very much. And I hope . . ."
She blinked back tears. "I hope that we can stay . . . friends. Stay
close, somehow, after my full transformation."

"Of course, Becky. Thank you, I shall count on that."

"Yes. Yes, that will help me through it all." She kissed him on
the cheek, and then she walked away.

Mishima Takamura sighed and joined Jakes and Kii as the
alien began to discuss the incredible spaceship that was taking
them back to their home planet.

If only he had received that radiation, instead of Kemp.

And the hell of it was, Phineas Kemp really didn't deserve it.
And certainly he didn't deserve Becky Thalberg.

No, he thought. The universe just wasn't fair.

"Well," he told Barkham as they looked down at the alien
patterns of lights, "at least we've escaped."

"Huh?" said Barkham. "Oh yeah. And you can bet your ass I
don't want to see another dinosaur in my entire life!"

Takamura smiled.

"There is that silver lining, isn't there, Jim? No more dinosaurs!"

EPILOGUE

COLONEL PHINEAS KEMP lay in the cubicle, strapped down.

He realized that he was changing, inside and out—and yet he wasn't becoming violent, as Timothy Linden had. He felt a little pain, he felt dizzy, and he wasn't precisely comfortable. . . . But it felt more like a hangover than any real illness. It had the feeling to it, the promise of departure. . . . Soon . . . soon . . .

He was barely conscious when Mikaela Lindstrom came in. Her voice revived him rapidly.

"Phineas? Phineas, are you still awake?"

"Mikaela? Yeah . . . Yeah, I'm okay. There was a strange time there for a moment."

"That was when the ship went into hyperspace."

"Then we've made it?"

"Yes. We're headed back for Earth."

"Thank God."

"Yes."

There was a long time of silence, then Mikaela said, "I'm so glad you made it back, Phineas."

"You know I'm going to change, don't you?"

"Yes."

"I'm going to look like Linden."

"Yes."

"Think you'll still love me with a kisser like that?"

"Oh yes, I'll still love you, Phineas. But you know, don't you, that things . . . things will have to be different."

"Yes. Yes, I suppose so."

"You'll be different and you won't have the same feelings toward me. . . . I know that. . . . I can perceive that."

Kemp nodded. "I'm going to need your help."

"And we'll all need yours. . . ."

"Just imagine . . . Phineas Kemp, transforming into a superior form of humanity."

"And you always thought that you had already made it that far," said Mikaela, a laugh in her voice.

"Yeah. How true. Oh well, nothing for arrogance like a good dose of radiation, I guess."

She squeezed his hand. "I look forward to getting to know the new you."

"So do I."

Mikaela looked up and out the door. "Ah. Yes, I just wanted to tell you that . . . to tell you that we'll all be here to help you as you change, Phineas."

"Thanks. That means a lot to me."

"There's someone who's come to talk to you, Phineas. . . . I've got to go now, but she'll take care of you. And you've got to take care of her as well."

"Thanks, Mikaela."

Mikaela kissed him on the cheek and then she left.

Someone else walked through the door.

And although his vision was bleary and foggy, he somehow did not need it to sense who it was. . . . He could reach out and touch her with something else . . . some new part of him.

"Hello, Phineas."

"Hello, Becky," he answered.

"We made it."

"Yeah."

"But we've got a long way to go yet. . . ."

"I don't want to think about it."

"We can do it, Phineas. I know we can. But we've got to do it together. We've got to be there for each other. . . . There's always been that between us. There's something. . . . And it's something we're going to have to build on. This time, though, it won't just be for our selfish selves."

"Yeah," he said.

"You're being awfully monosyllabic, Phineas Kemp."

"There's not much more to be said, is there, Becky?"

"No, I suppose not. It's going to be a strange future, Phineas."

"Tell me about it. I'm scared absolutely shitless."

"Yes. And so am I."

Becky came to him and lay beside him.

"When I dreamed of going to the stars, I never dreamed of this," said Phineas Kemp.

"No," said Becky. "But I think I did."

He laughed and put his arm around her, and her warmth was more than welcome.